A sly, funny, action-packed t...
iconic spy duo, ...
New York Time...

Skwerl and Cheese are down on their luck. Skwerl, who is resourceful like a squirrel (Marines win battles, not spelling bees), used to work for the CIA's elite paramilitary wing. He was unceremoniously fired after a raid went bad in Afghanistan. 'Big Cheese' Aziz, a legendary pilot – his nation's Maverick – is equally hard up. So Skwerl recruits Cheese into an anonymous network of so-called sheepdogs, who operate in the shadowy moral grey zone between predator and prey.

Their first mission? To repossess a private jet stranded on a remote Ugandan airfield. Their fee: a commission on the jet's $5 million value. But *nothing* about the job seems to add up. Their contact goes missing. Their handler is as mysterious as the real source of the money. And when the women in their lives get involved – one pregnant wife and one dominatrix – the stakes skyrocket overnight.

From the jungles of Kampala to a glamorous hotel in Marseille, from a veteran-run pizzeria in Kyiv to a Panera in northern Virginia, Skwerl and Cheese must navigate an increasingly tangled set of loyalties where no one and nothing is what it seems. Globe-trotting and page-turning, full of heart and humour, *Sheepdogs* is a wild ride through the underbelly of modern war and intelligence.

Hardback | 9780241772546 | Viking | 21 August 2025 | £16.99

For publicity enquiries please contact
Laura Dermody: ldermody@penguinrandomhouse.co.uk

© Huger Foote

ELLIOT ACKERMAN is the *New York Times*-bestselling author of
the novels *2054, 2034, Halcyon, Red Dress in Black and White,
Waiting for Eden, Dark at the Crossing* and *Green on Blue*, as well as
the memoirs *The Fifth Act: America's End in Afghanistan* and *Places
and Names: On War, Revolution, and Returning.* His books have
been nominated for the National Book Award, the Andrew Carnegie
Medal in both fiction and non-fiction, and the Dayton Literary Peace
Prize, among others. He is a contributing writer at the *Atlantic,*
a Senior Fellow at Yale's Jackson School of Global Affairs, and
a veteran of the Marine Corps and CIA special operations, having
served five tours of duty in Iraq and Afghanistan, where he received
the Silver Star, the Bronze Star for Valor and the Purple Heart.
He divides his time between New York City and Washington DC.

SHEEPDOGS

SHEEPDOGS

ن ام رک ی

Elliot Ackerman

VIKING

an imprint of

PENGUIN BOOKS

VIKING

UK | USA | Canada | Ireland | Australia
India | New Zealand | South Africa

Viking is part of the Penguin Random House group of companies
whose addresses can be found at global.penguinrandomhouse.com.

Penguin
Random House
UK

First published 2025
001

Copyright © Elliot Ackerman, 2025

The moral right of the author has been asserted

Set in 13.5/16pt Sabon
Printed and bound in Great Britain by Clays Ltd, Elcograf S.p.A.

The authorized representative in the EEA is Penguin Random House Ireland,
Morrison Chambers, 32 Nassau Street, Dublin D02 YH68

A CIP catalogue record for this book is available from the British Library

HARDBACK ISBN: 978-0-241-77254-6
TRADE PAPERBACK ISBN: 978-0-241-77253-9

www.greenpenguin.co.uk

For Drifter and Pigpen

War is a racket . . . Only a small "inside" group knows what it is about. It is conducted for the benefit of the very few, at the expense of the very many.

—SMEDLEY D. BUTLER, MAJOR GENERAL,
U.S. MARINE CORPS

SHEEPDOGS

Prologue

THE OFFICE

EVERYONE AT THE OFFICE WINDS UP WITH AT LEAST FOUR names.

The first is your true name. The one on your birth certificate. The one you enlisted with at eighteen or nineteen, standing formation on the Island's yellow footprints, scared shitless, your head fresh-shaved, bald as the day you were born. True names don't get used much around the Office. Which brings us to your second name.

This is your pseudonym—or *pseudo*. A name randomly generated for all undercover officers. Contrary to popular belief, this isn't everyone in the building. Not even the majority. If undercover officers corresponded in their true name instead of their pseudo, every email they sent—to include asking a colleague to grab coffee in the cafeteria—would be classified because that email, no matter how innocuous, would reveal the undercover officer's identity. So you get a pseudo.

The computer that generates the pseudos has always seemed to have a sort of a borsch-belt sense of humor, like when it assigned Wan C. CURR and Hugh D. MUNGUS to a couple of new hires. Mostly, though, the pseudos just don't line up with the personality of whoever they're assigned to, like the tweed-coat-bowtie-wearing forensic accountant in Counter Proliferation Division whose pseudo, Tony T. TATALIA, made him sound like a mob boss, like the type of criminal he used to hunt down before he moved across the Potomac from Treasury. A final point on pseudos: you know it's a pseudo because the last name is always all caps, and the middle initial always stands for nothing.

The third name you'll get is your alias, which the team at All-Docs creates. Your alias appears on your passport. Note that I didn't say *fake passport* because the passport isn't a fake; it's real, made for you by the State Department. It's a *fake* name but on a *real* passport. Typically, you use only one name per country, which is why everyone winds up with at least four names, but sometimes as many as a dozen. For the paramilitary guys, who work with the indig troops, they used to try to keep the first name the same on alias passports and only change the last name. This would keep some indig rifleman in Somalia from knowing you as "Mr. Joe" while another indig squad leader in, say, Afghanistan knew you as "Mr. Bob."

If this system sounds confusing, it is. You might think you're having a conversation about three different people (Joe Blow, Clark C. KENT, and *Bob Barker*) only to realize that they're all the same person (true name, PSEUDO, and *alias*).

This is where your fourth name comes in, and it doesn't appear on any birth certificate, email system, or alias passport. Typically, the use of a fourth name is specific to the paramilitary world, where most guys already have nicknames from their time in SOCOM. Your nickname would be what everyone in the Office knew you by, as well as the indig, at least the ones who'd worked on our programs awhile. Some of those nicknames sound cool. Like the retired CAG master sergeant who, strangely, was the doppelgänger of David Howell Evans, better known as The Edge or simply Edge, the guitarist for U2. So that master sergeant was forever known as Edge. Cool or uncool, all nicknames hold fast to a single rule, one you break at your own peril: never, ever try to give a nickname to yourself.

Mike Ronald tried to give himself a nickname. As a young sergeant, he'd passed MARSOC selection and checked in at 2d

Raiders in Lejeune from 3d Recon in Okinawa. Going from Recon to the Raiders was a step up. The week after his arrival, he was on the flat range at Stone Bay, working through transition drills between his M4 and Colt 1911, an old-model .45 caliber pistol that only the Raiders still used because, although unwieldy, its subsonic slug would punch a grapefruit-sized hole into your enemy's chest. Mike was doing pretty well, too, keeping up with the drills, tight shot-groups, quick hands. He even had the guys on his team calling him by the nickname he'd picked for himself— "Delta Mike." Of course, he hadn't told them that he was the one who'd picked this nickname after leaving Oki. He'd convinced his new teammates that on Oki *everyone* had called him Delta Mike because he could hold a soda-can-sized shot-group with his M4 at a hundred yards and the same with his 1911 at fifty. He'd then punched a few more dime-sized holes out of the silhouette target— double-tapping center mass and drilling one through the head—as if the last shot proved the point, like how you put a period at the end of a sentence.

After a week on the range (and a week of everyone getting used to calling Mike Ronald Delta Mike) his team was finishing up at the end of the day, doing a brass call. As they picked up fistfuls of shell casings off the grass, none of them noticed the arrival of their ops chief, Ted McDermott, a master sergeant everyone called "Mac" (not all nicknames are clever). While cleaning up, they hadn't noticed Mac's arrival and one of them stood up to ask Mike Ronald a question, "Hey, Delta Mike . . ." But before that Marine could get out his question, Mac cut him off, "Who the *fuck* is Delta Mike?" From across the range, Mike Ronald double-timed over to Mac, who he knew by reputation alone. That reputation included the following: that Mac had earned a Navy Cross and a Silver Star; that he'd been shot three times in two different wars; and that he ran Ironman triathlons on weekends, having completed his fifteenth two days ago. Which was why, as of yet, Mac hadn't met "Delta Mike" Ronald.

When Mac asked "who the fuck" gave Mike Ronald his nickname, Delta Mike was quick to explain that back in Oki, at 3d Recon, *everyone* had called him Delta Mike. When Mac asked why, Delta Mike—with probably a little too much pride— explained he'd *earned* the name on the range. He nodded toward his target and, with a mouthful of false modesty, said he supposed it was because, like the Delta boys at CAG, he was a skilled operator. When Mike Ronald said the word "operator" Mac had made a face like tasting spoiled milk. "Naw," he said, shaking his head mournfully and quietly laughing. "Your name ain't Delta Mike . . . No way . . ." and then, raising his voice so everyone on the range could hear, Mac declared, "Your name is Dickhead Mike." And so it was: he became Sergeant "Dickhead Mike" Ronald. Or, to his friends, simply "Dickhead."

Dickhead Mike never made it to CAG, or to the Office. A year later, out in Helmand, Dickhead and some of his teammates got themselves into an ambush, a nasty one on a raid near Now Zad. Within the first few minutes, a sniper shot him through the neck. Belly down in the dirt next to Dickhead was another guy, an older guy from the Office who'd been a Raider. He also had a nickname, "Skwerl." The bleed was bad, a severed carotid artery fire-hosing all over the place, so hopeless—you can't cinch a tourniquet around someone's neck—but Skwerl had tried to stop the bleeding nonetheless, holding a first and then a second soaked compress over the gunshot wound. Dickhead hadn't said much, he didn't scream or even complain really. He'd simply looked up and asked Skwerl his name, not his nickname but his true one. "Jay Manning," Skwerl had said quietly, realizing he hadn't given anyone that name in a long time. Dickhead had muttered, "Jay, would you mind . . ." but he didn't finish, and Skwerl was saying, "Stay with me, Dickhead, stay with me, buddy," over and over as he watched the lights . . . slowly . . . go . . . out.

People called him Skwerl because he was resourceful and could get you anything you needed, like a squirrel. They spelled it S-K-W-

E-R-L because Marines can't spell for shit, and when his nickname kept popping up spelled that way (on rosters, on his gear, anywhere someone had to write it) the spelling stuck. Like Dickhead, Skwerl had been a Raider. He left that unit when Uncle Tony, the recruiter for the Office and later his boss, had approached him about a career change. Skwerl didn't know it at the time, but the mission where Dickhead Mike was killed would be his last, ending six years of working for Uncle Tony. Skwerl got himself in a bit of trouble after that. Something about seeing that kid shot through the neck, bleeding out, and Skwerl saying his name over and over and that name being Dickhead; it set something off in Skwerl—like maybe *he* was the dickhead.

Anyway, it'd been a bad mission, and Skwerl made the mistake of talking to the press not only about the mission itself but also about the Office; and he'd made the even bigger mistake of not calling the Office "the Office" but of calling it by its other name, its true name: Ground Branch of the Special Activities Division.

They'd fired him for that.

Chapter One

SKWERL & CHEESE

THREE YEARS AFTER LOSING HIS JOB, SKWERL STOOD KNEE DEEP in a swamp. He was one hundred meters outside a jungle airfield with Cheese, his partner in a new venture. And Cheese was about to quit.

"How much longer are we supposed to wait for this guy?"

Their liaison, who'd met them earlier that day and introduced himself simply as "H," had gone up ahead, to check the perimeter fence. Skwerl assured Cheese that H would be only a few more minutes.

"He's got five," said Cheese through the darkness of the swamp. "Then I'm leaving . . . I'm serious this time."

Skwerl glanced at the luminescent hands on his watch, a Rolex he'd have to sell for cash if this plan of his didn't work. It was a little after 2 a.m. Their flight from Charlotte to Kampala had landed the morning before, and he and Cheese hadn't slept in two days.

"He'll be back," Skwerl said in a whisper. He glanced through the darkness in the direction H had walked off, to where the airfield's arc lights glowed, casting a fringed halo above the treetops. "H got you past that immigration officer, didn't he? Have a little faith."

"I never should've let you convince me—" and Cheese bit off the end of his sentence. The problem he'd encountered at immigration coincided with the reason Skwerl had needed to do very little convincing to get Cheese to come on this trip. Cheese was a pilot, an Afghan pilot no less, one who'd flown everything from Russian-made Mi-17s for the Office to a private jet for President Ghani. For years, Cheese had imagined that if Kabul ever fell, he'd be able to fly himself, his young wife, and their extended family out with plenty of time, either on a helicopter or a jet—Cheese could fly anything. But it hadn't gone down that way. When the end came, Cheese had been stunned to find himself at Kabul International, afforded no special treatment, stranded like everyone else. Because the work he'd done for the Office was secret, the Americans had refused to help him. He had been able to travel through Uganda, only him and his wife, another blighted pair of refugees living on cots in a gymnasium. This was the betrayal of betrayals, a humiliation for Cheese. The only reason he'd agreed to speak with Skwerl was because he'd known that somewhere along the line the Office had screwed him, too.

It was Cheese's prior stay in Uganda that had caused that morning's unforeseen delay at immigration. Cheese had popped up as "nationless" in some database, a passport from the Islamic Republic of Afghanistan no longer holding much currency. Fortunately, a well-placed phone call from H had cleared things up.

Skwerl was pleading in the darkness for Cheese to stay put. "Don't be an asshole . . . Just stick around so we can get this thing done."

This thing, as Skwerl had explained it to Cheese, was a Challenger 600 private jet parked on a runway less than a half-mile away that they needed to steal. When Skwerl had visited Cheese in a suburb on the fringes of Austin, he'd made the mistake of using that word, "steal." Sitting in the one-bedroom apartment Cheese shared with his wife, Skwerl had quickly corrected himself: "Repossess," he'd said as Cheese's wife, Fareeda, hovered over the tea service slitting her eyes. "That's when you steal something back." She'd poured Skwerl a second glass of sugary tea with a courtesy that was its own aggression. When Cheese asked, "From who?" Skwerl asked whether it mattered; and, as Cheese considered the question, he realized it didn't. What mattered was that Skwerl had promised that the two of them would split the repossession fee. Which was twenty percent of the jet's value. And that value was just under $5 million. So a cool million split down the middle. When Skwerl said the number, Cheese had taken one look around his overcrowded apartment and agreed: Skwerl would get them to the airfield, Cheese would fly the plane. The two of them shook hands. They were partners.

A week later, their partnership had led them into the knee-deep waters of this Ugandan swamp. Before they left the U.S., when Cheese had asked Skwerl a few follow-up questions—Who they were repossessing the plane from? How had Skwerl gotten this job in the first place?—Skwerl had told Cheese that no questions asked was also part of the deal. But now, in the dark water, something long slithered past Cheese's leg. Cheese imagined a python . . . crocodile . . . or any variety of equatorial creature he'd only seen in movies . . .

He'd had enough.

If Cheese was going to stay in this swamp a minute longer, he wanted answers. Except the truth was Skwerl didn't have answers. Or at least not many, except to assure Cheese that "This job came from a network I trust."

Up ahead, near the fence line, a dog barked. Before those barks could form a cadence, there was a high-pitched yelp that seemed to swallow itself and then abrupt silence. Skwerl and Cheese glanced at one another. One of the many assurances Skwerl had given to Cheese and his wife in their living room the week before was that no one would get hurt—Skwerl hadn't said anything about dogs getting hurt. "You don't have any clue where H is from?" Cheese asked with a nervy ring to his voice.

"Not really."

"You didn't ask?"

"He's not asking us questions, so I'm not asking him questions."

"But your *network* says you can trust him." Cheese pressed down on the word skeptically. H's appearance—at least to Cheese—didn't inspire trust. A blond-haired, blue-eyed Übermensch, with skin the palest Wonder Bread shade of white, H would've been perfectly cast in *Die Hard* as one of Hans Gruber's Germanic henchmen. Skwerl's slightly manic squirrel-brain, the part of his genius that made unlikely associations, had a tendency to fixate on movies, which was why he'd mentioned *Die Hard* to Cheese—making a joke about the Nakatomi Plaza Christmas party and *Ho, Ho, Ho, now I have a machine gun*—but Cheese didn't laugh, and it wasn't because he hadn't seen *Die Hard*.

"He doesn't sound German," said Cheese. "His accent, it is more Afrikaans."

"Afrikaans? Maybe."

"Definitely. Every time H opens his mouth it's like he's about to say"—and now Cheese slid into his best parody of a white Afrikaner—"'That Nelson Mandela is a real wanker' . . . or 'A German shepherd is a *very* fine animal . . .'"

A rustling in the brush up ahead was followed by a single, pulsing light.

This was the signal they'd been waiting for. Skwerl smacked Cheese playfully on the shoulder, as if to say I told you he'd come back. Whether H was German, Austrian, or South African, it hardly mattered. They'd get this plane off the ground, hand it over to H's colleagues at a friendly airstrip, and collect their million.

"C'mon," Skwerl whispered.

SKWERL AND CHEESE SLOSHED THROUGH THE SWAMP. THEY climbed its near bank and met H at the edge of the jungle. The shadows ended where a band of arc lights fell on a clearing before the airfield's perimeter fence. As Cheese and Skwerl approached, H's gaze was fixed ahead. "There," he said with an accent that turned every *th* into a *z*. H formed his hand into a small, decisive karate chop that he thrust toward a breach in the chain-link fence. "We'll get in through there, and then it's a sprint to the jet." H did a second chop toward an open hangar, where the Challenger 600 sat on a landing pad, immaculate and gleaming, distinctly out of place on so remote an airfield. Clearly, someone was hiding it. As to why, Skwerl had no idea. And he knew not to ask questions, not if he hoped for his payday.

H checked his watch. "The guards change in four minutes. You have the flight plan ready?"

From his cargo pocket, Cheese removed two laminated cards hung on a binder ring. Typically, the details of the flight plan would be entered into the plane's onboard computer. To avoid detection, Cheese would fly with only the most rudimentary avionics switched on. Meticulously written on a template in permanent pen was his flight plan, the headings and speed for each leg of their journey, the radio beacon frequencies they'd navigate from instead of GPS, every detail he'd need to take them to their destination, JetEx, an FBO at Aéroport Marseille in the south of France. Total flight time, three hours, forty-six minutes. After that, Cheese and Skwerl would fly home commercial. Some other crew would take the Challenger 600 to its final destination, which neither Skwerl nor Cheese needed, or wanted, to know.

Four minutes passed. H gave a single nod and the three of them ran at a crouch toward the fence. As they approached the sheared-through section that was peeled back, Skwerl noticed it was too large for H to have cut himself. Clearly, H had someone on the inside. Whoever this was had not only helped him with the fence but also was helping him coordinate their arrival, so it fell between guard shifts. As they sprinted up to the flat expanse of the airfield, there wasn't a guard in sight. Skwerl understood the importance—on any mission—of compartmentalization. Everyone had their job. And everyone got their percentage. Cheese's job was to fly the plane. Skwerl's job was to deliver Cheese, an off-the-books pilot, to the airfield. This was, in many ways, the same as Skwerl's job when he'd worked for the Office. Back then, he'd managed off-the-books armies for the U.S. government. Not much had changed. Everyone was still getting their cut.

H led the way as they angled their bodies through the fence. They jogged a few steps and then Cheese stutter-stepped. Lying in a heap on the ground was a dog. Blood flecked its mottled brown-and-white coat. Its tongue lolled out the side of its mouth, its head half splattered. Little pieces of brain and skull sifted into the grass. When that dog had barked, H must've blown its brains out with a silenced pistol.

Cheese stood gazing down at the dog. Skwerl bumped into him. "Let's go," he whispered in a single impatient breath, and they continued to run toward the Challenger 600, catching up with H as they covered the last hundred meters. But the sight of the dog also gave Skwerl pause. Not because he was an animal lover. Because he didn't have a gun. Neither did Cheese. And H did.

A few steps short of the hangar, H held up his hand. The three of them lined up one behind the other, forming a stack near the broad double doors. H craned his neck forward, peering inside. Without unlocking his gaze from the jet, H waved at Cheese and Skwerl. They ran into the hangar bay. The aircraft hatch was open, its retractable stairs slung onto the ground. H and Skwerl climbed aboard. Cheese remained outside. He began circling the jet. A pilot through and through, no matter the circumstances, Cheese wouldn't take up an aircraft without at least a cursory pre-flight inspection. He was, some had argued, one of the best pilots in Afghanistan. That was why the Americans called him Cheese—as in "The Big Cheese." He ran his palm over the trailing edge of the right and then left wing, searching for dents that might affect the jet's aerodynamic performance . . . he kicked the tires on the landing gear, to make sure both were fully inflated . . . he manually rotated the left and then right aileron . . . everything looked good.

Cheese grabbed a ladder from a nearby maintenance station

littered with tools—socket wrenches, spanner wrenches, replacement bearings and bolts. When he leaned it against the back of the Challenger 600, so he could check for obstructions in the twin turbofan engines, H muttered, "He's taking too long."

Skwerl agreed. He stepped toward the cabin hatch. Before he could poke his head outside and tell Cheese that they needed to go—as in *right now*—an exit door creaked open on the far side of the hangar. Tracks of overhead halogen bulbs blinkered on in a dark corner.

Cheese froze on the ladder.

Skwerl crouched inside the skin of the plane. Carefully, he peeked through one of the portholes. A guard, wearing the nondescript uniform of a private security contracting company—black polo shirt, khaki cargo pants, black ball cap—ducked into a corner office. In this moment, Cheese began climbing down the ladder one cautious step at a time. He'd only made it halfway before the guard reappeared with a rifle slung over his shoulder—he must have retrieved it from the office. He carried the rifle casually, the way a woman might carry her handbag. It wasn't a very good rifle, an old model AK-47 with a wooden as opposed to composite buttstock, with no modifications or pickatinny rail to mount an optic. The guard took two steps into the hangar. He saw Cheese balanced on the ladder, frozen in place, dangling four rungs from the ground.

"Can I help you with something?" the guard asked rather politely.

Inside the aircraft, Skwerl remained crouched at the window. He glanced over his shoulder at H, who was also frozen in a crouch. How had H screwed this up? The guards weren't supposed to be on shift. How come this guy hadn't gotten the word? H shrugged his shoulders, as if he knew what Skwerl was thinking.

"Just finishing up pre-flight," Cheese said with an overlay of casualness.

The guard seemed confused. "We don't have any departures manifested until the morning." He'd taken a few steps closer. He'd also repositioned his rifle, so it wasn't slung over his shoulder anymore. He'd punched his left arm through its three-point sling, so he was wearing it cross-body, in the ready carry, its muzzle pointed toward the ground, its buttstock nestled near his right shoulder, his palm brooding on the pistol grip. With a single movement, he'd be ready to fire.

Cheese stepped down from the ladder, which he pulled away from the back of the Challenger 600. "Must be a mix-up," he said as he stowed the ladder amongst the maintainer's wrenches, bearings, and bolts.

"I'm going to need to see some identification."

Inside the jet, when H heard this, he made a move, as if this was enough and he would now take matters into his own hands. Skwerl remembered what H had done to the dog. He positioned himself between H and the hatch. A standoff ensued. Which, outside the jet, gave Cheese enough time to hand over his pilot's license.

The guard gazed down at the plastic card. A smile spread across his face, as if recognizing an old friend. He glanced up at Cheese and then down again at the card, shaking his head side to side. "Chi tor hasti, Commandance Iqbal?"

"Khob, tashakor," said Cheese, a little startled, answering the guard's greeting of *How are you?* with a simple *Good, thank you.* Cheese transitioned away from his native Dari and back to English: "I'm sorry, but do we know one another?"

"You're Commander Aziz Iqbal, yes? . . . The one the Americans called Big Cheese Aziz. You flew out of Eagle Base, in Kabul. I worked security at the airfield."

Cheese clasped the guard warmly by the arm. "Yes, of course . . . Now please remind me of your name."

With a single movement, the guard rotated his rifle, so it wasn't slung across his body and once again hung casually on his shoulder. "Ali Safi." When Cheese offered his hand, Ali Safi took it. But then he brought Cheese closer, pinning him to his chest. The two shared an awkward embrace, a kind of overly familiar bro-hug. "I'm sure there's been a mix-up, Commandance. Allow me to place a phone call and we'll have you on your way."

"And how did you wind up here, in Kampala?" Cheese asked Ali Safi. Not because he was interested but because he was playing for time. Cheese's eyes darted up at the fuselage, at the portholes from where H and Skwerl were no doubt watching this exchange.

Ali Safi's posture slumped, as if to answer this question required the shouldering of a physical burden. And he began his story, explaining how, like so many others, when the Taliban had entered Kabul, he fled to the airport. Because Ali Safi hadn't worked for the Americans in an official capacity, he wasn't evacuated to the U.S. He'd wound up—like Cheese—in one of those third countries that immigration officials called "lily pads." The governments of these countries (an ad hoc assortment, from Mexico to Montenegro to Uganda) had decided it was good policy to grant the U.S. this favor, trusting that one day it might be returned.

"Three times, the U.S. embassy has rejected my application for a visa," said Ali Safi. "But, Mashallah, I'm better off than others. I am safe from the Talibs. I have a roof over my head. And I've found work." Ali Safi glanced down at his shirt, at the crest embroidered over his left breast pocket. A Fairbairn-Sykes dagger, the symbol of commandos the world over, stabbed through the globe. The script beneath read *DRCA Global* in block letters.

"How long have you worked at D-R-C-A?"

"Quite a long while. But today is only my second day at this airfield." Ali Safi announced this detail as if it was proof that some hidden hand, some minor providence, was the architect of their encounter. For Cheese, it answered a different question, which was why this one unfortunate guard had shown up at the hangar when the others had gotten the word to stay away.

Then Ali Safi noticed the legs of Cheese's trousers, where he'd waded through the swamp—they were soaked. He asked Cheese how this had happened.

Cheese, trying to buy more time, struggled to think of anything to say.

He wouldn't need to.

INSIDE THE JET, AMONG ITS PLUSH SURROUNDINGS—THE SEATS upholstered in latte-colored leather; the polished mahogany surfaces; and the service, a mix of heavy crystal tumblers, delicate champagne flutes, and fine porcelains so intricately painted one could see the flimsy brushstrokes—it was here that Skwerl and H continued their standoff.

Skwerl had placed his body between H and the hatch. Neither spoke; they couldn't for fear of tipping off the guard outside. But H's cold blue eyes were calculating angles, his body moving imperceptibly to gain advantage so that he might barrel past Skwerl. At which point H would kill the guard, much as he'd killed the dog at the gate. Skwerl knew this was what H would do. It wasn't that Skwerl was squeamish about killing—he'd done plenty of it over the years. But he hadn't come here to kill anyone. Which was why he was blocking the hatch.

H shifted his weight to the left. Skwerl followed. And then H exploded to the right. Skwerl flung himself at H, catching him from behind at the waist.

"WHAT'S THAT NOISE?" ALI SAFI ASKED.

He took a first and then a second step toward the jet. In those steps two things happened: first, Ali Safi glimpsed H, who stood in the hatch but was unable to take another step as if an invisible tether fixed him inside; second, H was reaching for his waist. Ali Safi wouldn't have understood this second gesture—*What is this angry blond man reaching for so desperately?*

But Cheese understood . . . the barking dog at the gate.

He never would've worked with H—or even been in the same room with H—if Skwerl hadn't vouched for him, and, truth be told, if Cheese hadn't so desperately needed the commission that came with this job. Five hundred grand for a few days' work. How could he refuse? If the difference between a soldier and a mercenary is that a soldier kills for a cause while a mercenary kills for money, Cheese had stopped being a soldier a long time ago. But he wasn't ready to see Ali Safi killed, at least not yet, and not for five hundred grand.

H had his pistol drawn by the time Ali Safi took his third step. The pistol, a palm-sized Glock 43, no larger than a toy, had a black suppressor affixed to its muzzle. That suppressor, a carbonite cylinder that was longer and heavier than the pistol itself, was unwieldy at close quarters, throwing the pistol out of balance. This gave Cheese an extra fraction of a second. Ali Safi turned around, his eyes shiny and wide, his mouth frozen, his expression captured by fear as if set in a sculptor's cast. His pleading eyes fixed on Cheese, who already gripped a DeWalt 8" all-steel adjustable wrench. He had snatched it from the mechanic's kit.

In a single motion, Cheese knocked Ali Safi on the head.

THEY HADN'T KILLED HIM.

The wrench fell from Cheese's hand, clanking to the ground. He bent over Ali Safi. A strong steady pulse. Not too much blood. Inside the Challenger 600, Skwerl released his grip from around H's waist and toppled onto the plush carpet. H was standing over Skwerl, his pistol leveled. All it would take was a flick of his finger. But H thought better of it. He leaned out the hatch and aimed his pistol across the hangar, in the direction of the unconscious Ali Safi. But Cheese was in his line of sight.

"We don't have time for that!" Cheese shouted at H before he sprinted back over to the jet, pulled the chocks, climbed through the hatch, and hoisted up the stairs behind him. He took a final look at Ali Safi, who'd had quite the second day on the job. He would wake up with a crushing headache and, hopefully, a bout of short-term amnesia.

Cheese folded himself into the pilot's seat. H sat beside him, not because he could pilot—or even copilot—the jet, but to keep an eye on Cheese. They didn't need to put on their headsets; there was no tower they'd be radioing, no permissions they'd be requesting. The engines fired. The gyros hummed. The Challenger 600 trundled forward, out of the hangar, onto the runway.

Not a soul in sight.

Skwerl, who sat comfortably in the back, was thinking that aside from Ali Safi everything had more or less gone according to plan. They'd land at JetEx in Marseille. Another crew would take over. He and Cheese would get a wire for a half-million each. They'd board flights home—him to his farm outside of Philly, Cheese to his apartment outside of Austin. Then Skwerl remembered the dog, its mottled fur splattered with blood, the little flecks of its skull sifted into the grass—okay, he thought, aside from Ali Safi *and the dog* everything had gone according to plan.

When they got to the edge of the runway, Skwerl stepped into the cabin. With his left hand on the back of Cheese's headrest and his right hand on the back of H's, he craned his neck forward. The three stared straight ahead, their eyes adjusting to the darkness. The stillness created an intimacy between them. Cheese edged the throttle forward while, like a dancer, he rolled on the balls of his feet, depressing the rudder pedals, holding the brakes as the engines came to full power.

Then he released. They hurtled down the runway. Cheese didn't have to check his instruments to know when they hit rotation speed. He could feel it through the shuddering controls and through his seat, that moment when the jet becomes aerodynamic, when its wings lift. Cheese pulled back on the yoke. They floated up, airborne, the runway receding behind them, the dark smudge of jungle expanding beneath, a rash of stars overhead.

H was sitting beside Cheese—his silenced pistol balanced on his knee.

"You going to put that thing away?" asked Cheese with his gaze fixed out the cockpit and into the night.

H leaned forward, tucking the pistol back into the holster on his waistband.

"No one said anything about shooting anyone."

"No one got shot," said Skwerl.

"He was going to shoot that guard."

"I wasn't going to shoot him," said H. "I was simply going to scare him."

"Yes, by shooting him."

"Quite a coincidence that Ali Safi would recognize you," said H, who'd clearly been paying attention to the exchange in the hangar. He spoke these words as a challenge, as if Cheese and Skwerl had as much explaining to do over this unfortunate encounter as H did.

"Not so remarkable," said Cheese. "Where do you think soldiers go when the war is over? We still need to make a living. That someone like Ali Safi has to work as a guard is no different than me. Why do you think I'm flying this jet?"

"You don't need to lecture me on being a soldier."

Because H mentioned the subject, Cheese asked him about his time soldiering. Where was he from exactly? Which army had he served in? H told Cheese that perhaps he should focus on flying, that the three of them would go their separate ways once they landed in Marseille, that it was best not to know too much about the other. But Cheese wouldn't let it go. He told H that he couldn't place his accent. Was it Afrikaans? Or perhaps Rhodesian? With this question came an implied accusation, that H had served in the armies of one of those criminal regimes. Was this why H played so coy with his nationality? On and on they went.

Skwerl left Cheese and H to bicker. He was tired and hungry and climbed into the back of the jet. He collapsed onto one of the plush executive seats. It was wide and luxurious, as fine a chair as Skwerl had ever seen, even as nice as the La-Z-Boy ProMax currently installed in his home office, a gift to himself years ago after a particularly rough deployment when he worked at the Office. Skwerl removed his hiking boots and socks, which were wet from the swamp. Like an idiot he'd worn jeans. He rolled them up over his calves with difficulty. Skwerl was messing around with the footrest—trying to get it fully parallel, like his one at home—when he noticed a wicker snack basket tucked into a small galley kitchen. He ambled across the cabin, squinching his toes together on the plush carpet underfoot. The snack basket—very high-end, from Fortnum & Mason—was bountiful. Skwerl picked out a wedge of Manchego cheese, a circle of gouda, sliced prosciutto, a salami, there were some olives too (Castelvetranos, his favorite), a little bottle of red from a vineyard he'd never heard of (whatever, probably still good), apricots, dried cherries, some crackers, and sliced baguette rounds.

Above Skwerl, in a lacquered wooden cabinet, were three dozen intricately painted plates. He took one down and loaded it with food. Then he took another one down, filling it as well. He also took one of the crystal tumblers, which he balanced on top of the second plate, and returned to his seat. Barefoot, he sat with his legs extended, a feast laid before him. Using a palm-sized buck knife and one of the plates as a cutting board, he hacked off a slice of salami, paired it with a cracker, and ate the mini sandwich in a single bite. He washed it down with a mouthful of wine. He shut his eyes and even wiggled his toes, delicious.

The bickering between H and Cheese in the cockpit had petered out. The Challenger 600 proved a remarkably quiet aircraft. Aside from the gentle, almost Zen-like hum of its engines, the only sound was Skwerl. He continued with his little picnic. The knife smacking down as he cut the salami and cheese. Him contentedly crunching his crackers and slurping his wine. Until H wandered into the cabin.

"What do you think you're doing?"

Skwerl's mouth was full. "Eating," he said, blowing crumbs onto his shirtfront. "Want some?" He firmly gripped the salami and slammed down his knife, which clinked loudly against the plate. A fleck of porcelain chipped off its rim. "Whoops." Skwerl finished constructing the cracker sandwich and offered it to H.

H reached toward him, but it wasn't for the sandwich. He snatched away the plate. Skwerl's picnic dumped across the table.

"What the hell you do that for?"

H ignored Skwerl. He was holding the plate at eye level, examining it with a jeweler's fastidiousness. He began to curse in his native language, uttering quick guttural words as if he were conjuring a Nordic spell. Then he leaned in close to Skwerl, holding the plate up to his face. "Look what you've done." With his fingernail, H traced a crack that began at the plate's center and ended on its rim, where, among a brocade of hand-painted flowers, Skwerl had scratched both the porcelain and segments of the pattern, the damage no doubt caused by the blade of his knife.

"Bad luck," said Skwerl. "Sorry about that."

H dumped the food off Skwerl's other plate. He disappeared into the galley, where Skwerl could see him giving both plates a more thorough examination before wiping them clean and returning them to their place, secure in the wooden cabinet. H returned with a plastic plate; this must've been what the crew ate off. With bare hands, he heaped Skwerl's picnic from the table and back onto this cheaper plate. "There," he said when he was done, brushing his palms together. "Eat off that, and please don't make such a mess. This isn't our jet."

Skwerl was tempted to ask, *Whose jet is it?* But he caught himself. That impulse, to ask a question he wouldn't receive an answer to, had gotten him in trouble in the past. No good would come from pushing H any further. Skwerl needed that commission. A half-million would solve a lot of problems for him, the mortgage on his farm back home being the least of them. Don't lose sight of what's important, he thought. The only time in his career that he'd ever opened his mouth, he'd come to regret it.

H climbed around the cabin, shutting out the overhead lights, sliding down the window shades. He reached beneath his seat and removed an amenities kit, like the ones in first class on a commercial airliner. A little more than three hours remained in their flight and H seemed determined to put them to good use. From the kit, H replaced his shoes with a pair of socks, the kind with rubber treads on the bottoms. He held his shoulder-length blond hair back with his strong hand while slotting a foam earplug into each ear. Finally, he slid on a plush sleep mask that tastefully matched the jet's interior. He lay on his back, fully extended, with his hands folded over his chest. He appeared medieval, a crusader laid out for his funeral rites.

Tired as he was, Skwerl couldn't sleep. And the idea of sitting in the dark interior of the plane with H didn't appeal. He grabbed his snacks and climbed into the cockpit beside Cheese.

"You must be starving."

Cheese was gazing into his instruments. "Sure, I could eat."

Skwerl pulled out his knife. He made one of his cracker sandwiches, which Cheese reached for without breaking concentration. Cheese took a bite, chewed a couple of times. "This is good, what's in it?"

"Manchego. Sausage."

"Pork sausage?"

Before Skwerl could answer, Cheese was spitting out the food into his cupped palm. Skwerl began to apologize. "Oh Christ, you can't eat that, can you? Shit, sorry . . . I always forget this little stuff."

Cheese looked at him, bewildered. He thought to himself: *That's why you assholes lost the war.* But instead he said, "Don't worry about it."

LIKE AFTER ANY HEIST, THEY SPLIT UP. ON LANDING IN
Marseille, Cheese stayed with the Challenger 600 at the airport,
sleeping the night in its cabin, while Skwerl and H left for two
separate hotels in the city center. H had arranged everything,
a reservation for him at the InterContinental and a second
reservation for Skwerl at the Comfort Suites. Skwerl hadn't stayed
at the InterContinental in Marseille before, but he'd stayed at other
InterContinentals, and he was certain that, unlike the Comfort
Suites, their rooms didn't reek of wet cigarettes or have slightly
discolored pillowcases on the bed. Skwerl's room did have a view
of the water. It looked directly out onto the Château d'If, the island
fortress and prison facing the city. After considering the view,
Skwerl left his blinds closed.

Skwerl decided to explore the city, checking the banking app on
his phone hourly while he waited for his commission to arrive by
wire transfer. It wasn't his first time in Marseille. His last visit had
been nearly a decade before, on a port call. For forty-eight hours,
he and half a dozen Marines had canvassed the bars around the
Old Port. They'd met some girls on their second and final night.
The girls hardly spoke English (and they hardly spoke French), but
language had little to do with what each was looking for as they
paired off with a discernment no greater than who happened to be
sitting next to whom. The girls had invited them from the bar to a

dance club. Skwerl couldn't remember the club's name anymore. If he could've, he might've tried to find it in this fit of nostalgia as he wandered the city.

What Skwerl did remember about the club was that it had a dress code. No shorts allowed. And, of course, he'd been the only one in their group wearing shorts—jean shorts. He'd been in a panic as his friends (or supposed friends) ordered a pair of cabs. The French girl who'd assigned herself to him seemed appropriately disappointed. Of course, this wouldn't keep her from leaving Skwerl and going with his friends to the club. This is what she seemed to be explaining as, in halting English, she stitched together a pursed, red-lipsticked apology that Skwerl couldn't quite understand. Then, as she was stepping toward the exit and the cab that awaited, salvation arrived. A second group of Marines. This included Mac, who Skwerl had deployed with once before. Mac had famously earned a Silver Star for pulling two Marines out of an ambush in Nasiriyah. His Navy Cross would come later. But on that night, Mac performed what, in Skwerl's memory, was his single greatest act of valor. When Skwerl asked to swap his jean shorts for Mac's khakis, Mac agreed. No hesitation. They'd done it right at the bar, garnering an "Ohhh-la-la" from the girl with the red lipstick.

If Skwerl was thinking about Mac, it wasn't only because of his return to Marseille. He was thinking about Mac because it was Mac who had introduced him to Sheepdog. And Sheepdog was the reason Skwerl had made this trip.

Introduce might be too formal a word. About a year ago, not long before closing arguments in a civil case between Skwerl and the Office, Skwerl had bumped into Mac at a business conference for veterans turned entrepreneurs. By this point, Skwerl had become a controversial figure. His dispute with the Office—a claim of "on-the-job negligence" made by his boss, Uncle Tony, who by then was the chief of Ground Branch—was shrouded in the wildest rumors. This was why Skwerl was particularly grateful Mac had so willingly approached him, hand outstretched, a ready smile, eager to talk about old times and little else. Mac had transitioned out of special operations and started a company, Cyberdyne Security, which already had half a dozen lucrative contracts. "I just hit it at the right moment," Mac had said before asking Skwerl about his own fledgling business, in rope manufacturing.

"Rope?"

With the proper machinery, a rope business could be completely automated, or so Skwerl explained. It was perfect for him; once he'd set things up, secured accounts with a few reliable clients, he'd hardly have to work at all. "Also, there's not a single major rope manufacturer left in the United States. Not one. This isn't just rope. It's *American* rope."

"Enough to hang yourself with, Skwerl?"

"Ha. Ha."

His joking aside, Mac loved the idea, or at least had told Skwerl that he did. He'd asked about his customer base, who his clients were. When Skwerl explained that he was still building the foundations of his business, Mac offered up a contact of his. "Well, not a single contact," he'd explained, "more of a network. About a year ago, I was at another one of these conferences, this was when I was getting my business off the ground. I bumped into Tubes, remember Tubes?"—this was an Air Force combat controller Skwerl had worked with years ago—"He started this aviation supply company and he's already got contracts with Lockheed, Boeing, the big boys. Just killing it. He'd scored most of the contracts through a guy named Sheepdog."

"Sheepdog? Never heard of him."

"Me neither, but he runs something called 'the network.' Tubes got me signed up." Mac had then offered to do the same for Skwerl. All he needed was an email address and to have another network member vouch for him. Which Mac was happy to do. Skwerl took Mac up on the offer, and for the past year Skwerl had been getting messages from Sheepdog with his email address blind-copied along with other members, each message formatted the exact same way: *Sheepdogs, A member of the network* . . . and then the request. Most of these were anodyne: *A member of the network needs a reliable contact at the Embassy in Lisbon* . . . *is looking for medical supplies to ship to Ukraine* . . . *is hosting a fundraiser for a Congressional campaign.* But every fifth or sixth request was something outside the norm: *A member of the network is searching for a company that sells used F-16 parts* . . . *is looking for a flamethrower from WWII, operational or non-operational, for a charity event.* Skwerl, who in those years after leaving the Office felt increasingly at odds with the special operations community, would've unsubscribed from the network if it wasn't for these quirkier requests. He'd shown them to his girlfriend, Sinéad, who wasn't typically quick to laugh, and even she got a kick out of them.

Skwerl never thought he'd respond to one of these requests. But then he received a message that read: *Sheepdogs, A member of the network is searching for a commercial pilot with special operations experience for a short-term project, good pay. Inquire direct.—Sheepdog.*

Skwerl's rope business was struggling. He had unpaid legal bills and, after losing his civil suit for workplace negligence in spectacular fashion, the Office also had an eight-figure claim against him. Skwerl suddenly found himself considering Sheepdog's request. He figured whatever he earned on this "short-term project," presumably, would be off-the-books, not reportable W2 income, or business income the Office could repossess to fulfill its financial claim. He would be able to keep this money free and clear. He'd already gone through his savings and was living off whatever mattress money he could scrounge together, and he needed a little more. When Skwerl replied to Sheepdog, a response landed in his inbox in minutes. Over the next few days, Sheepdog made all the arrangements. He'd paid for Skwerl's flight to Austin so he could convince Cheese to come, and then he'd put them both on a commercial flight to Uganda, business class, with instructions that on landing they call a cellphone and ask for someone named "H."

At every stage, Sheepdog had acted decisively, with no delay. Which was why by the time Skwerl had finished walking around Marseille that first day he was increasingly concerned. The wire with his money still hadn't arrived. From the little Skwerl knew, this was very unlike Sheepdog.

THAT SECOND MORNING SKWERL COULDN'T DECIDE IF HE should pay H a visit at his hotel. All this waiting was making him nervous. He went for another walk, a little more sightseeing to clear his mind. He ambled past the Basilique Notre-Dame de la Garde built onto a spur of the old city overlooking the sea, and then he descended a warren of cobblestone paths toward the columned front of the Opéra Municipal, which seemed as good a destination as any. Walking north, on the Rue Paradis, through a canyon of prosperous little shops, he was lost in anxious thoughts when a certain display caught his eye. Among rows of porcelain tableware, a plate stood out—its pattern matched the plate he'd cracked on the jet.

A little bell chimed above the door as Skwerl stepped inside the shop. A fastidious gentleman, professorial in bearing, wearing wire rim glasses and a blue bowtie studded with white polka dots, intercepted him in the doorway. Taking an unbending glance at Skwerl, he forewent French and spoke directly in English, asking in a voice laden with skepticism whether he could be of assistance. Skwerl pointed to the plate in the window. He asked if he could look at it. A plan was already forming in Skwerl's mind. He'd bring the plate as a peace offering to H's hotel, replacing the one from the jet's collection that he'd cracked. It might not have been the perfect excuse, but it was a good enough excuse to get Skwerl over to the InterContinental. The gentleman, who introduced himself as the shop manager, handed Skwerl the plate. "These are the same motif of a service once used at Versailles," he said proudly, the name alone conjuring those mirrored and gold-pilastered halls. The shop manager then dipped behind a display case and returned with the manufacturer's catalogue, which he read, his voice assuming a new resonance, like that of a tour guide:

> "*At the Petit Trianon, Marie-Antoinette succeeded in creating the intimate setting that suited her. She overlooked no detail. Wanting to live among flowers, she had them woven, embroidered, recreated in gauze or porcelain. In 1781, she commissioned from the Manufacture Royale de Sèvres a service adorned with her two favorite motifs: cornflowers and pearls. Airily festooning the rims of plates and dishes, the decoration of the Marie-Antoinette service weds simplicity and refinement.*"

"That's some plate," said Skwerl. He flipped it over in his hands and the shop manager flinched, as if ready to dive to the floor after it. Skwerl shot him a disdainful glance before reading the manufacturer's name: *Bernardaud* painted in gold in a precise sans serif font on the back. The plate—with what he'd now learned were cornflowers and pearls banding its rim—was an exact match. "How much?"

Instead of saying the price, the shop manager wrote it discreetly in a looping cursive on a scrap of paper: *2,980 euros.*

"For a fuckin' plate!"

The shop's few patrons swept their eyes in Skwerl's direction. The shop manager, lowering his voice to a distinctly more discreet register, said, "No, monsieur. That is the price for the dinner service, which is a set of ten."

"Okay," said Skwerl, exhaling. "So how much for just one plate?"

"Monsieur, they are not sold in ones and twos. The service is purchased as a set . . . my apologies."

"One plate should be about three hundred." Skwerl took out a billfold and began peeling off euros.

"Please, monsieur. Dividing the set is not permitted."

"Alright then, four hundred." Skwerl made a cursory inspection of the shop. He grabbed a porcelain sugar jar, checked the price on its bottom, and placed it on the counter. "And I'll take this too." Skwerl placed a fifty-euro note beside the jar. He knew Cheese's wife was still upset that they'd run off together on this job; it'd be a nice touch, Skwerl thought, to deliver a souvenir, a peace offering for Fareeda.

The shop manager glanced anxiously at his other customers, who were now ambling toward the exit, seemingly disinclined to witness the remainder of this vulgar display; yet another American abroad with a conviction that everything had a price.

As the customers left, the shop manager followed them to the door. Skwerl thought he was going to plead quietly that they remain, but he simply stood there as they departed. When the last of them walked around the corner, he shut the door and bolted the lock. He flipped the shop's sign in the window from *open* to *closed*. The shop manager pivoted on his heels, stepped back inside, and, rather officiously, said, "Follow me, monsieur."

He dipped behind a heavy velvet curtain. This led to a storeroom. Stacked on railed metal shelves from floor to ceiling were boxes, each the dimensions of a vinyl record and thick as a paperback novel. Skwerl could read on their spines the high-end brand names—*Asprey*, *Ginori*, *de Gournay*—until he saw *Bernardaud* etched on stacks of turquoise boxes. "Help me a moment, please." The shop manager told Skwerl to hold the boxes steady as he removed one from near the bottom. Skwerl did as instructed, balancing two or three dozen plates—tens of thousands of dollars of merchandise—while the shop manager removed a single box from the stack, sliding out the plate inside, and then reinserting the empty box in the same position as before.

The shop manager stood, plate in hand; it was the Marie

Antoinette service Skwerl had been admiring. "You said four hundred, yes?"

Skwerl nodded.

"You understand why I can't include the box?"

Skwerl understood and handed over the fold of bills, which the shop manager re-counted before tucking them into his own pocket. He began rummaging around the storeroom again and returned with a plain white box. He lined this with old newspapers and nestled the plate inside, giving it to Skwerl. They exited the storeroom, returning to the front of the shop from behind the curtain. Sitting on the counter was the porcelain sugar bowl for Fareeda. "I'd also like to buy this," said Skwerl, again sliding over the fifty-euro note. The shop manager told him he could have the bowl for free. The owner of the store, his boss, sold them for forty euros apiece but made them for two euros at a little workshop down the road. "The owner's price isn't an honest one," he said. "Better that you just take it."

THE FOUR STORIES OF THE INTERCONTINENTAL HOTEL overlooked a descent of neighborhoods whose red-tiled roofs led to the Old Port. Cradled into the south-facing nook of the hotel's H-shaped footprint was a veranda the size of a soccer pitch where patrons lounged over mixed drinks and mayonnaise-y club sandwiches. The view faced the port, toward the yachts that lazed at anchor, their masts like the upturned lances of a chivalric order. Waiters shuttled through two side doors, while guests came and went by a single main entrance. This is where Skwerl had installed himself, watching that entrance, waiting for H to appear.

A first and then a second hour passed. Skwerl was confronting the prospect of a third when he decided to allow himself a minor indiscretion. He flagged down his waiter and gave a description of H: the Aryan jaw, the blue eyes, the shoulder-length blond hair. Had he, perhaps, noticed such a guest at the hotel? The waiter, who spoke halting English, stitched together his eyebrows. "He is like the model Fabio, but very white-skinned, yes?" Skwerl thought the henchman in *Die Hard* bore a stronger resemblance but *whatever*. Had the waiter seen him recently? "Oui, monsieur. He returned to the hotel perhaps an hour before you arrived." Skwerl tipped the waiter handsomely. He was about to offer a far larger tip in exchange for his friend's room number when, passing behind the waiter's shoulder, he recognized a face.

Skwerl could hardly believe it. He followed the man, who from behind carried himself with a head-up, shoulders-back dignity, advancing into the hotel at a slow, ceremonious walk. Skwerl then caught a longer look at him in profile waiting at the bank of elevators in the lobby. It was definitely him. Any doubt Skwerl had about the man's identity vanished when he glimpsed a white adhesive bandage affixed to the base of his skull, right where Cheese had struck him two days before with a DeWalt 8" all-steel adjustable wrench.

Ali Safi was dressed elegantly, which initially threw Skwerl off. His suit, a deep shade of midnight blue, was double breasted, immaculately tailored with peaked lapels. His brown leather shoes had a shine, and he wore a silk knit tie, expertly knotted, that jutted out from his collar proud as a man's chin. Tucked beneath his arm was a leather attaché, a rich, almost marbled shade of auburn, much like his shoes. In stature and poise, he appeared indistinguishable from a corporate executive, except for the bandage at his skull.

The elevator chimed as it arrived. Ali Safi stepped inside, alone. The doors shut and Skwerl gazed above them, to where an antique elevator dial swept its hand up to the third of the InterContinental's four floors; here, it stopped. Skwerl crossed the lobby and shouldered open a door that led to a nearby stairwell. With his shopping bag cradled beneath his arm, he took the steps two at a time.

Skwerl was on the third-floor landing in a matter of seconds, only slightly out of breath. Through a sliver of a window at the stairwell door he glimpsed Ali Safi walking casually down the corridor until he stopped at a corner room, number 317, likely a suite. Ali Safi didn't knock, and he didn't remove his room key. He glanced up and down the corridor a final time and reached into his attaché. He removed what looked like a dry erase marker, crouched low, and inserted its tip into the base of the door's electric key card reader. Back when Skwerl had worked for the Office, he'd attended several courses run by the Directorate of Science and Technology on "non-permissive entry," a euphemism for breaking and entering on behalf of the U.S. government. A basic circuit with a pre-programmed microcontroller could defeat ninety percent of these hotel locks. All you had to do was plug the microcontroller into the port on the bottom of the lock. The circumference of that port was about the size of a dry erase marker's tip.

Ali Safi slowly turned the door's handle while dropping the dry erase marker back into his attaché. As he leaned into the door, it only opened partway. The chain lock was on. Ali Safi didn't miss a beat. He reached back into his attaché and removed a large rubber band. Skwerl knew exactly what this was for, he'd learned the same technique himself. With his shoulder leaning against the door, Ali Safi looped the rubber band around the chain, so his trigger finger was threaded through both ends of the rubber band. He then slammed the door shut, keeping the handle depressed so it wouldn't lock again, while simultaneously yanking the rubber band. This caught the chain, causing it to fly off its latch. Before any reaction came from inside, Ali Safi had stepped into the room, firmly shutting the door behind him.

THIRTY MINUTES BLED AWAY AS SKWERL STOOD ON THE staircase landing, waiting for Ali Safi to emerge from what must have been H's room. Skwerl harbored no particular affection for H, but he was praying that when the door to the room opened both he and Ali Safi would appear. Imagining this best of possible outcomes, Skwerl thought he might sprint back down the staircase to the lobby, intercept them both, and figure out why he and Cheese had yet to get paid; and, with this settled, he'd be happy to receive no further explanation as to the strange relationship that existed between H and Ali Safi. But this wasn't meant to be.

When the door to room 317 did open, only Ali Safi appeared. He remained neatly dressed, every hair in place, his tie still perfectly knotted—no sign of a struggle. As he strode down the corridor, a young couple, perhaps newlyweds, approached from the opposite direction. They were rushing to their room as if to unburden themselves of some irresistible urge. Ali Safi offered them a broad, knowing smile, which, in the moment he delivered it, caused the young woman to clutch the young man a little tighter.

Still wearing that smile, Ali Safi disappeared into the elevator, and the couple disappeared into their room, which was next door to 317. The corridor was empty again, and Skwerl finally stepped out from the staircase. He approached the door to H's room, moving as quickly as he could without breaking into a run. He placed his ear to the jamb, not a sound inside. He knocked on the door gently with the knuckle of his middle finger, again not a sound (though he could now hear the urgent little gasps of the couple one room over). Unlike Ali Safi, he didn't have a microcontroller, let alone one that neatly fit into the body of a dry erase marker. However, in his wallet, he had a debit card. At the same non-permissive entry course where he'd learned about the dry erase marker, he'd also learned that, in certain cases, a debit card strip, if properly remagnetized, could fool an e-card reader. Skwerl was struggling to recall the technique, though he remembered a diagram of a rectangle of tinfoil held in place by Vaseline on the card's back—*was that right?*

Skwerl didn't have any Vaseline. He did have some ChapStick in his pocket. He didn't have any tinfoil, but he had a piece of foil-lined wrapping paper in his shopping bag. He smeared the

ChapStick, which was cherry flavored, all over his debit card. Then he neatly folded that debit card inside the wrapping paper as if it were a gift. He was making a cherry-scented mess right as one of the maids appeared behind him, ready to begin the evening turndown service.

He froze.

The maid left her cart in the corridor and walked directly toward him with a scold cemented to her face. She glanced at Skwerl, who had stuffed the foil-wrapped debit card into his pocket, and then at the key card reader, which was smeared with ChapStick. But her scold had little to do with him; rather, it was for the young couple whose muted "ohs" and "ahs" escaped into the corridor. "I hope you weren't planning to take a nap," said the maid, arching a well-plucked eyebrow as she glanced at their door before unlocking 317 with the master key tethered to her apron. With complete disinterest in Skwerl, and utter fatigue in her own work, she returned down the corridor, disappearing into a room on its far side, the towels, soaps, and shampoos in her cart jingle-jangling as she dragged it behind her.

The drawn shades . . . the sparse light . . . the already stale air . . . Skwerl didn't need to take two steps into the room to tell that someone had died here. H lay in the bed, the white comforter tucked up under his arms, his hands folded neatly over his chest, his legs outstretched, his body arrayed in the same crusader funeral pose as before, the one he'd slept in on the flight to Marseille. Skwerl could recognize death at a glance, though he still checked for a pulse, placing his index and middle finger to the still warm skin above H's carotid artery. The eyes were wide open, his opalescent gaze fixed to the ceiling. A froth, like a child's depleted baking soda volcano, bubbled from his lips.

Skwerl stomped around in the gloom, making a quick inspection of the hotel room. He noticed a daub of blood staining the hem of the comforter. Carefully, Skwerl pulled back where it was folded beneath H's armpit. This revealed a freshly adhered bandage not much larger than a postage stamp. Given the location and dimensions, Skwerl thought he knew what this was: a meat tag. Two decades ago, before his first deployment to Iraq, the ubiquitous tattoo parlors around Lejeune used to give them. The idea was to ink your name and service number (in case of Americans your SSN) onto your body. That way if you wound up shredded by an IED, or burned beyond recognition when your Humvee, or Bradley, or Stryker's gas tank torched, you could be promptly identified. For a grunt of any nation, a meat tag was an article of faith. It was like the "little black box" on an airplane. No matter how bad the crash, that part of you would survive.

Except in this case.

When Skwerl peeled back the bandage from H's side, it didn't reveal a meat tag but a missing strip of skin, no larger than a clothing label and cut away as if with a scalpel. Ali Safi had not only known the exact identity of his target, but he'd also known the precautions to take to erase that identity, and if Ali Safi was willing to take these measures against H—to include carving up his body—then he'd certainly do the same to Skwerl; and—it also dawned on Skwerl—he'd do the same to Cheese.

Skwerl sprinted out of H's room, down into the lobby, and to a taxi.

He had to get to the airport.

THE TAXI COULDN'T DRIVE FAST ENOUGH. IF ALI SAFI HAD killed H that meant he was also coming for Skwerl and Cheese. The only question was in what order. Ali Safi had left the hotel about ten minutes before Skwerl. If he'd chosen to travel directly to the airport, there was no way Skwerl could beat him there, no matter how fast he coaxed his taxi driver to go. But if Ali Safi stopped at Skwerl's hotel first, to ambush him in his room as he'd ambushed H, then Skwerl had a chance.

Skwerl checked his watch. It was nearly 5 p.m. He would call the Comfort Suites in another ten minutes. This would give Ali Safi ample time to arrive from the InterContinental across the Old Port, at which point Skwerl would inquire with the front desk as to whether "a friend of his" had come around, ". . . well-dressed, a blue double-breasted suit, leather attaché, an Omar Sharif–looking fellow . . ." *Dr. Zhivago*, *Lawrence of Arabia*, even *Top Secret!* . . . Sharif at his best!

Focus, thought Skwerl, as he reeled in his squirrel brain. And what if he beat Ali Safi to the airport? The taxi driver had taken Skwerl's encouragement to heart. The speedometer on the dash was edging north of 160kph as they passed one car after another on the outside lane. He called Cheese and it went to voicemail. Skwerl listened to the recording, the opening bars of Kenny Loggins's "Danger Zone," followed by Cheese saying, "Leave a message," a beep, and then the cell carrier announcing that the voicemail was full. He tried a second and third time before giving up.

Skwerl began to think . . . If he reached Cheese first, they'd need a plan . . . But where would they go? . . . A hotel wouldn't do . . . Ali Safi would track them down, and neither knew the city well enough to hide out . . . Also, they would lose their commission on the jet if they left it behind . . . That was a lot of money . . . And so, the plan became obvious . . . They'd use the jet, simply take off and go; they could worry about where once they'd gotten in the air. Skwerl stared vacantly out the window and soon caught himself humming, ". . . highway to, *the danger zone* . . ."

As Skwerl sped north on the A22, he glimpsed a squadron of freighters out his window trundling around the commercial port. The afternoon sun held at an angle behind them, casting narrow silhouettes of the freighters across the wind-disturbed Mediterranean. Inside the port, longshoremen stacked and restacked shipping containers, their Sisyphean work like the ceaseless founding and raising of an uninhabited city. The port soon disappeared over Skwerl's left shoulder. The airport was only fifteen minutes away.

Skwerl dialed the Comfort Suites. He asked whether anyone had called for him or if a man meeting a certain description— double-breasted suit, bandage on the neck—had recently visited. Skwerl was passed from a receptionist to someone in reservations and finally to a woman at the front desk, who said that a man meeting that description had only just left.

"When?"

"Perhaps two minutes ago."

Skwerl glanced at his watch again. The drive to the airport was twenty-five minutes. As the taxi driver pulled up to the JetEx main office, Skwerl was calculating that this gave him a twenty-minute lead on Ali Safi. Not a ton of time, but enough to find Cheese and get up in the air. As luck would have it, Skwerl wouldn't have to search far. When he stepped inside the JetEx office, Cheese was signing forms at the reception counter. Skwerl sauntered up beside him, placing his shopping bag with the porcelains—the plate and sugar bowl for Fareeda—beside Cheese. In the calmest voice Skwerl could muster, he said, "C'mon. We gotta go."

"What are you doing here?" Cheese handed the forms to a member of the ground crew, who handed him a receipt in carbon copy.

"Are we fueled up?"

"Yes," said Cheese, glancing down at the receipt like it was a lottery ticket he wasn't sure he should toss or play. "What's in that bag?"

"Some dishes."

"Dishes . . . ? How about our money? Did you bring that?"

"H is dead."

This brought Cheese to silence. He glanced at the member of the ground crew, a kid with a sunken chest and greasy hair in coveralls who couldn't have been much more than twenty. The kid averted his eyes, but he'd clearly heard Skwerl.

"Alright," said Cheese. "Let's go."

The Challenger 600 was parked in a low-priority spot a few hundred meters down the tarmac. As Skwerl and Cheese headed for the door, the kid offered to save them the walk and drive them in a golf cart. The ride was brief, a little over a minute, a fact Skwerl noted as he was closely monitoring the time. After dropping them, the kid headed back to the JetEx main office. Skwerl hurried aboard the jet while Cheese began circling its fuselage, checking the landing gear, running his hands down the surface of the wings, just as he'd done in Kampala, conducting his final pre-flight inspection.

"C'mon, we don't have time for that."

Cheese told Skwerl this would take another two minutes. "We've got that much time, don't we?"

Skwerl glanced again at his watch. They did, but not much more. As Skwerl climbed into the cockpit, he passed the galley kitchen; that's when he glimpsed the dishes, to include the plate he'd broken, and suddenly realized that he'd forgotten his shopping bag on the reception counter inside JetEx. This included the gift for Fareeda. No sooner had Skwerl realized this than he heard the hollow, high-pitched sound of a horn blaring from the taxiway. Skwerl climbed to the jet's hatch. When he stuck his head outside, he saw the kid from before. He was honking his golf cart's horn, calling out to Skwerl and Cheese, while driving with one hand. With his other hand, he was holding the shopping bag aloft like a lantern, intent that they not leave without it—wherever it was they were going.

Skwerl checked his watch.

The kid parked his golf cart in front of the right wing, so it blocked the jet. "You almost forgot this." He clambered out of the golf cart, a little out of breath and unduly relieved to have caught them in time. He handed the shopping bag to Skwerl. "What's in there?"

"Dishes."

"Dishes?" The kid laughed; had he known he might not have made a fuss.

Cheese had by now climbed aboard the jet. Skwerl thanked the kid again, and explained they needed to get on their way, so would he mind moving his golf cart.

"Oh yeah, sure . . ." But the kid froze. He glanced back at the JetEx office. "You guys have got full tanks, right? I was wondering where you're heading." Again, the kid glanced back at the office; but this time, Skwerl noticed how the kid did it, as if maybe he'd rushed out here for a reason aside from the shopping bag—after all, they could have mailed that along, people are always forgetting things in airports, so why this whole production? Was there some other reason? Like if, perhaps, just as Skwerl had called along to the Comfort Suites to check the state of play, if Ali Safi had done the same, if Ali Safi had—after not finding Skwerl at his hotel—called ahead to JetEx and heard from the kid that they were there. No doubt Ali Safi would've told the kid to stall, to keep him and

Cheese from leaving. This is what the kid was doing, and it was why he'd parked in front of the wing.

"I need you to move that golf cart."

"Yeah, of course. But you never said where you were headed . . ."

Unlike some, Skwerl didn't relish violence. But he was certainly capable of it, and so he thrust his arm forward, his grip extended like a pair of calipers. He grabbed the kid by the throat, backpedaling him into the golf cart and slamming him across its front seat. The kid made the first of a few gurgle-gasps as Skwerl pressed harder and harder. Between the kid's sputters, a trickle of his drool dripped over Skwerl's thumb knuckle. Skwerl might not have stopped except that he glimpsed a black Mercedes E-Series pull up to the airfield's chain-link fence.

The kid sat up, gasping.

Skwerl muttered, "Oh, Christ," as the driver's side door opened and Ali Safi stepped outside.

SKWERL HAD RUN OUT OF TIME. HE LEFT THE KID IN THE driver's seat of his golf cart wheezing and hacking. Skwerl sprinted into the jet, hauling up the retractable stairs. Cheese, who'd seen the altercation from the cockpit, was asking what the hell was going on as Skwerl barreled into the copilot seat. "Get us out of here, *now*."

Nothing else needed to be said. Cheese fired the engines. The kid had abandoned his golf cart and was running toward the black Mercedes as it bore down the taxiway. Cheese leaned his palm against the throttle, gunning it to two-thirds, while stomping the right rudder pedal to the floor. The leading edge of the starboard wing knocked down the golf cart. The collision made a horrible scraping sound as the jet skidded a ninety-degree turn on the tarmac, the maneuver creating a clear path to the nearest runway.

Skwerl came forward in his seat. Pressing his face to the cockpit glass, he couldn't quite see the damage to their right wing. He glimpsed the Mercedes. He couldn't make out who was driving, but he could see Ali Safi on the passenger side. He was leaning out his window. To shoot out their engine wouldn't have taken much, a few well-placed rounds into the jet intake. But for some reason, Ali Safi decided against it. He leaned back into the Mercedes.

"Sit down." Cheese put a hand on Skwerl's chest. "I can't see," and Cheese leaned forward, ensuring that the runway was clear.

He brought them to full throttle.

The Mercedes receded from view. As did the runway. The ancient port of Marseille. And, eventually, the city itself.

Safely cocooned in the jet, Cheese brought them to cruising altitude.

Cheese looked angry, his shoulders hunched over the flight controls, like he needed a minute to process what'd happened. Skwerl disappeared into the cabin. He found the shopping bag with the Marie Antoinette plate, which he'd managed to grab from the kid without breaking it. He placed the plate with the others. He also took out the sugar jar, which he decided to bring to the cockpit as a peace offering. "I bought this for Fareeda," he said meekly. "I thought she'd like a souvenir."

"What the hell was all of that?" asked Cheese, ignoring the souvenir.

"All of what?"

"That Mercedes, that little chase back there."

"Where do you want me to start?"

Cheese turned away from Skwerl. Arcs of sweat ringed his armpits. His gaze was fixed out the cockpit, as if their destination, which neither of them had discussed, existed somewhere on that cloud-banked horizon. "How about you tell me who Sheepdog is . . . Let's start there."

Chapter Two

SHEEPDOG

IN THE DAYS BEFORE HE LEFT WITH AZIZ, SINÉAD COULD hardly stand to hear Jay talk about Sheepdog anymore. Three years they'd been together, and she'd mostly broken him of the habit of referring to his many old friends (and sometimes to himself) by these ridiculous nicknames—at least around her.

"You're grown men," she would explain to him for the umpteenth time. "Referring to yourselves this way is the manifestation of regressive juvenile ideation . . ." This was typically the point in a conversation when Jay would loop his arm around her waist, or kiss her cheek, or grab her elbow and tell her that he loved it when she talked like a shrink, that it turned him on, and then he'd beg her to call him Skwerl. She'd give him a playful slap on the head or dig her fingernails into his arm. But he'd beg and beg, and she'd always wind up calling him Skwerl in the end.

On the day he left for Kampala, when this episode played out on the way to Philly International, she hadn't said or done anything after Skwerl reached for her.

"What's wrong?" he'd asked as she parked her Acura at the kiss & ride.

Sinéad stared straight ahead, out the windshield. Her hazard lights made a ticking sound. "Just be careful, okay?"

"I will."

"I mean don't do anything stupid."

"I won't."

"Freud believed that an assumption of recurrent and unnecessary risks is typically rooted in an underlying trauma. So, unless you . . ."

"Toots, I'm gonna be late."

God, she hated all his nicknames . . . except for this one which he'd given her. *Toots* . . . To relax on deployments, he used to read celebrity biographies. *Toots* had been Jack Nicholson's nickname for Anjelica Huston. Sinéad liked that, not only to think of herself as sophisticated and dark, like Huston, but to think of them as that type of a couple, one brutally in love. Sinéad glanced at herself in the rearview mirror. She set her jaw. When she turned to face him, he offered her a thin smile. She planted a kiss on his lips. Then she pulled away and took a breath. "I left a note in your bag," she said. "Read it on the plane. And I slid a treat in there for you too."

"A treat? What is it?"

"Ever heard of the marshmallow test?"

"You got me marshmallows?"

"No, that's a test about delayed gratification."

Behind them, a car began to honk. A traffic cop was walking up the sidewalk.

They had already agreed they wouldn't talk while he was gone. The risk of his cellphone being traced to hers wasn't worth it, so this would be goodbye for the week. She had the details of his return flight and would be at the airport to pick him up. He couldn't help but say they'd be half a million dollars richer then. Unlike him, she kept herself from mentioning the half a million. That money was what the note in his bag was about.

Sinéad had met Skwerl online three years before (she would come to know him as Jay later). When he arrived at her door and offered that strange name, this was what she'd called him, no questions asked. This was because Sinéad had a no-questions policy between her and her clients. They could call themselves whatever they wanted so long as they called her by her work name:

Mistress S.

Skwerl and Sinéad had, technically, met on an online dating site: Eros.com. But it was a dating site where one side paid and the other got paid. This was back when Skwerl still worked for the Office. His life had a tempo then. Seventy days deployed. Thirty days home. And that tempo had taken its toll. Between trips to warzones for Uncle Tony—Iraq, Afghanistan, Yemen, Somalia—Skwerl had come to live so precariously that a single misstep might at any time tip him into the void. He drank too much. He gambled online. He never had time to meet a girlfriend, so he'd begun to pay for companionship. Which had led him to Sinéad's door.

Except Sinéad didn't sleep with her clients. She never had and never would.

"Then what are we gonna do?" Skwerl had asked. He was perched naked on the side of what looked like a gym's incline bench in a Spartan barn, an hour outside Philly, with no carpets, only a cold wood floor. His tattoos—a winged skull over his chest, a scroll on his arm with the names of his dead buddies, even the meat tag with his own name, blood type, and social security number inked neatly on his ribs—had appeared ridiculous to Sinéad, so self-serious. To her, his tattoos seemed as inconsequential as the doodling of a bored little boy.

"I'll show you what we're gonna do," she'd said, planting herself in front of him with one stiletto-heeled boot and then another—*click, clack*. These boots ended at midthigh, and she could feel his wide-eyed gaze traveling up from the zips that started at her ankle, to the crotch of her black bikini bottoms, to her leather bodice, to her choker, to her over-the-elbow gloves in red latex, and then, finally, to her face.

When Skwerl's gaze met hers, Sinéad raised the riding crop she gripped in her right hand. She'd leveled it at him, allowing the little black leather tongue on its end to dangle in front of Skwerl's nose for a fraction of a second. Then she'd clocked him as hard as she could across the cheek.

"Owww! Christ! What are you doing?"

Sinéad continued to beat him with the riding crop—*whap!* ". . . you little . . ." *whap!* ". . . you think you can just . . ." *whap!* ". . . I'm going to . . ." She took wide, fully extended overhead swings. Skwerl covered his face, howling, while Sinéad continued with a torrent of well-scripted insults, starting with Skwerl's impudence at daring to gaze directly at her, Mistress S. She called him a pervert, a piggy, a weakling. She questioned his manhood. Her insults were, of course, carefully calibrated. Sinéad took great pride in her work, which, as she saw it, was to help people—men and women alike—to confront and release their anxieties. Those who sought her out had deeply repressed appetites, which manifested in their lives as unbearable stress. Through her sessions, she'd seen many a client cured. Not cured of their sexual preferences. But cured of those preferences being a burden they had to carry.

"Safe word!" Skwerl shouted. He was pancaked on his stomach, spread-armed against the bare floor like his body had been staked out. Sinéad had her stilettoed heel planted between his shoulder blades.

"Safe word?" she said as if wanting to spit out such a rancid idea. "You pansy. I never gave you a safe word." She laughed and struck him again, the riding crop making a *whap!* as it landed on the fuzzy, tender backs of his thighs.

He howled, covering his face with his hands. "*Safe word* is my safe word!!!"

"That's two words, dummy." *Whap!*

"Safeword . . . safeword . . ." he said, trying to conjoin the two parts into one. He was whimpering now.

She took her boot off him.

Skwerl was still facedown on the floor, his arms cradling his head. Slowly, he peeked through shut fingers. Sinéad was sitting on the leather bench, her stance wide, her elbows perched on her knees, her body angled forward like a ballplayer resting between halves. Her riding crop was gripped loosely by her side. When she saw Skwerl looking at her, she snapped at him, "You came to the wrong place."

"Can't we just have sex?" he said so pathetically that the words themselves revealed the impossibility of that outcome.

"I already told you," she said. "That's not what I do."

Skwerl was off the floor now. He'd stepped across the room, where the terrycloth bathrobe he'd changed into after undressing hung on a peg by the door.

"If you'd read my online profile," Sinéad said. "You would've known *that's* not what I do. Why did you even come here?"

"Because . . ." He was facing the wall. He didn't want to say it.

"Listen, why don't you just—" She was going to ask him to go.

"Because I thought you were pretty." He turned away from the wall and cinched down the tie on his robe. He was looking at her.

"Christ, sit down."

Skwerl crossed the room barefoot and sat next to her. The leather riding crop rested between them on the bench. "So, if you don't do *that*, what is it you do?"

"I help people."

Skwerl lifted the riding crop. He brought it down painlessly across the side of Sinéad's leather boot, *whap*, giving her a little taste of her own medicine.

Finger by finger, she took off her red gloves. Skwerl noticed two thin lines tattooed on her right forearm, the first an inch above her wrist and the second two inches above that. He told her that he liked her tattoos. "What are they?"

"The first," and she pointed to it with a manicured finger, "was the furthest I'd ever reached inside a man's ass. I never thought I'd beat that record. But with another client, I did, so got the second tattoo. He was a regular, a used-car dealer turned politician, which probably explains him being so limber." With her hand, she made a talking motion like *blah . . . blah . . . blah . . .* "I wore him like a sock puppet."

"Jesus . . ."

She shrugged. "I'm like any other mental health provider."

Skwerl didn't say anything.

Sinéad pinched the zipper tab on the inside of her thigh, running it all the way down to her ankle, taking off each of her boots. "I'm not much different than a psychiatrist," she said, now sitting next to Skwerl barefoot. "We both beat the shit out of people to ease their anxieties. One of us accepts health insurance, that's all."

Sinéad took the riding crop back from Skwerl. When she offered to refund Skwerl's money, he refused. He asked if he could stay for a bit longer. She again explained to him that they wouldn't be having sex. He understood and asked, maybe, if they could just talk a little. And so they began talking, at first him, and then, eventually, her.

Hours had passed on that first day and, three years later, they hadn't stopped talking. Since he'd left for Kampala the week before, Sinéad had missed him fiercely. They had, quite improbably, built a life together. Imperfect though it was at times, she was hesitant to see that life disrupted. This is what her note to Skwerl had been about.

That note, written in a distinct and stylish rightward-sloping cursive that Skwerl (and most everyone else) struggled to decipher, with teacup handles on the capital letters, attested to Sinéad's love and the pride she felt for all they had built together. She had, in the last year, taken over Skwerl's sometimes-solvent rope business. He'd managed to transfer ownership to Sinéad before the government could claim it as part of their settlement against him and she was rapidly turning the business around. Sinéad had identified an underserved market: patriotic working girls like herself who, in addition to their riding crops, thigh-high boots, and bodices, needed quality rope, preferably American-made. After a little legwork pitching the business to a few new accounts, mostly in various red-light districts, Sinéad had delivered their first profitable quarter earlier that year. Sinéad had then had the idea to rebrand the company. Business was now exploding. They had become the single top-rated manufacturer of BDSM rope on Amazon (with over 125,000 five-star reviews and an average produce rating of 4.7 stars). Customers raved about the rope's vivid selection of colors, its wide variety of textures—from *Wicked Witch of the East* (coarse) to *Dorothy* (supple)—even its tensile strength was favorably mentioned in these reviews. In short, everyone loved the American-made rope produced by this new, upstart company: *Knotty Pleasures*.

Well-versed as Sinéad was in psychology, she understood that her succeeding where Skwerl had failed might be hard on him, a blow to his ego. She was attuned to his emotions in this way and, in her letter, implored him to be careful. "Whether you come back with half a million bucks or with nothing," she wrote at the end of the letter's third page, "we'll figure it out." And then she again warned him about Freud's theory of "the assumption of recurrent and unnecessary risks rooted in an underlying trauma" before telling him that she loved him.

In addition to the letter, she'd also packed him his treat, her favorite candy, which had also become his: black licorice whips.

CHEESE COULD HARDLY BELIEVE IT: SKWERL HAD NO IDEA WHO Sheepdog was. The two of them flew from Marseille toward a sunset that took hours, their westward progress causing the ribbon of orange, yellow, and blue to stall on the horizon while Skwerl confessed that he had never met, seen, nor spoken to Sheepdog. Nothing. "We traveled halfway across the world to steal a plane based on an email?"

"We're not stealing this plane," Skwerl reminded him. "We're *repossessing* it."

They passed into a bank of clouds, and, for just a moment, Cheese lost the horizon. He then pulled back on the yoke. They gained altitude, punching through those clouds. A carpet of overcast spread beneath them while they again flew toward this seemingly unending sunset.

"What if we found out H's identity," said Skwerl, "that could lead us to Sheepdog. There can't be that many albinos in the repossession business."

"H wasn't an albino," said Cheese. "He was just pale. Albinos are nearsighted, a lack of melanin in the eyes. H couldn't have served in the military as an albino."

"That's kinda ableist, Cheese."

"Ableist? . . . Growing up, an old albino lived in my village. He was half blind."

"You can't be an albino and Afghan."

"That's kinda racist, Skwerl."

Cheese said he was hungry. Skwerl stepped into the back of the plane. He rifled around in the galley but couldn't find any food. However, he didn't return to the cockpit empty-handed. "What you got?" Cheese asked as Skwerl sat back down in the copilot seat. He opened a bag of black licorice whips, which they shared as they began to weigh their options.

Fortunately, Cheese had refueled in Marseille. With full tanks, they could range half the planet. Where to go wasn't their problem. Where to stash the plane was. Also, on takeoff, they'd damaged the right aileron when they'd rammed into the golf cart. Cheese was keeping an eye on that shuddering aileron. If it tore off the wing, he could still steer the jet by manipulating the throttle of the two turbofan engines. Each was powerful, generating 7,500 pounds of thrust, but this was a dangerous and awkward way to fly. They both agreed they needed to get back to the U.S., and Skwerl thought it made sense to put the plane down near where he lived, so they could plan their next move. Using an online directory, he found an FBO outside of Philly, in Chester County, Aero Services Aviation. Cheese glanced at the details—its operating hours, hangar capacity, landing requirements—and he agreed that it would suffice. The only problem—and this wasn't specific to the FBO Skwerl had picked—was that the tower would log their tail number as soon as they landed.

"We've got to figure out how to make this plane disappear," Cheese said. "At least for a bit."

Skwerl and Cheese sat together, neither talking. When the sun, which for hours had hovered on the western horizon, finally dipped below it, Skwerl turned to Cheese. "I've got an idea," and, in the darkness, he laid out his plan.

THE CHIEF OF BASE IN MARSEILLE HAD CALLED THE CHIEF OF station in Paris who'd called Uncle Tony that morning at his northern Virginia office in Tysons Corner. When the call came in, it interrupted Uncle Tony as he was mixing his post-workout shake. This was a precise blend of legal and semi-legal supplements mixed with cocoa powder and beet juice in his favorite shaker, the one with a sticker from his old unit, SEAL Team 4, plastered to its side. The sticker featured a jacked bullfrog flexing a tattooed bicep (the tattoo being a fouled anchor, of course) with a cigar stub chomped in the corner of his mouth and a sailor's white dixie cup hat jauntily balanced on his head. The French Direction générale de la Sécurité extérieure, or DGSE, their external intelligence service, had reported to Paris Station the death of a shared asset in a hotel room at the InterContinental in Marseille. He was a fifty-two-year-old Rhodesian-born but naturalized Russian citizen, Hendrik Hofstede. Uncle Tony inquired as to the cause of death.

"The authorities have done us the courtesy of listing this as a suicide," the chief of station curtly explained, "though it sounds like there's more to it. Hofstede had a strange incision on his rib cage, someone had flayed a strip of his skin. The French probably wouldn't have IDed him except they had his prints on file, seems he'd once done a stint in the Foreign Legion. His name popped up as a onetime asset of ours run by your office, so I thought

I'd let you know." Uncle Tony could hear the *clickety-clack* of a keyboard on the other end of the line. "I've got his 201 file right here . . ." A little more typing . . . "Syria, Libya, Afghanistan . . . *a lot* of Afghanistan. Most recently Africa. Looks like this fellow was operating under non-official cover, a security company called D-R-C-A, Defense Response and Coordination Associates. Are you familiar?"

"Yes," said Uncle Tony, shaking his protein shake hard in its mixing cup. "I've heard of *Derka*."

"*Derka* . . . ? Is that how you say it?"

"Yeah, like *derka derka*. You know, that's how they talk."

"How who talks?"

"The indig." A silence, which was a little judgmental, held the line. Uncle Tony rolled his eyes. He took a long pull on his protein shake and thought to himself, *Fuckin' cake-eater,* before saying, with all the patience and politesse he could muster, "*Derka derka* . . . It's a joke from *Team America*. You ever see that movie?"

"No, sorry Tony. I have not."

"You ever been downrange?"

The chief of Paris Station hadn't spent time downrange, either; and he asked Uncle Tony if there was anything they should pass along to the French authorities about DRCA given that the DGSE had done the courtesy of alerting them. He also suggested that Uncle Tony review Hendrik Hofstede's 201 file, a catalogue of every cable written on him, just in case. "Sure thing," said Uncle Tony, rather unconvincingly. "I'll get right on it," and then he hung up the phone.

As the head of the Office, Uncle Tony retained administrator rights over all his assets' 201 files. It didn't take him long to pull up Hofstede's, and even less time to archive it—about as long as it took him to finish his protein shake.

SKWERL AND CHEESE LANDED AT AERO SERVICES AVIATION

around midnight. After they paid an extra thousand-dollar fee to park the Challenger 600 in a private hangar, Skwerl stepped outside, to call Sinéad at their barn, twenty minutes east down Route 30 in Chadds Ford. The call rang and rang, going to voicemail. He tried again. Same result. Sinéad wasn't expecting him until tomorrow. When Skwerl stepped into the hangar, he found Cheese beneath the right wing, inspecting their damaged aileron. "It's in bad shape," he said. "We're not going anywhere until we fix it."

"How long will that take?"

"They've got to order the part, and then we've got to find a mechanic . . ."

Skwerl started to rub the back of his neck. "I'm guessing all that gets logged."

"It's tough to make a plane disappear."

Skwerl glanced at his watch. They still had a few hours until the daytime maintenance crews arrived. If he couldn't figure a solution, he thought Sinéad could. He told Cheese to stay put, that he'd head home and be back first thing in the morning, hopefully with some ideas.

"No way," said Cheese. "You left me with the plane last time and nearly got us both killed. I'm coming with you."

"You should *really* stay . . ."

Cheese was adamant, no way, not again.

Skwerl lacked the energy to argue with Cheese. A simple, "My wife sees clients at night," was all he could muster as fair warning.

Less than an hour later, an Uber dropped them off in his gravel driveway. It wound down to a stone barn with a broad sloping roof. The barn was silhouetted darkly against the clear night sky and its eaves sat nearly three stories tall. A couple of first-floor lights were on. Skwerl didn't enter through the front door, but through the garage, an ancient, shingled outbuilding where he seldom parked. The garage was reserved for clients so no passerby would glimpse their cars from the road, their discretion being Sinéad's utmost concern. Bags of hemp and other raw rope-making materials sat stacked in the corners. Like any garage, tools hung from shelves. But what caught Skwerl's eye—and confused Cheese—was what was parked in the garage: a buggy drawn by a single pony. The pony swished its tail, hardly noticing them, preoccupied as it was by the feed bag it had quietly buried its nose into.

"Is that yours?"

"No," said Skwerl. But he knew exactly whose it was.

At the back of the garage, beyond the door that led to the barn and the industrial-sized winding, stranding, and coiling machines, as well as dying vats that made up their rope business, Skwerl could hear familiar, muffled sounds. He glanced back at Cheese, who wore a puzzled expression, seemingly less sure of what he was listening to. Then a series of *whaps!* fell one after another in quick succession. A whimper followed, like air squeezed out of a balloon, also some name calling—"pervert," "piggy," "weakling"—and then more *whaps!* Skwerl glanced over his shoulder, at Cheese, who shot his gaze toward the back of the garage, as if he was about to bolt past the pony and buggy and out into the night. Skwerl cracked open the door into the main barn, not opening it entirely, but enough so his voice would project inside.

"Toots . . . *pssst* . . . hey, Toots . . ."

Silence.

Skwerl shut the door and stood arms crossed over his chest with his back to it, waiting for her. He offered a thin-lipped smile to Cheese, who averted his eyes. On the other side of the door there was a noise like a long chain falling to the ground in a pile and then a gasp of relief. When the door to the garage opened a crack, Sinéad wore a plush terrycloth bathrobe; it was one half of a Pottery Barn "him & hers" set Skwerl had ordered as an anniversary present the year before. When Sinéad saw Cheese, she clasped the robe tight at her neck, hiding her black leather choker. She stepped into the garage. "I thought you got back tomorrow . . ."

"Change of plan," said Skwerl. "You working?"

"No . . . I just thought I'd get all dressed up and do some

cleaning around the house . . . What does it look like? Of course I'm working." Cheese, whose eyes were still fixed on the ground, had found himself staring at Sinéad's feet, specifically the toes of her leather thigh-high stilettos that peeked from under her robe. "You must be Aziz," she said. "I'm—"

But before she could properly introduce herself, a cry from inside the barn interrupted them. "How much longer, Mistress S?"

With the fury of a drill instructor, she flung open the door and barked back that this client of hers would wait as long as she damn well pleased, and that another peep out of him would earn more time "on the rack" (whatever contraption that was). She shut the door behind her, turned to Cheese, and finished her introduction, saying, "I'm Sinéad. I've heard so much about you from Jay."

Cheese managed to heave his gaze off the floor, look Sinéad in the eyes, and shake her hand. Her auburn hair was pulled into a tight ponytail. Her mouth was lipsticked as red as a fruit. Every inch of her visible skin was powdered white and her eyes were lined black. Cheese had never been at this range with a woman like her, one who was equally terrifying and beautiful.

Skwerl spoke quickly, summarizing the last couple of days, from what'd happened at the airfield in Kampala, to bumping into Ali Safi in Marseille, to the dead man, H, at the InterContinental, and how they'd fled here in the Challenger 600, which was parked at Aero Services Aviation. "It's got a busted aileron," said Skwerl. "Also, we've got to do something about its tail number. Right now, we're easy to track, and it'll only be a matter of time before Ali Safi or someone else shows up looking for that jet, and for us."

"I'm glad you came here." Sinéad was still clasping her robe together, but with her other hand she had clasped Skwerl's.

"If we can fix the jet and sort out the tail number, I've got an idea where we could hide out, at least for a bit—"

As Skwerl said this, a creaking sound, like a person stepping on a loose floorboard, came from the other side of the door. In a single motion, executed with the violence and precision of a well-practiced martial arts move, Sinéad flung the door open so hard it slammed into whoever had crept up to its other side. Standing in the threshold, wearing nothing but a towel around his waist, a man was bent over clutching his elbow. "*Arghhh* . . ." His thick reddish-brown beard was shaved around the mouth and cheeks in the Amish style. "You hit my funny bone." He stomped his feet at the ground until the pain dissipated. He'd been wearing a straw hat with a black band around the base, which he now picked up off the floor. He brushed the dust from its brim before placing it back on his head. "How ya doing there, Jay?"

"It's Skwerl to you, Ephraim. Only she gets to call me Jay."

When Sinéad had flung open the door, her robe had also flung open. She stood on the threshold like a superhero—boots, gloves, bikini bottoms, bodice—with her Pottery Barn robe billowing behind her like a cape. Skwerl, Cheese, and Ephraim all stood slack jawed, staring at her, before she muttered, "The three of you get enough of a look," and then she disappeared inside the house.

Ephraim called after her, "So we're done, Mistress S . . . ? Should I be coming back next week then . . . ?" But Sinéad didn't reply.

When Cheese finally asked Ephraim and Skwerl how they knew each other, Ephraim didn't answer. He patted his pony on its flank and reached into his buggy, removing a coarse white shirt, dark trousers with buttons (zippers strictly forbidden), and calf-high boots. Skwerl answered instead. "He's one of Sinéad's clients."

"A loyal one, too," added Ephraim. "Ain't that so, English?"

"I told you, call me Skwerl."

"If I'm not to call you by your Christian name then I'll be calling you English." Ephraim finished buttoning his trousers and tucked in his shirt. Standing erect, he was at least a head taller than Cheese and a few inches taller than Skwerl. He pulled his suspenders over each of his shoulders. They snapped against his back, raising a smile; he clearly enjoyed the little jolt of pain.

Sinéad returned to the garage. She had changed into a cable

knit sweater and jeans. "I've got an idea," she said. "Let's head to the airport." Then she turned to Ephraim. "You're coming too."

"Am I now?" This didn't seem unexpected to Ephraim, who was in the midst of unfastening the feed bag from his pony's bridle. But it did confuse both Cheese and Skwerl. What could they possibly need Ephraim for?

"Your aileron's busted, right? And you've got to switch out your tail number, which will require some careful repainting."

"Toots . . . Ephraim isn't a flight mechanic."

"No, he's Amish. They can fix anything. Ain't that right, Ephraim?"

By now, he'd finished haltering his pony and was climbing onto the driver's box of his buggy. *"Go up to the mountains, bring wood and rebuild the temple, that I may be pleased with it and be glorified, saith the Lord."*

"What's that supposed to mean?" asked Skwerl.

"That he can fix anything, like I said."

When Sinéad spoke, Ephraim glanced in her direction, adding, *"For all have sinned and fall short of the glory of God."*

Now Sinéad was the confused one. "What's that mean, Ephraim?"

He smiled in much the same way he'd done a moment before, when his suspenders had snapped against his shoulders. "The Bible teaches that kindness must be repaid by kindness . . ."

"I'll give you one free session," Sinéad said curtly.

"Three sessions."

"You're pushing it." Sinéad took a heavy breath. "Two sessions, but you leave your buggy and pony here and drive with us, so we're not up half the night waiting for you."

Ephraim balanced his driving whip across his legs. He leaned forward and considered his pony for a few seconds as he thought over Sinéad's offer. Then he patted his pony on its flank and vaulted down from his buggy. "That's a deal," he said. "But I've got one other condition."

Sinéad had already extended her hand, but she was slowly beginning to retract it. "What's that?"

"The front seat," said Ephraim. "I drove in a car once, but never sat up there. If I come with you, you let me sit in the front seat." Again, he was smiling.

AFTER UNCLE TONY DEALT WITH HENDRIK HOFSTEDE'S 201 FILE, he made a lunch plan. He phoned the corporate headquarters of Cyberdyne Security, which was only about a ten-minute drive away, and housed in a northern Virginia office park as equally nondescript as his own. He got the CEO's assistant, who explained that her boss was in a meeting. Uncle Tony declined to leave a message. He called a second number, which got him Mac after the first ring.

"Hey Tony, how's things?"

"I hope this isn't an inconvenient time."

"Nope, not inconvenient at all . . . Just hold on a second."

Uncle Tony could hear background noise. Mac stepping out of a room. His hand cupped over the receiver telling his assistant—the same woman Uncle Tony had just spoken to—that he'd be right back, and to make sure no one left the meeting. When Mac came up on the line again, Uncle Tony said, "You're sure I'm not bothering you." He was toying with Mac, a little game as if to underscore that no matter how successful Mac had become, no matter how many contracts Cyberdyne Security had landed—from Boeing to Lockheed to General Dynamics, the very spinal column of America's military-industrial Goliath—Mac would always have to take Uncle Tony's call. ". . . because if you're busy, I could call back."

"I'm in a meeting about the DRCA payroll shortfall, but I can talk."

"How's that going?"

"Tony . . . cut the shit. You know how that's going. What do you want?"

He laughed. "You free for lunch?"

"I'll have my office book us a place." Mac was clearly trying to preempt Uncle Tony from making a suggestion.

"Let's just meet at Panera."

"Christ, again?"

"Yeah, again."

Uncle Tony had always liked Mac. Maybe it was because Mac, unlike most others in this line of work, had limited patience for dumb games. "You play stupid games, you win stupid prizes" was a Mac-ism that Uncle Tony had always appreciated. Yes, he knew about Mac's combat record, the Navy Cross, the Silver Star, his reputation in special operations, but it was Mac's forthright (no bullshit) nature in a profession based on deception (bullshit) that was the reason Uncle Tony had recruited him. When Mac had retired from the Raiders, he had approached Uncle Tony about a job at the Office. "I've still got some good years left in me," Mac had said. Uncle Tony didn't doubt it, but he had greater ambitions for Mac than being third banana on some paramilitary program in the Near East, Middle East, Far East, or even eastern Europe. Uncle Tony didn't need more guys he could rely on out *east*. No, what he'd needed was more guys he could rely on at home.

"I wouldn't join us at Ground Branch," Uncle Tony had explained. "It's too small for you." Mac had an ego. He liked being told this, so he'd listened. "SOCOM is the same as high school, understand? The Green Berets, they're like the Voc-Tech kids. Not too smart, but useful and lots of them. The SEALs, they're like the swim team. Big and beefy, spend all their time in the pool. The JSOC guys from DevGru and Delta, they're like the rich kids with fat allowances. They show up at school in the fancy cars their parents bought them. Everyone hates their guts because they get all the cool toys and pussy. So where does that leave us? Where would that leave you if you joined the Office? Paramilitary officers, we're like the guys who graduated last year but just come back for the parties." Then, in his best Matthew McConaughey voice, Uncle Tony said, "'Alright, alright, alright,'" and then asked, ". . . Do you really want to be that guy?"

That riff had proven enough for Mac to consider and then accept Uncle Tony's alternative offer. This included a fully funded two-year MBA at Harvard, which Mac went on to finish in fifteen months. While at Harvard, he'd founded Cyberdyne thanks to some generous seed funding Uncle Tony had helped secure. The only string attached was that Mac provide "sensitive, nonpublic information" when Uncle Tony or any of his colleagues asked. The lawyers had even placed language to this effect in the zero-interest loan documents Mac had signed shortly after Uncle Tony had recruited him into the CIA's QX program, a constellation of U.S. citizens working as assets in the highest echelons of business. Mac had, of course, asked what QX stood for, and Uncle Tony had told him the truth: it stood for nothing. The digraph was meaningless, a random pair of categorizing letters designed to disappear as quickly as they'd appeared. "Kinda like our work together," Mac had said. To this, Uncle Tony hadn't replied.

This string of events is how Mac landed at Panera with a bowl of autumn squash soup on a tray searching for a free table. As the CEO of Cyberdyne, he thought he should've been at the Palm or Café Milano; or, barring a better lunch date, powering down the C&O canal's towpath on his seventy-five-hundred-dollar Ventum One, the road bike he'd treated himself to the month before. The Challenge Wanaka Ironman in New Zealand was coming up. He could hardly wait, a little vacation he was planning with the latest in a string of girlfriends. Yet Mac was in none of these other places. He was here. Bowl of soup on a tray. Uncle Tony in the corner, waving him over to a sticky table that hadn't been wiped down.

"What you got there?" asked Tony.

"Bowl of autumn squash."

"You didn't want to make it a bread bowl?" Tony glanced down at his own tray, a bread bowl overflowing with heart-stopping creamy broccoli cheddar soup.

"Naw, I'm good."

"It's only seventy-nine cents more." Uncle Tony dipped the lid of his bread bowl into the broccoli cheddar. While Mac was still stirring his soup, Uncle Tony had taken a first bite, which was too hot.

"You take all those supplements and then you eat like garbage."

"I'm a man of contradictions," said Uncle Tony. He had reached for his drink, a bottle of pink lemonade Snapple, taking a gulp before adding, "Just seems a waste not to order the bread bowl."

Mac dropped his spoon on his tray. He interlaced his fingers together, holding his hands above his soup. "Am I here so you can lecture me about the cost of bread bowls?"

"No," said Uncle Tony. He spooned up a second bite of the hot soup, blowing on it more carefully than the first. "Just want to make sure you're not getting too used to the good life at Cyberdyne."

"And what if I am?"

"I suppose there's nothing wrong with that. So long as you remember who butters your bread."

"You mean who buys the soup."

"Exactly."

"What do you want, Tony?"

Uncle Tony had again taken a too hot bite. He formed his mouth into an O, blowing from the back of his throat, as he managed to say, "Sheepdog," before taking another gulp of lemonade. "You know him, right?"

"I'm part of his 'network,'" said Mac. "I get the emails. But I don't *know* him."

"You've introduced people to him."

"I introduced Skwerl to him—" Mac bit off the end of his own sentence, as if immediately regretting what he'd said. Slowly, carefully, he added, "Is Skwerl in some kind of trouble?"

"He took something," said Uncle Tony. "And now he's disappeared."

"You mean he stole something."

Uncle Tony didn't answer.

"Can you blame him?" Mac added. "You guys screwed him over pretty hard. How's the guy supposed to make a living?"

"Maybe he should've thought about that before smoking two dozen civilians."

"Don't feed me that line," said Mac. "I was in-country when it happened. Two dozen people might've gotten smoked on that raid, but they sure as hell weren't civilians. If you guys hadn't hung Skwerl out to dry, particularly after he had to watch Dickhead Mike bleed out, he would've stayed quiet, and you wouldn't have had to lie and say they were civilians."

"That's one theory," said Uncle Tony. "Too bad the FISA judge didn't buy it."

"Yeah, too bad. And now Skwerl's out stealing stuff, causing you problems, because you already robbed him blind."

"He's not really stealing stuff," said Uncle Tony. "He's repossessing stuff."

"I'm failing to see the difference."

"Possession is nine-tenths of the law. And we're a nation of laws."

"Okay," said Mac. "But you still fucked him."

"Skwerl's in way over his head. I might be the best friend he's got."

"If that's the case then he really is screwed."

"If you hear anything—from him, from Sheepdog, from anyone—let me know."

"Did you try his house?"

"Yeah, but it seems like we just missed him there."

"You're not going to find him if he doesn't want to be found."

"Maybe," said Uncle Tony. "But I'm not the only one looking for him."

FAREEDA IQBAL'S PHONE RANG AFTER MIDNIGHT. SHE SAT UP on the sofa in the living room of her one-bedroom apartment. She'd fallen asleep with the television on. Her husband was gone, but the number came from his work, the landline at the Esso station on Route 290. The store manager, an octogenarian named Luther Nesbit, was on the line. Despite owning the station and a dozen others, Luther liked to take the occasional graveyard shift. "Keeps me honest," he would say whenever asked about this curious habit. But Nesbit sounded spooked. "A lawman just left here," he said in his thick Texan drawl. "No uniform. He was looking for your husband."

"Where was he from?"

"Not from here," said Luther. "He flashed a badge, but I didn't get a good look and wasn't asking him to stick around so I could get a better one."

"What did you tell him?"

"Nothing," said Luther, as if mildly insulted by Fareeda's question. "I'm not in the practice of speaking to out-of-state lawmen. But I thought you should know . . . Your husband in some kind of trouble?"

She drew silent for a moment before saying, "I'm not sure."

Fareeda hung up the phone. When she went to turn off the television, an ad for the ASPCA was playing. Malnourished puppies and kittens. Old dogs leashed outside in the snow. All of them staring piteously at the camera through chain-link fences, pleading, pleading, for someone, for *her,* to help. A QR code flashed on the screen. She had succumbed to their pleas before, much to Cheese's chagrin. She couldn't help it. She missed her home, the strays who she used to feed, the dogs and cats of her old neighborhood. "For $19, you can save a life," the ad said. She scanned the QR code, made her donation, felt a little closer to home, and hoped that Cheese wouldn't notice—but as tight as their finances were of course he would.

Fareeda wandered from the living room to the bedroom, which would double as the nursery for the baby that'd arrive in four months. Her husband's work as a pilot used to take him away so often that his absence had become an unspoken but always felt precondition of their lives. If the fall of Kabul had robbed Fareeda of her home, those unsettled months as refugees had given her the longest uninterrupted stretch she'd ever known with her husband. This was when she'd at last gotten pregnant, and so the fall of Kabul had also given her a child. Her pregnancy had been easy, aside from the occasional Braxton-Hicks contraction, which worried her husband far more than it did her or her OB. When she and her husband arrived in the United States, he returned to work, though not as a pilot. She found these new separations more difficult. Before, when he'd been gone for weeks or even months, and in extreme danger, she hadn't missed him the way she missed him now. Back then, she'd known he was doing what he loved. This made their separations easier. But in the U.S., he was working six nights a week at the Esso station and spending days at South Austin Community College eking out an accounting degree one soul-crushing class at a time. Under these conditions, it felt unbearable to be apart.

Except for now. Ever since Aziz had left with Skwerl, Fareeda noticed that she missed him less. He was flying again, so this made sense. The happiness of each was contingent upon the happiness of the other. Their emotions attuned.

This was why—as Fareeda sat in the silence of their apartment, afraid and wondering what to do about this officer who'd come looking for her husband—it didn't surprise her when her phone rang: it was Aziz.

SKWERL HAD BEEN ABLE TO GO HOME AND SEE SINÉAD, SO Cheese thought it only fair that he be allowed to phone Fareeda, simply to tell her that he was okay. Skwerl was skeptical. "I don't know, Cheese. It's a risk." They were on their way to the FBO. Sinéad was driving her Acura with Ephraim in the passenger seat (as agreed upon). In the backseat, Skwerl and Cheese debated the point.

"No bigger risk than you seeing your wife."

"I'm not his wife," Sinéad announced like a lawyer filing an objection in court.

Cheese glanced at Skwerl.

"What? . . . She's not."

"Which is all the more reason I should be allowed to call Fareeda." The sentence caught in Cheese's throat. That word: *allowed*. Ever since arriving in the U.S., Cheese had noticed it crept recurrently into his speech. This psychology of asking permission, it was the psychology of a guest, of not living in one's own home. Given his migrant status, would he be *allowed* to sign a lease on an apartment? Would he be *allowed* to work legally? And, most important of all, would he be *allowed* to remain in the U.S.? On the airport tarmac after Kabul fell, embassy officials hadn't been exactly handing out green cards. Cheese and Fareeda had fled to the U.S. under a specific State Department program known as Humanitarian Parole. This gave him two years, provided he remained on good behavior. Stealing (or repossessing) a luxury jet probably didn't fall into the category of good behavior in his adopted country. But having five hundred grand in his bank account did. Cheese understood this much about America.

Ephraim began playing with the automatic windows, rolling them up then down, as if to remind everyone that this was his second-ever ride in a car. The wind was blowing right into Skwerl's face. "Will you knock that off."

Up, down. Up, down. Ephraim ignored Skwerl.

"I'm calling home," Cheese announced. "I'll keep it brief."

"I can't stop you." The wind tussled Skwerl's hair annoyingly like an uncle at a family reunion. "But I wish you'd wait a day or two, until we get settled."

"Settled where?" asked Ephraim.

Skwerl kicked the back of Ephraim's seat. "Stop screwing with the windows!"

Ephraim rolled them up. "Where?" he asked again.

"I can't say."

Ephraim began to play with the windows again. Before Skwerl could cuss him out, a metallic clunk sounded. Sinéad had engaged the child safety lock. Ephraim *click-clacked* the switch on his door. Sinéad clapped him on the back of the head, "Knock it off," and Ephraim smiled like he'd just tasted something delicious. He then announced, "I'm hungry," as if getting smacked by Sinéad had awakened a cascade of appetites. He wanted to take full advantage of the car ride, having never eaten at a drive-thru. Ephraim asked if they could grab something.

Skwerl glanced at his watch. He and Cheese hadn't eaten since the licorice whips on the plane. "You hungry?" he asked Cheese.

"Starving."

They pulled off the road at the next exit. Left was Taco Bell. Right was McDonald's. They put it to a vote. Sinéad abstained, she wasn't hungry. Cheese lost 1 to 2. They made the turn for Taco Bell. The drive-thru window was broken; a sheet of paper with *out of order* taped across the intercom spoiled the possibility of yet another new experience for Ephraim. Undeterred, he and Skwerl ambled inside. Cheese waited in the car with Sinéad. Turning to Cheese, she said, "You should really eat something."

"I'd rather not."

"Don't be a bad sport."

Cheese mumbled, "I'll grab something later." He was tempted to tell Sinéad the reason he had vowed to never again eat at Taco Bell. He cringed each time he thought of it, this memory that was among his most awkward as a new immigrant. It happened at the

Taco Bell a half-mile from his job at the Esso station. This was only weeks after he and Fareeda first landed in the U.S., having cycled through camps in Uganda (where he could hear cicadas at night outside his tent), in the UAE (where he could see the skyline of Dubai), and, lastly, at a holding facility at Fort Hood (among the American soldiers who on certain days he blamed for his troubles and who he imagined blamed him for losing a war). For Cheese, finding that first job at the Esso station had felt like an act of providence. Crime had spiked along the lonely strip of Route 290 where Luther Nesbit had bought the station a decade before. Two armed robberies had caused the last two attendants to quit. A robbery—or even a pair of robberies—hardly bothered Aziz. He'd told Mr. Nesbit that an inch and a half of bulletproof glass was more protection than he'd ever had flying his Mi-17. Luther Nesbit had laughed and clasped Aziz on the shoulder, hiring him on the spot.

Once Fareeda became pregnant, supporting the two of them on the state's minimum wage of $7.25 meant snacks at the Esso station were out of Aziz's price range—the Jack Link's beef jerky in aisle three might as well have been Beluga caviar. Still, he had to eat something. On his first night at the station, he'd asked the daytime attendant what the cheapest nearby place was. "That'd be Taco Bell," he'd said, pointing a half-mile down Route 290. So, at a little after midnight, when Cheese was afforded one of his shift's three fifteen-minute breaks, he locked up the service station and jogged down to Taco Bell. The restaurant was closed, but the drive-thru window was open. Cheese—much like Ephraim—had never been to a drive-thru. He didn't see the intercom, where the menu was posted, and walked directly up to the pickup window. Back in Kabul, where the restaurants often had no menu, their names typically advertised their signature dish. If you go to Khalil's Shawarma you order the *khalil shawarma*, if you go to the Baghdis Qormah House you order the *baghdis qormah*; and, as Cheese assumed was the case in the U.S., if you go to a place named Taco

Bell, you order the . . .

"I will have one *taco bell,* please," he announced to a sleepy (and startled) twenty-something attendant who was working the same graveyard shift as him, chewing a piece of gum.

"You wanna what?" she'd asked.

"A taco bell."

"What's that?"

Cheese took a step back, glancing up at the enormous neon sign with the purple bell. "This is Taco Bell, yes?"

"Menu's back there, bubba," said the attendant.

Bubba?

A pickup truck had pulled in behind Cheese, blocking his way. The driver peered over his steering wheel. He tilted up the brim of his cowboy hat with two fingers, his face set in an expression of mild disgust, as if he'd returned home to find a dead rodent stinking up the living room. The driver looked ready to run him over.

"What's the cheapest thing on the menu?" Cheese asked in a hurry.

"That'd be the Cheesy Bean Burrito."

Cheese reached into his pocket, removing a few bills and coins. The attendant said, "That'll be eighty-seven cents." It was taking Cheese a moment in the darkness to sort through his change. "You'll need three of those big ones," she said, pointing to Cheese's open palm. "That one little one, and two of those copper ones."

Cheese thanked her. "And a water, please."

The attendant placed a Dasani on the counter.

"Sorry, tap water."

She took back the Dasani and gave him a plain white cup, different than the soft drink cups, which in his sudden poverty felt aspirational. By this time, the man waiting in the drive-thru line had the fender of his truck so close that Cheese could feel its engine giving off heat. Cheese took his single brown sack, his cup of water without a lid, and sat on the painted curb along Route 290. He counted the bites to finish his burrito (seven) and was picking bits of cheese off its wrapper as he watched the attendant hand two heavy sacks of food to the man in the pickup truck.

Cheese was deep in this memory as he sat outside the Taco Bell with Sinéad. "I know it's none of my business," she said, snapping him back into the moment, "but Jay's wrong. You should call your wife, to make sure she's okay. Just keep it short. If you use my phone, no one's going to flag the call."

"He'll be angry." Cheese glanced through the windows of the Taco Bell, at Skwerl. He was placing his order with the cashier while Ephraim stood a few steps behind, gazing dumbfounded at the extensive backlit menu like a man in mid-abduction by a UFO.

"I love Jay," said Sinéad. "But he's always a little pissed about something." She placed her phone firmly in Cheese's palm. "It might as well be you." Sinéad reached into the glove box. She fished around inside, taking out a lipstick and some mascara. She tilted down the rearview mirror. "Why don't you step outside. Take that phone with you while I freshen up."

Cheese opened his door and stepped around the back of the Acura. Leaning against the trunk, he dialed home. After a few rings, Fareeda answered, "Hello?" Cheese felt an immediate release of anxiety on hearing her voice. He spoke in rapid fire, wanting to tell her everything he could with the little time he had, that his "trip hadn't gone according to plan," that "it'll be a few days at least until I'm home," that "I'm safe, so don't worry." Fareeda couldn't get a word in. Finally, she was able to tell Cheese that someone had shown up at the Esso station asking about him. "This man," she said ominously. "He had a badge."

"When was this?"

"A day ago," she said. "Mr. Nesbit came by to tell me. I didn't say anything about you. Nothing about where you were or the jet you stole."

"*Repossessed,*" Cheese shot back. Why had he agreed to Skwerl's stupid scheme? He glanced up at the Taco Bell, its neon sign flashed as if to remind him of what it felt like to eat a meal for eighty-seven cents.

Cheese apologized to his wife.

Fareeda asked if it was safe for her to stay in their apartment.

No sooner had she uttered the question then there was a knock at the door. "Is someone there?" Cheese asked, but Fareeda didn't answer. "Whoever it is, don't let them in . . ." Aside from Fareeda's short, nervous breaths, she didn't reply. The knocking started again, a steady pounding. Then a crash, like a door coming off its hinges. A shout, his wife. And silence.

Cheese stood in the parking lot, his palms sweating, the silence ringing in his ears. He called back. No answer. He called back again. Still no answer. He called back a third time and a man's voice answered Fareeda's cellphone. "You have something of mine," he said, and in those words, Cheese vaguely recognized the voice. "And now I have something of yours."

The line went dead.

UNCLE TONY'S JOB AT THE OFFICE WAS TO RUN AMERICA'S OFF-the-books armies. But no army is ever, truly, off-the-books, so at least once a month he had to meet with a select group of bookkeepers in Congress. One such meeting was on his calendar that afternoon, after his lunch with Mac at Panera.

Technically, these sessions were considered Congressional testimony. Whenever Uncle Tony would mention to the uninitiated that he had to testify before Congress, he noticed how eyes would widen, how thoughtful nods would commence. Such testimony conjured oak-paneled briefing rooms, legislators arrayed down a long dais, the Great Seal of the United States of America hanging on a curtained wall, its eagle clutching arrows in one talon, an olive branch in the other, with its ferocious attention on a hair trigger, poised to turn away from the olive branch (peace) toward the arrows (war) at a single inopportune word.

But, like most things in life—and especially in politics—reality proved less glamorous. Uncle Tony's testimony had never once occurred in the U.S. Capitol, beneath its magisterial dome. He was always tucked away next door, across Independence Avenue, in the bowels of the Rayburn House Office Building.

That afternoon, Uncle Tony was running late. A dip in temperatures had turned a cold, steady rain into sleet, and then into snow, and then into a three-car-pile up on Chain Bridge

Road. Briefers from Langley typically had access to parking spots on the Capitol grounds, but when Uncle Tony flashed his blue headquarters badge to the Capitol policeman, he was informed that those spaces were being used today by a delegation. "From which country?"

"No country." A splotch of wet snow slid off the sleeve of the police officer's rain jacket as he handed Tony back his badge. "They're brand ambassadors . . . influencers . . . InstaTokers, TikAgramers, those types. A few Hollywood people, too. It's a get-out-the-vote thing for Congress."

"For which party?"

"I dunno," said the police officer. "Does it really matter?"

Uncle Tony thought about it for a second. "No," he said. "I suppose it doesn't."

Out of his side mirror, Uncle Tony glimpsed a minor commotion. A young woman, thirty-ish, eye-catchingly beautiful, was crossing the street trailed by Congressional aides. Uncle Tony had seen her before, in some forgettable movie on an airplane. She was sheathed in a designer navy pantsuit, as if cast in the role of "socially conscious starlet" and shipped to Washington. Walking beside her was a man in a far dumpier suit, the same shade of navy, who was nodding at her every word. His lapel pin identified him as a member of Congress, as did the aides who'd formed a protective bubble of umbrellas over each of their heads so they might walk and talk unmolested by the sleet and snow.

The police officer pulled a voucher off a pad he'd kept dry by tucking it into his rain jacket. "There's a private lot on South Capitol, right below E Street, that we're using." He handed Uncle Tony the voucher. "You can park there, just get someone to validate that."

As Uncle Tony pulled away, a chauffeur stepped out of a black SUV on the Capitol grounds, just beyond the police barricade. The SUV was parked in what should've been Uncle Tony's spot. When the woman in the navy suit approached, the chauffeur held open the door for her, gripping it with both hands. But she and the congressman weren't done talking. Both seemed equally fascinated by the other.

This mutual fascination didn't surprise Uncle Tony; it mirrored the relationship of their two industries—politics and entertainment. It'd often been said that Washington, D.C. was Hollywood for ugly people, and that the two one-industry towns were sister cities. If asked which city was more decadent, Uncle Tony would've said Washington (not that anyone had ever asked him). In Hollywood they were just making movies. Their decadence didn't hurt anyone, aside from themselves. In Washington, they were making policy. The stakes were higher. Dysfunction in Hollywood was accounted for in the glossy pages of gossip magazines. Dysfunction in Washington was accounted for in the grim black-and-white headlines of national newspapers.

Uncle Tony parked his car and walked five blocks from the lot to the lobby of the Rayburn Office Building. A staffer from the House Permanent Select Committee on Intelligence, the HPSCI (pronounced the *hip-see* by those in the know), escorted him to the SCIF, a secure and windowless briefing room in the basement. Although Uncle Tony would provide Congressional testimony, not a single member of Congress was present. A dozen staffers—a mixture of the HPSCI's permanent staff as well as the staffs of the individual House members—had arrayed themselves around a U-shaped table.

Most of the faces were recognizable to Uncle Tony, some he'd known for years, a few for decades, though he wasn't fool enough to consider any his friends. Even those he didn't know or had only met once or twice felt familiar because they were all of a certain breed. Their ghostly, blue-white complexions were the result of days spent locked in SCIFs without ever seeing the sun. Their sunken, bloodshot eyes were proof of overtime hours spent scouring highly classified cable traffic. They carried a weighty, blitzed-out look, like scientists who'd spent years in the lab, perpetually on the brink of some great yet elusive discovery. Their dowdy, ill-fitting clothes evidenced their meager pay, an insulting sum completely disproportionate to the responsibilities entrusted to them. Many of the staffers shared the same name. There were three Toms, two Johns, and three Marys. Uncle Tony could never keep them all straight.

After the exchange of some minor pleasantries, Uncle Tony settled into his seat at the mouth of the conference table. One of the Toms asked him to raise his right hand and swear to "tell the truth, the whole truth, and nothing but the truth," so the testimony could begin. Uncle Tony then unlocked the clasp on a secure leather attaché, removing a laptop. He logged on to the wireless network. This linked his laptop to a projector at the back of the room. The lights dimmed and he began walking the HPSCI members through a cascade of Microsoft Excel spreadsheets. Each represented the accounting of a paramilitary program run by the Office. This was the bookkeeping for the off-the-books programs. Uncle Tony maintained programs in dozens of countries, from Shiite SWAT teams in Sadr City who killed Islamic State operatives to exfiltration squads in Scandinavia who recovered Russian agents. His reach was global, his resources vast. His entire testimony was really a reconciliation, a kind of audit. He would open his books and the HPSCI would open theirs, the theory being that each would keep the other honest so that they could lie and obfuscate to the rest of the world.

Up on the screen, Uncle Tony was briefing the activities of one of the Office's proprietary companies in Finland. This was a fishery of four boats that, in addition to harvesting cod and haddock in the Barents Sea, had also deployed seismic listening devices in the waters near Russia's submarine fleet in Kaliningrad and had, most recently, conducted the failed exfiltration of a compromised asset. That asset, a young woman mothering the illegitimate child of a senior SVR official, had been granted a cushy secretarial job in exchange for staying quiet about the affair. Her little boy was even at daycare a few doors down from her office in the Kremlin. But there was no way this arrangement could last. Understanding this, and the need to put away money for her and her boy's future, the young woman began smuggling classified documents out of the building. She would visit her son's daycare on her lunch break, placing the documents in the diaper bag's compartment for soiled diapers. In the afternoons, this allowed her by all appearances to leave the office empty-handed.

The documents had been a goldmine, and headquarters in Langley paid her handsomely through deposits to a Bahamian bank account. Her reports touched on everything from Russian troop movements to satellite launch schedules. Uncle Tony had been particularly interested in Russian assessments of former indig soldiers, those Afghans, Iraqis, Yemenis, Somalis, who'd once been on the Office's payroll but who'd now found work fighting alongside the Ukrainians in the International Legion. The intel arrived for months until another mother, in a mix-up, took home the wrong diaper bag. The next day, the asset didn't come into work. Three nights later, Uncle Tony's people had picked her and her son up on a freezing beach an hour outside of Saint Petersburg. Two hours later, a storm blew in. No one had heard from her, her son, or the crew of the ship since.

Uncle Tony finished telling this sad little story with a curt, "Next slide."

"Hold on," said one of the staffers. Uncle Tony didn't recognize her, but the name on the placard read *Janice* and she worked for a junior congressman, a former used-car salesman from Pennsylvania who was new to the committee. She was peering through a pair of reading glasses perched on the end of her nose. "I see you've archived all the 201s"—*archive* being a nice euphemism for moving not only the woman and her son, but also the paramilitary officers who'd tried to exfil her, from the category of those who were *active* (alive) to those who were *inactive* (dead)—"but what I don't see is that you've removed the ship you've lost from your inventory."

Uncle Tony indexed his finger on the screen, scrolling down the columns of his Excel spreadsheet, past rows and rows of equipment and personnel, all of which were part of this Finnish agent exfiltration operation posing as a fishing business.

He found the ship on his spreadsheet. She was right, he needed to remove it and place it in the archive. With all the magnanimity he could muster, Uncle Tony said, "I've made a note of it. Thanks, Janice."

"It's Ja-NIECE, accent's on the second syllable."

"Got it," he said, offering the barest of smiles, making another note.

CHEESE WAS PACING AROUND THE CHALLENGER 600 WITH Sinéad's phone clenched in his hand, trying Fareeda every five minutes. Skwerl sat nearby in the hangar, on a picnic table where ground crews ate lunch during working hours. Sinéad was beside him, also watching Cheese. Both were concerned, and both agreed that the last thing Cheese should do is go home. Cheese disagreed, at least at first. When he'd heard the voice on the other end of the line tell him, "And now I have something of yours," Cheese had insisted that they drive to Philly International so he could board the next commercial flight to Austin.

This was, of course, a bad idea. Cheese was the only one who could pilot the Challenger 600. Also, it was the middle of the night, so it'd be hours until he could get a flight. And if Cheese traveled through an airport, TSA would flag him instantly. Skwerl reminded Cheese that whoever had taken Fareeda had a badge, so was tied in with the authorities, and likely had his name too. "Take a deep breath," Skwerl said, "and try to calm down."

Cheese stopped his pacing. He turned toward Skwerl and took a breath.

"Better?"

Cheese rotated his hips, pivoted on the balls of this feet, and landed his cocked fist on Skwerl's jaw, spinning him like a top. "I never should've let you convince me about any of this! If we don't get Fareeda back . . . ! If we don't . . . !" Cheese turned away, bowing his head.

Skwerl got back on his feet, massaging his jaw, running his tongue over his teeth. ". . . Better now?"

Cheese nodded. "Sorry."

"I sorta deserved it."

Cheese took a step toward Skwerl. He pointed to his own chin. "Land one on me. Fair is fair."

Sinéad interrupted, "Boys . . . we don't have time for this."

Cheese pointed at his chin again, inviting Skwerl.

"She's right. I'll tag you later." Skwerl opened his arms, inviting Cheese to give him a hug. "C'mon," he said, motioning with his cupped palms.

Cheese hesitated.

"C'mon . . ." Skwerl went in, hooking an arm under and the other over Cheese's arms, slapping him on the back twice. "Two slaps on the back," he said, "just like that, so it doesn't get weird."

Cheese returned Skwerl's two slaps on the back.

TWO HOURS PASSED AS UNCLE TONY WALKED THE STAFFERS through each program, comparing his lists to theirs, at times dropping hints of daring operations successfully executed or failed operations nobly attempted. Although he punctuated his briefing with little, exciting anecdotes, the atmosphere turned monotonous and boring. These were the exact conditions Uncle Tony was waiting for when it came time to brief the largest of his archived assets, Defense Response and Coordination Associates. "You'll note," Uncle Tony began, "that last quarter we completed the transfer of DRCA assets into private hands. As of today, the Office has entirely divested itself from that partnership."

Uncle Tony paused. He would allow the appropriate few

seconds to pass before moving on to the next slide. But before he could, there was a question from across the room. "DRCA . . . is that the security company implicated a few years back in the Now Zad raid?"

"Correct," said Uncle Tony. "After Now Zad, our government stopped working with DRCA."

"I see most of DRCA's assets transferred to private ownership," said the staffer, flipping through her notes, "a majority stake is now owned by . . . Cyberdyne."

"Given the controversy surrounding Now Zad, we had to clean house, so we decided to—"

The staffer interrupted Uncle Tony. "Like thirty people were killed on that raid," she said. "Lots of them civilians."

"It was a little more complicated than that . . ."—and Uncle Tony peered at the name card on the desk, this staffer was also named ". . . Janice."

"It's pronounced JA-niss," she said. "Not Ja-NIECE." She glanced across the room at the other Janice, the one from Pennsylvania. "Just FYI."

"Okay . . ." Uncle Tony took a breath. "It's pronounced *Derka,* not D-R-C-A. Also, just FYI." He turned back toward his briefing. "After Kabul fell, the last of our assets who'd worked for DRCA came off the books. DRCA has no outstanding contracts with the U.S. government, so their operations are really none of our concern. But, if it's of interest to this subcommittee, I'd be happy to ask around and give you a fuller briefing on their current activities, *JA-niss.*"

She took a long, hard look at Uncle Tony. "That won't be necessary."

Uncle Tony flipped to his next slide.

"A last question," said Janice. "If you wouldn't mind going back a slide." Uncle Tony pushed the button on his clicker like he was crushing a bug between his fingers. "Thank you." She reached into her purse, removing a laser pointer. Its red dot floated on a single name that appeared on the roster of assets: *Hendrik Hofstede*. "Before this meeting, I saw that his 201 had been archived just this morning."

"Correct."

"What's the story there?"

"No story," said Uncle Tony. "At least not anymore. Hofstede is dead."

Janice fingered a folder with a red coversheet with a *TS/SCI* classification on its front, one of many such folders littering the U-shaped desk. Uncle Tony pursed his lips and slitted his eyes. His glare conveyed a single message, like a bureaucratic Dirty Harry armed with a retractable pen instead of a .44 Magnum: *Go ahead, Janice. Make my day.*

Uncle Tony knew what was in that folder, Hendrik Hofstede's recovered 201. Hofstede had been working both for DRCA and the U.S. government when he was killed. No one on that subcommittee wanted those details recorded in Congressional testimony. Yes, these HSPCI staffers wanted the truth. And they wanted to know secrets. But only up to a point. They'd been complicit in building secret armies. In recent years, they'd disbanded those armies, fired them, sent them out into the streets, into the fields, back to wherever the hell they came from, issuing edicts for them to get regular jobs while having no idea what that might mean to men like these. These staffers and their bosses in Congress wanted to believe they could simply turn the page. To Janice (and the Toms and Marys and Johns around the U-shaped table) DRCA was evidence of an inconvenient truth: that armies last longer than the wars they're raised to fight. American-trained Afghans, Iraqis, Somalis, Yemenis, Kurds were turning up in odd and unseemly places. Their unique skills sold to the highest bidder, whether that was Assad's Alawite hit squads, Wagner's Libyan training cadres, or Russian separatists in the Donbas. Hofstede had served as a bag man for DRCA, a jack of all trades and master of none, tasked to handle odd jobs. The details of his life and work were in that file.

All Janice had to do was ask about it, put it on the record. Uncle Tony would gladly provide her the answers. But they were answers that she—and her colleagues and the legislators they worked for—didn't want to hear.

Janice left the folder closed.

Not much of Uncle Tony's briefing remained after that. He presented slides on a defensive driving course his officers were running in central Florida for female operatives of the Saudi General Intelligence Presidency (a high accident rate had forced them to switch insurance carriers three times, putting the course over budget). He'd also briefed an embarrassing incident with the Pakistani embassy (the Office had submitted student visa requests for six of its operatives all at once, so six thick-necked, bearded, tattooed thirty-somethings allegedly interested in studying the microbiology of the North-West Frontier Province). Uncle Tony had apologized for those screwups. Congress had accepted, glad to have an apology for something.

With that, the subcommittee adjourned.

The staffers gathered up their materials and began to head back to their offices. Before they could leave, Uncle Tony asked whether any of them could validate his parking. He held the voucher in his hand, making eye contact with Tom, Mary, Janice, and the rest of them. But no one seemed to have a clue.

It was still snowing and sleeting when Uncle Tony returned to his car. In the end, he had to pay the twenty-six dollars in parking from his own pocket.

Man, it pissed him off.

WHILE THEY WAITED FOR EPHRAIM TO REPAIR THE CHALLENGER 600, Sinéad explained her plan. She knew how to find out who had taken Fareeda. One of her clients had recently run for office and, somewhat improbably, won. Charles Mangrove was now a first-term congressman, but he'd been seeing her as a client since the days when he sold used cars. Mangrove had given up Sinéad during the campaign, the way a good Catholic might give up sweets for Lent. But only a few weeks ago he had reappeared, inquiring whether he and Mistress S might discreetly schedule a session. When Skwerl asked about him, Sinéad didn't provide a description so much as a diagnosis. "Mildly delusional. Definitely bipolar. Probably a narcissistic sociopath." To which Cheese had replied, "Do you think he could help us?"

"Definitely."

"How can you be so sure?"

Sinéad pointed to the line tattooed nearly three inches above her wrist. "Because that's Mangrove. I'll pay him a visit at his office tomorrow."

The prospect of Sinéad visiting with the congressman seemed to calm Cheese, at least enough so he could focus on the task at hand, which was getting the Challenger 600 back in the air. Ephraim was in a corner of the hangar hunched over a workbench, having detached the remnants of the aileron from the wing. The transatlantic flight had exacerbated the damage, shredding a two-by-four-foot segment of the aileron. Although the damage was bad, it was largely contained to that single segment. Ephraim, rummaging around in the back of the hangar, had found a similarly sized plank with a couple of nails sticking out its end; it had come off a shipping pallet, one built sturdy and used to transport engine parts.

"This'll do nicely." Ephraim sighted down the plank like it was a rifle. With pencil in hand, he traced a curve onto either end, a measurement to guide him as he began to shape the wood.

"Are you kidding me?" Skwerl said.

Ephraim locked the plank into a vise on the workbench, ignoring Skwerl.

Cheese understood the genius of Ephraim's plan. "What do you think aircraft were originally built from?" he said to Skwerl. "The rest of the wing is made of carbon-fiber-reinforced plastics, which is light and strong. But there are plenty of woods that are equally strong. It's just that they're heavier. But it won't matter if it's only the aileron." Turning to Ephraim, Cheese asked, "What type of wood is that?"

Ephraim had found a handsaw and sanding block. "Birchwood," he muttered between grunts. With each powerful stroke slivers of wood flew in all direction, clattering to the floor.

"Ephraim's talented," Sinéad whispered to a still skeptical Skwerl. "Also . . . he's Amish. They can build anything out of wood." Some of the dungeon furniture in her studio—as well as a dovetail-jointed desk and chairs in her Knotty Pleasures administrative office—had been built by Ephraim when he was short payment for a few of their sessions.

If Skwerl needed more convincing, Cheese added, "One of the largest planes ever built, the *Spruce Goose,* was made of birchwood."

"Then why'd they name it *spruce*?"

For once, Cheese didn't have an answer.

Skwerl asked about the tail number. How would they fix that?

Ephraim paused his sawing. He gazed up at the tail section, as if considering it for the first time. He silently mouthed the tail number, as if solving an equation. "You should be changing that 3 to an 8, and that 4 to a 9." Ephraim gestured to a corner of the hangar, toward a can of black paint, white paint, some thinner and brushes. He commenced with his sawing, which he soon finished. Next, he began to sand and shape the segment of wood while Sinéad and Skwerl wheeled a platform ladder around to the tail section. The two of them climbed the ladder. From this vantage point, they could see through a pair of second-story hangar windows that looked out at the darkened runway.

They began to paint, levering open the can of thinner, cleaning the brushes, and carefully manipulating each number so the change wouldn't appear too obvious to the tower as they taxied down the runway.

"Have you figured out yet where you're going to stash the plane?" Sinéad asked. The two of them had begun work on the tail, her handling the 3 and him the 4.

Skwerl nodded.

"Are you planning on telling me?"

He knew Sinéad wasn't going to like the answer.

"Where, Jay?"

Skwerl made a couple of more brushstrokes before mustering the courage to say, "Colorado . . ."

"You're kidding." She pitched her brush into the can of thinner. "Not him . . . Not J.S."

"Do you know anyone else with their own landing strip?"

"He's a lunatic."

"Would he have his own landing strip if he wasn't a lunatic?"

"Does Cheese know?"

"Yes."

"And he's going along with this?" Sinéad dropped her voice an octave. Cheese and Ephraim were beneath them now. They'd finished transforming the two-by-four into a segment that matched the original aileron and fit into the wing's oblong airfoil. They'd been able to reuse the titanium brackets and were turning the last half dozen screws to complete the repairs.

Skwerl said, "What choice does he have?" also dropping his voice.

Cheese tugged on the aileron. The brackets seemed secure. He told Ephraim to climb into the jet. Cheese wanted him to manipulate the controls so he could make a visual inspection of the aileron in motion. "Sit in the pilot's seat, that's the left one," Cheese explained. "Then turn the yoke to each side." Ephraim gave Cheese a questioning glance, as if he weren't quite sure whether sitting in the cockpit with the jet off and manipulating the controls would violate certain religious dictates. With a shrug, Ephraim climbed aboard.

Cheese shouted "Left!" and the birchwood aileron went down.

Then he shouted "Right!" and it went up.

As Cheese was finishing the last of these checks, Sinéad spotted a car crossing the runway in their direction. "Do you know who that is?"

Skwerl had no idea.

SINÉAD SCURRIED DOWN THE LADDER. WITHIN SECONDS, SHE was outside the hangar, standing on the runway, ready to intercept whoever had come to pay them a visit. Skwerl watched out the high windows from where he remained on the ladder's platform. When the car pulled up beside Sinéad, Skwerl glimpsed a logo on its side—*Night Shield*—some type of budget, rent-a-cop security company. The guard stepped from his car. He gestured to the hangar, saying something to Sinéad. Skwerl could only watch. He had to have faith that Sinéad would figure a way to convince the guard to turn around, to leave them alone, that there was nothing worth seeing inside the hangar.

The guard again pointed toward the hangar. Skwerl ducked, glancing down to where Cheese stood beneath the wing. "This thing ready to fly?" he whispered.

Cheese gazed up at him, a little confused but increasingly used to leaving airports in a hurry. "Yeah . . . time to go?"

"Maybe . . ." Skwerl looked back out the window. Sinéad was still chatting up the security guard, who, at least for the moment, had halted his progress toward the hangar. He remained parked on the runway, deep in conversation with Sinéad. Skwerl couldn't imagine what they were talking about. But he also knew—from his own experience—that Sinéad could get anyone to open up to her.

Sinéad placed her hand on the guard's forearm. Whatever she was saying compelled him to stay where he was. The guard fixed his gaze in Skwerl's direction, as if considering a proposition, and then he nodded, turning his back on the hangar. Sinéad climbed into his car. They drove across the runway toward a cluster of buildings on the far side of the FBO, near the tower, where the lights came on one by one.

Sinéad had bought Skwerl the time he needed.

"YOU'RE COMING WITH US," SKWERL TOLD EPHRAIM. "I CAN'T have you wandering off after Sinéad." He had already pulled the wheel chocks and opened the hangar door. Cheese was in the cockpit, running through his pre-flight, firing the engines, toggling on the avionics. For Ephraim, a trip in Sinéad's Acura and a visit to a drive-thru were one thing. Flying in a private jet was a heresy of another order of magnitude. Ephraim asked about his pony, the one he'd left haltered to his buggy in the garage. "I'm sure Sinéad will look after her," Skwerl said. "And we'll have you home in no time. But for now, take a seat in the back."

Ephraim couldn't figure out the seatbelt, so Skwerl had to help him with it. Before climbing into the cockpit, Skwerl also shut the window shades, assuming this would make the experience of flying a bit less overwhelming for Ephraim. "He going to be okay back there?" Cheese asked as they began taxiing out of the hangar.

Skwerl glanced over his shoulder. Ephraim sat as rigid as a man strapped to an electric chair. "Yeah," said Skwerl. "He's good."

Cheese radioed the tower, calling in their new (fake) tail number. "Chester Tower, Romeo 8195K, Runway 23, ready for takeoff."

There was a pause. Unlike in Marseille, where they'd almost immediately entered international airspace once in flight, they'd now be flying across the continental United States. If the tower didn't clear them, they'd appear unregistered on FAA-monitored air traffic control systems. They needed this clearance. Skwerl glanced out the window, in the direction of the tower. The security guard's car was parked at its base. Sinéad was likely up there, too.

Cheese repeated his call.

The radio crackled to life. "Roger, Romeo 8195K, Runway 23, cleared for takeoff." Then the unfamiliar voice added, "Have a nice flight, fellas."

Cheese glanced at Skwerl. "What do you think she told them?"

"I have no idea."

Cheese brought the Challenger to full throttle, keeping one eye down the runway and the other on the retrofitted aileron. They climbed smoothly after takeoff and were not yet at their cruising altitude when Ephraim appeared in the cockpit. "What are you doing up here?" said Skwerl. "Get back in the cabin." When he turned over his shoulder, he could see that Ephraim had raised all the window shades so he could look outside.

"The view is even more amazing up here," said Ephraim. At that moment, they punched through a cloud and Ephraim gasped and then laughed like a child. "Where are we going?" he asked. His stare remained fixed out the cockpit as if convinced that should he look away for even an instant this magic of flight would vanish and they'd all tumble from the sky, back to earth.

"Colorado," Skwerl announced.

"Colorado . . ." Ephraim repeated. "I've never been to Colorado."

"No," said Cheese. "I suppose you haven't."

"What's in Colorado?"

"A friend of ours," said Skwerl. "J.S."

"J.S.? This is a nickname?"

"Kind of . . . it stands for 'Just Shane,'" but as Skwerl turned around he noticed Ephraim didn't look quite right. "You feeling okay?"

Ephraim had turned a sudden and greenish pale. Little beads of sweat had congregated on his forehead and on his shaved top lip. He'd begun working his jaw side to side, complaining that his ears felt clogged, a new experience for him, having never been at this altitude. Then his eyes widened and became shot with panic. He clasped his hands over his mouth, but there was nothing he could do to stop it.

He threw up in the cockpit.

Chapter Three

JUST SHANE

THE HALF-DOZEN MEN WHO'D APPEARED AT FAREEDA'S DOOR had been exceedingly polite. They first apologized for frightening her, but then explained that she would be taking a trip for a few days. If she wanted them to gather some items for her—a change of clothes, nightgown, toothbrush, toothpaste, etc.—they would happily do so, but she would need to remain sitting in her living room and not move around the apartment. Unfortunately, they couldn't permit her to bring any electronics. But if she had a couple of books she'd like to take along, she need only to tell them which ones and they'd place those into the suitcase they were packing for her.

One of the men did most of the talking. Fareeda thought she could place his accent. Its tones were Iranian, but a little off. Listening more closely, she felt increasingly certain it wasn't inflections of Farsi she was hearing, but inflections of Dari, making him an Afghan like herself. He was very good-looking, almost like a movie star, impeccably dressed, with a small bandage on the back of his neck. Once Fareeda's bag was packed, he escorted her downstairs; there, a windowless van was parked outside her apartment.

He apologized profusely when, with thick plastic zip ties, he flex-cuffed her wrists together. "So sorry, sister. Required precaution." Next, he pulled a black hood over her head and eased her into the back of the van. She sat braced against its side, on a foam mattress. Less than an hour later—she couldn't say exactly how long the drive had been—the back doors of the van were flung open. The only thing Fareeda could distinguish from beneath her hood was light and dark. And it was definitely dark outside. It was also noisy, the air filled with the high-decibel squeals of jet engines, a sound that would always remind her of the night she and her husband had fled Kabul airport.

A steady wind blew against Fareeda's face. Two men marched her across a runway, each gripping one of her elbows. She climbed a few stairs, arriving in a bright, low-ceilinged space. The floor beneath her was softer, thickly carpeted. One of her escorts pushed firmly on her shoulder, instructing her to sit down (unlike the men at her apartment, he sounded European). She tumbled backward into a luxurious recliner. A door shut, not a regular door, but a hatch. It was almost entirely silent now. She could tell she'd arrived in the back of an airplane, a very nice one. Fareeda wondered if her husband knew how to fly this type of airplane. She suspected that he did.

Fareeda sat up in her seat a little straighter. *My husband . . .* she said to herself, *can fly anything*. She could sense that someone was sitting across from her. Even with a hood over her head, she glowered at whoever that was.

ALI SAFI WAITED UNTIL THEY WERE OVER WATER BEFORE snatching off Fareeda's hood. She was still blinking into the light as he introduced himself. "You must be hungry," he added. "Eat something . . ." He gestured to a basket of fruit—bananas, apples, grapes—as well as an ornate serving dish crowded with packaged snacks that had come from a galley kitchen at the front of the jet, near the sealed cockpit doors. "When we land," he said, "I'll make sure you receive a proper meal."

Fareeda didn't reply.

"You must eat." Ali Safi gestured to her abdomen. "For your child's sake."

She lifted her bound wrists above the table.

"My apologies." Ali Safi swiftly unbuttoned his tailored suit jacket, reaching for his belt. He removed a knife, a stiletto sharpened on both sides and tapered to a point, its grip large enough to fill his entire palm. Ali Safi reached across the table, cutting off Fareeda's flex-cuffs with a swipe of the blade, freeing her hands. As Ali Safi leaned back into the seat across from Fareeda, she glimpsed his pistol. Its black polymer handle dangled beneath his left armpit in a chest holster.

With her hands free, Fareeda began to pile fruit onto a napkin embossed with a globe superimposed above a dagger, the corporate logo of whoever owned this plane. "Where are we going?"

"Marseille," Ali Safi said casually. "Your husband was supposed to steal a jet and deliver it there. Unfortunately, he backed out on the deal. Which is why you find yourself in this situation."

"My husband wasn't hired to *steal* a jet," said Fareeda. "He was hired to *repossess* one."

"*Repossess?*" Ali Safi seemed genuinely perplexed by this word. He began to laugh. "What's the difference?"

Suddenly, Fareeda wasn't sure.

"May I ask, sister, who hired your husband to *repossess* this jet?"

"Someone called Sheepdog."

"Sheepdog . . ." Ali Safi made a slight smacking sound with his mouth, as if he needed a sip of water to rinse out an unpleasant taste. "That's an odd name?"

The night after Skwerl had appeared in Fareeda's apartment with the prospect of quick money, she had asked her husband about the meaning of their unseen partner's name. She now offered Ali Safi that explanation. "There are three types of people in this world," Fareeda began haltingly, floating her gaze up toward the ceiling. "Sheep, wolves, and sheepdogs. Those who believe that evil doesn't exist in this world to threaten them are the sheep. When that evil arrives, they are the ones unprepared to protect themselves and loved ones. Then there are those who use violence to prey on the weak. These are the wolves, predators who steal and murder. But then there are those who, like the wolves, also understand violence, except they use that understanding to protect others. These are the sheepdogs."

"And this Sheepdog, who protects his flock of sheep from the evil wolves, he does this by having your husband steal—sorry, *repossess*—luxury jets?"

"You're making fun of me."

"No," said Ali Safi. "I'm making fun of a person who thinks they are a sheepdog."

Fareeda held up the napkin with a logo on it. "What about you?" she asked. "Aside from kidnapping pregnant women and taking them to the south of France, what is it that you do?"

Ali Safi gave a sharklike grin. "I'm a security guard."

"A security guard with a jet . . . ?"

Ali Safi crossed his arms over his chest. He wouldn't be explaining further, so Fareeda tried another question: "Have you always been a security guard?"

"Before, I was a university student."

"What did you study?"

"Mathematics," he said, considering Fareeda for a moment before deciding to say more. "Logic to be exact. My specialty was in model theory, the study of systems. Three years ago, my brother was killed. I had to return home to support my family. That's when I became a security guard."

He seemed done answering her questions, though Fareeda ventured one more. "How was your brother killed?"

At first, Ali Safi seemed to ignore the question. He was fiddling with the paper napkin, folding it over itself into smaller and smaller squares, as if maybe it was possible to fold it so many times that it might disappear. When he'd folded the napkin so tightly that he couldn't fold it any more, he laid it flat on the table, smoothing out its creases. He glanced up at Fareeda, tracing the embossed logo with his finger. "He was killed working for the owners of this jet."

Fareeda suddenly turned away. She began to breathe heavily with her gaze fixed out her window. It sounded like she was hyperventilating.

"No need to be afraid," Ali Safi said.

Fareeda took another half-dozen breaths, and then made one long exhalation. Slowly, her breathing became normal. Her attention returned to inside the plane. "I'm not afraid," she said with contempt, and then placed her hand against her stomach. "I was having a contraction."

"A contraction?" Ali Safi edged forward in his seat.

"Braxton-Hicks," she said. "They're practice contractions."

"Practice?" Ali Safi sputtered.

"It's my body preparing for the baby, not the baby coming."

"Oh, that's good." Ali Safi eased back into his seat.

Fareeda then added, "But you never know."

Now it was Ali Safi's turn to gaze out the window. Minutes passed in silence as he contemplated the Atlantic below and the possibility—planted into his imagination by Fareeda—that he might have to deliver a baby. Eventually, he turned his attention back inside the cabin. Fareeda had shut her eyes, trying to sleep, or at least to keep herself relaxed. Ali Safi rummaged around in a compartment near the galley and came back with a blanket, which he offered.

"You know," Ali Safi said, settling back across from her, not seeming to care if he kept Fareeda awake a little longer, "it's not just sheep, wolves, and sheepdogs in this world."

"No . . . ?" muttered Fareeda. "Who else then?

"Wolves in sheep's clothing." Ali Safi pulled his own blanket up to his neck. Shutting his eyes to sleep, he reminded her, "You've also got to watch out for those."

EPHRAIM HAD GONE TO THE BACK OF THE JET TO LIE DOWN. He'd thrown up twice more and was now sleeping, reclined in his seat, wrapped in a blanket. Skwerl had spent the past hour on hands and knees. With fistfuls of paper napkins and hand soap from the dispenser in the Challenger 600's single toilet, he'd been picking out little pieces of regurgitated Taco Bell. It was all over the carpet, stuck in the controls and avionics, completely disgusting. He and Cheese sat in the pilot and copilot seats, flying southwest, the collars of each of their shirts pulled over their noses.

"I can't take the smell anymore," Cheese said in a nasal tone—he was pinching his nostrils shut. "I need a break."

"Who's gonna fly the plane?" Skwerl's voice was equally nasally.

Cheese reached deep into the control panel. He touched a switch without flipping it. "Ugh, it's also wet," and he held his hand in the air until Skwerl could pass him a fresh paper napkin. Cheese wiped his hand and the switch clean. He dumped the dirty napkin onto an enormous pile that had accumulated between them near the throttle. He flipped the switch and the jet lurched before its glide path smoothed, as if it'd suddenly been placed on rails. "Autopilot is now on," Cheese announced. "Stay up here. If you see another plane or a warning light just shout back for me."

"Are you kidding? I can't fly this thing."

"You're not flying it, autopilot is."

"Cheese . . ."

"If I don't get some fresh air, you'll have two of us laid out back there."

Cheese disappeared into the jet's main cabin. Skwerl checked his watch. They had another couple of hours until they'd reach Just Shane's place, which was about an hour's drive outside of Little Neck, Colorado, a town with a population of under a thousand. Skwerl would have to wake Ephraim up soon, no matter how sick he was. Skwerl had a few things to explain, to ensure that everything would go smoothly when they landed.

The first of those things was that Skwerl was no longer from Pennsylvania—at least not while they were with Shane. So far as Just Shane was concerned, he and Skwerl were from the same hometown . . .

This elaborate fiction had begun a decade before, when Shane and Skwerl had been on the same special operations team, 8233, Hotel Company, 2d Raider Battalion, Combined Joint Special Operations Task Force—Afghanistan. Back then, Shane was a bomb tech, so a specialist and not a fully qualified operator. This meant he was subjected to a little more ribbing than most. To kill time, Skwerl had thought to play a practical joke on Shane. His idea was to convince him that they were from the same little corner of Colorado. ("Get outta here, Shane? You're from Little Neck . . . ?" "Sure am!" "I grew up nearby, not far from Hopkins Creek . . ." "Great trout fishing there!" "Sure is . . .")

The guys on 8233 got a pool going, how long could Skwerl keep up the joke? A week? A month? Two months? The whole deployment? ("We should organize a fishing trip when we get back, Skwerl, maybe even invite a couple of the other 8233 guys, show 'em Hopkins Creek.") Skwerl never lost his composure, not once. His teammates were another matter, and often they'd step out of a briefing or around the back of the Humvee to crack up when Skwerl got Shane going. This isn't to say that Shane never became suspicious of Skwerl. ("Hey, if you grew up near Little Neck, how come I never once saw you at Eldorado Elementary or Kit Carson High?") But Skwerl always seemed to have an answer ready. ("Ma and Pa were pretty strict, so they homeschooled me and Jo.") Everyone in 8233 agreed that Skwerl's introduction of little brother Josiah Manning into the story was some next-level joke-master shit. Skwerl had added this storyline to test the boundaries of Shane's gullibility.

During long patrols or on days off between raids, Skwerl would pass the hours with elaborate fictions all set around Little Neck and Hopkins Creek—*The Adventures of Skwerl and Josiah*, a multipart spoken-word epic worthy of anything Mark Twain ever wrote (at least if you asked Skwerl). By the seventh month of their deployment, Skwerl had dug himself a pretty deep hole. Shane was talking about post-deployment leave, how good it would be for him and Skwerl to travel home together. Skwerl knew he had to come clean, but the idea terrified him. Gullible and guileless as Shane could be, he had a temper. A violent one. This was why he was called Just Shane, or J.S. for short.

Rumor had it that when Shane had shown up as the junior bomb tech on his first team, the one before 8233, they'd tried to give him a nickname. Shane hadn't liked what his teammates picked. He insisted that they quit it with the name. But they wouldn't and kept badgering him. One day after work, in the team room, Shane snapped. He wound up putting a guy in the hospital (shattered jaw, crushed nose). A week later, when his teammates still didn't quit it with the nickname, he put a second guy in the hospital (fractured tib-fib caused by the butt of a rifle). A month later, that team deployed two operators short. Their commanding officer could've brought Shane up on charges. But he didn't. If he had, they would've headed overseas short a bomb tech and had to defuse IEDs themselves—no thanks.

After that, everyone stopped calling Shane this nickname. And no one thought to try to give him another. They would *just call him Shane* instead—as in *Just . . . Shane*. As for that other nickname, the one Just Shane hadn't liked, Skwerl had begun asking about it around the same time he'd started pretending he and Just Shane were from the same hometown. Out of fear, those who knew the offending nickname wouldn't dare utter it—lest Just Shane trace the source of its reemergence and snap, putting that person in the hospital. Needless to say, as Skwerl learned more of Just Shane's reputation he grew increasingly panicked. What would Just Shane do when he learned the truth about their hometowns?

Except Just Shane never found out. Before Skwerl could come clean, their team ran into an ambush. They'd been returning from a mission when the lead indig truck hit an IED, killing two Afghan soldiers and trapping two inside. When Shane's vehicle came up to investigate, they found that a second IED in the crater had failed to detonate. Shane didn't have time to get out his TALON, the IED-defusing robot he typically used. Instead, he went straight to work, down in the crater, bent over the IED with nothing but his Leatherman. The second IED was huge, three daisy-chained 155 artillery rounds. The dust from the explosion hadn't even cleared as Shane cut wires and tore out blasting caps and fuses from these rounds. When he was pulling out the last blasting cap, it clacked off. The high explosive inside the 155 rounds didn't detonate thanks to Shane's quick work, but the blasting cap mangled his right hand and sent frag into his left eye.

Within two days Just Shane was at Bethesda Naval Hospital. Two months later, he was back home in Little Neck. That's when the reporter from *Stars & Stripes* found him. Skwerl had less than a month left on his deployment when, on his firebase, he read the headline: *Hometown Heroes*. The piece featured a photo of a recuperating Shane standing in Hopkins Creek, fishing left-handed. It was a three-thousand-word profile, in which Shane went on at length about how hard it was to leave deployment early, "particularly as one of the other guys on my team is from Little Neck." It also had quotes from Just Shane's aunt, who'd raised him, including a line about how "sensitive my Shaney can be" and how it gave her solace to know that "he'd had a good friend from back home with him when he'd been crippled."

Skwerl could never tell Shane the truth after that.

The two had stayed in touch. Skwerl had successfully convinced Shane that his highly sensitive and classified work for the Office is what kept him from returning to Little Neck ("I don't want to lie to people back home about what I do . . . you can understand.") And Just Shane had nodded discerningly, appreciating that through his absence Skwerl was protecting the good people of Little Neck from nefarious forces, the same bureaucratic-capitalist forces that waged the endless wars that cost him his hand and eye. In the years since his injury, Shane had become more conspiracy minded. When he inherited the remains of a hefty 401(k) from that same aunt, he went completely off the grid. With that money and savings from his monthly VA disability checks, he bought a few hundred wooded acres from a bankrupt mining company in a fire sale. This included a small overgrown airstrip, occasionally used to resupply the mine but originally built by the 10th Mountain Division for their training camps during World War II. After buying the land, Shane had recleared the airstrip himself with a Bobcat.

Cheese had plugged those coordinates into the autopilot on the Challenger 600. They would arrive within the hour.

WHEN SINÉAD ARRIVED AT CONGRESSMAN CHARLES MANGROVE'S Philadelphia office, the receptionist was seated in the anteroom. On her otherwise empty desk was a computer and silent telephone. She stood and asked whether Sinéad had an appointment. Sinéad did not. But she felt certain that the congressman would want to see her. Mangrove's receptionist was less certain. She explained that the congressman's schedule was completely filled. "Perhaps you'd like to schedule an appointment online, through our constituent services portal?" Sinéad declined, saying that she'd wait. She took a seat. The receptionist made a production of settling in back behind her desk, resuming her busy work while keeping one eye on Sinéad from above her computer's monitor.

The office was on Walnut Street, housed in a modern glass-and-steel building with views of Rittenhouse Square. It was a significant upgrade from Mangrove's brick-and-mortar operation at the used-car dealership on Belmont Ave, in West Philly. Sinéad had only ever traveled there once, after Mangrove had thought it'd be cute to stiff her on payment for two sessions. She'd appeared in the showroom dressed as though she were going to work. That had been enough for Mangrove to sprint out of his office, shuttle Sinéad into a maintenance bay in the back, and write her a personal check on the spot. Although Sinéad wasn't dressed for work today—she still wore the jeans and cable knit sweater she'd left the house in yesterday—she was betting her appearance alone would gain her an audience followed by a favor or two from the newly elected (and newly respectable) congressman.

While she waited, Sinéad thumbed through the latest issue of *Time* magazine. Buried in the back of the issue, beneath one of their lists of 100 high-flying achievers that included Mangrove, Sinéad found a story about the war in Ukraine. It described how offensives launched by both sides had bogged down. The Russians, running short on manpower, had taken to recruiting felons out of their prisons and into their ranks. The Ukrainians, who were even more shorthanded, had augmented their ranks with foreign fighters, making the war in Ukraine a truly international affair that included Georgians, Latvians, Britons, Nepalese Gurkhas, to name a few. The journalist who wrote the story had even managed to find an older Ukrainian commander who had fought in the Soviet Army in Afghanistan in the 1980s. He now had Afghan foreign fighters volunteering in his ranks, some of whom had fathers and grandfathers who'd fought *against* the Soviets. When asked by the journalist whether he had a problem fighting alongside the children of those he'd once fought against, the Ukrainian commander was quoted as saying, "Why should it bother me? . . . Switching sides in a war is the oldest of military traditions."

Right as Sinéad was reading that line, the door to Congressman Mangrove's office swung open. He stood ensconced in a gaggle of his supporters, a half-dozen men and women clad in business suits, all agreeing with one another on some series of urgent points. As they stepped into the anteroom, Mangrove was offering to take a photo with his guests when he caught sight of Sinéad. Mangrove's secretary swiftly positioned him in front of a display of flags. She held up an iPhone. "Everyone smile."

Mangrove's attention was now fixed in the corner of the room, on Sinéad.

"Congressman . . ." his secretary said more forcibly.

Mangrove shot her a glance.

"Smile," she said.

The flash went off, and Mangrove hurried his guests out the door. "Come inside," he said to Sinéad, not so much as an invitation but as a command. When Mangrove's secretary protested, reminding him of his back-to-back appointments, he told her to cancel them. As he shut the door, he left strict instructions that under no circumstances should he be disturbed. Stepping into his office, Sinéad was already perched on the leather tufted sofa across from Mangrove's large oak desk.

"What the hell are you doing here?"

"Aren't you going to offer me something to drink?"

"Are you thirsty?"

"No," said Sinéad. "It's just polite to offer a guest something."

"A guest is someone you invite."

"I need your help."

Mangrove crossed his office to a well-stocked drink caddy. He poured himself a midday scotch served neat in a crystal tumbler. Instead of installing himself behind his desk, he plopped down on the sofa next to Sinéad. "We've got a session scheduled in a couple of days." He spread his arms along the back of the sofa. "Couldn't this wait until then?"

"A friend of mine's in trouble, or rather his wife is." Sinéad explained about Fareeda, how a man with a badge had come looking for her husband at the Esso station and that shortly thereafter she had been arrested—or kidnapped.

"By who?"

"Not sure, I need you to ask around. You sit on the HPSCI, correct? I need whatever info you can get me on a man named Ali Safi."

"Sinéad, you can't expect me to—"

"*Ali Safi*," she snapped back.

Mangrove flinched, his spine straightening as he spilled his scotch.

"Write it down, you pig."

He popped up off the sofa without cleaning up his drink. He was scrambling around his chaotic desk, searching for a pen, a pad of paper, anything to write with.

"And Mangrove . . ." He paused and glanced up at her. "It's not *Sinéad*. It's Mistress S to you. Got it?"

Mangrove nodded, and then he smiled.

THE MORNING AFTER UNCLE TONY DELIVERED HIS
Congressional testimony, the director of Special Activities appeared
in his office. Uncle Tony was still in his workout clothes and had
only just finished mixing his protein shake. His boss, Alejandra
Fedorov, was an old Russia hand, assigned to Special Activities to
babysit Uncle Tony and the other paramilitary officers before her
inevitable promotion to chief of Europe Division, known as EUR
at headquarters. She was what the paramilitary types called a cake-
eater, those case officers who dealt strictly in intelligence collection
and did not deign to sully their hands in the paramilitary world.
Cake-eaters were to CIA what fighter pilots were to the Air Force
or ship drivers to the Navy, a brahmin class convinced of their own
finer qualities; they ran the organization and weren't the types to
lift weights in the mornings or chug protein shakes or think very
highly of those knuckle-dragging Neanderthals, like Uncle Tony,
who executed their dirty work.

"The White Russian herself . . . to what do I owe the pleasure,
ma'am?" Uncle Tony moved a pile of yesterday's clothes off a chair,
offering it to Fedorov. If the first rule of nicknames is that you never
give one to yourself, Alejandra Fedorov was one of the few who'd
successfully circumvented that rule. Born and raised in the South
Bronx, she'd taken an early interest in Russian history, wasting
away whole afternoons at the New York Public Library reading

translations of everything from Tolstoy to Trotsky to Turgenev. She earned a scholarship to study Russian at Princeton, writing her thesis on the Romanovs (a forensic analysis of their finances) and eventually marrying her professor, a Muscovite descendant of that family. After case officer training at the Farm, she'd whizzed through advanced surveillance and tradecraft, graduating top of her class. Once assigned to EUR, she'd insisted on going after Russian targets inside of Russia, as opposed to going after lower-priority expat Russians in the Caribbean, South America, or African countries where she wouldn't stand out. After some back-and-forth with human resources, she got her way. By the end of her first tour at Moscow Station, she'd set a record for the most recruitments that, twenty years later, remained unbeaten. Jealous colleagues used to whisper her nickname behind her back. When she got wind of it, she chose it as her own and wore it with pride: *The White Russian* (who was Puerto Rican and Black).

Fedorov removed a pen from her blouse, using it to toss aside a dirty sock that Uncle Tony had missed. She sat carefully in the chair, placing her weight on its seat gradually as if half-expecting its arms and legs to collapse in a splintered heap. Once settled, Fedorov stared up at the wall behind Uncle Tony. It was elaborately hung with dozens of shadow boxes, each filled with maps, photos, and captured weapons, an impressive reliquary of commando operations. "That one's rather large, Anthony." Fedorov gestured to a scimitar, its thick upward-sloping blade mounted on a polished slab of mahogany. "Is it new?"

"No, ma'am. The Saudis gave us this, after QZSPLATTERBOX." This cryptonym referred to a restricted handling program from a decade ago. Operatives from the Office had embedded with Saudi hit squads in Yemen, taking out dozens of high-value Houthi targets. As Uncle Tony explained this, he lifted the scimitar off its mount, gripping it two-handed and planting his feet in a power stance like the lead guitarist for a metal band. "This type of blade is what Saudi executioners still use." He encouraged Fedorov to give it a swing. She politely declined.

As Uncle Tony placed the scimitar back on its mount, he knocked over a pair of satellite photos blown up and printed on cardstock that were leaning against the wall. "What are those?" Fedorov asked.

Uncle Tony brought them over so she might take a closer look. The images were black and white, seemingly taken through some type of thermal optic. In the top right corner was a timestamp. It dated each photo to the Afghan withdrawal, an event overseen by Fedorov's predecessor at Special Activities. Center-frame in the first photo was an aircraft, which looked like an American C-17 transport. Its ramp was down. A crowd swarmed its back. Behind them were abandoned vehicles, trucks, motorbikes, all strewn across the taxiway. Total chaos. "That's a satellite image of the last Afghan National Army unit to fly out of Kandahar."

Uncle Tony showed Fedorov a second photo, taken two days later from the same airfield. This aircraft was slightly different, an L-100. Favored by the Office for clandestine operations, it was the civilian variant of the military C-130. Its ramp was lowered. Behind it, two columns of soldiers, aligned in perfect order, as if on parade, were loading. With them was all their equipment. "This one is a satellite image of our indig soldiers boarding their last flight out of Kandahar."

"Quite the contrast," said Fedorov. "Impressive."

"I'm glad you think so." Uncle Tony took the two photos and leaned them back against the wall, so they faced away and he wouldn't have to stare at them from his desk. "I wish Congress had seen it the same. I briefed these photos on the Hill after the withdrawal. It was a huge mistake to fire our indig. Twenty years they worked with us—twenty years! We could've used them elsewhere. An insane waste of talent and capability. You take a unit like that, you build it, you train it, you create all this trust . . . and then you just send 'em packing. We could've kept these guys, retained their capabilities for a bargain. But Congress didn't listen . . . they never do."

"That's what I came to talk with you about," said Fedorov. "How'd yesterday's briefing on the Hill go?"

"If you're here, apparently not as well as I thought."

"A few HPSCI staffers had some follow-up questions. They called over to EUR wanting to know more about that murder in Marseille. And so, the gang at EUR called me."

"What does *EUR* want to know about the murder?" He blended the *E*, the *U*, and the *R*, so his pronunciation sounded like *ewww*—in Uncle Tony's world, EUR was ground zero for cake-eaters.

"This Hofstede fellow, the one who worked for DRCA, he had an incision on his rib cage, where someone had cut off some skin, right?"

"That's a meat tag." Uncle Tony stood from behind his desk and lifted his sweaty T-shirt, showing Fedorov his tattooed ribs. "I got mine when I first showed up in the SEAL Teams."

"Keep your clothes on, Anthony." He sat back in his seat, and Fedorov continued, "Turns out, Hofstede had quite a history. He fought with the Rhodesians—on the wrong side, of course. That led him to enlist for a stint in the French Foreign Legion—which is why DGSE flagged his murder. After that, he got into the private security racket, where he did some work for the Russians and for DRCA. This is why he's coming up in our system too."

"I briefed all that on the Hill yesterday. What's the problem?"

"DRCA's pretty active in Ukraine right now. The Hill staffers want to know if any of our old guys know anything about Hofstede."

"You mean the guys we screwed over and then fired? Since when does the Hill care about DRCA?"

"Since the French gave us a copy of Hofstede's autopsy. Cause of death: polonium-210. He ingested an enormous dose, 50 micrograms. That's a thousand times the median lethal dose." Fedorov reached into the inside pocket of her suit jacket, removing a copy of the report. She handed it to Uncle Tony, who leaned forward over his desk. He laid the half-dozen pages flat and began flipping through them.

"That's a poison the Russians have used," he said, arriving at the last page. "You think the Kremlin did this?"

"Don't know. Russia's not the only place where you can get polonium. My theory is that Hofstede was just a bag man."

"Why's that?"

"Because at the end of an operation, particularly one that doesn't go according to plan, the bag man always ends up dead."

"Is that what you're going to tell those HPSCI staffers?"

"I'll tell them the truth, that Hofstede was working for DRCA. I'll also remind them that we cut ties with DRCA after the Now Zad raid, speaking of an operation where the bag man took the fall."

Uncle Tony slid the autopsy back toward Fedorov. He planted both his hands on the desk. "Ma'am, with due respect, you weren't on the Now Zad raid. You weren't even in Special Activities back then. When Skwerl took his story to the press, he tied our hands. After that, the Office never got a chance to—"

Fedorov cut him off. "You wouldn't have helped Jay Manning even if you could have. In Now Zad, you needed your own bag man. You might not have dosed Manning with polonium-210, but I've read the classified transcripts from the FISA Court. You murdered him reputationally and financially . . ."

"What's your point, ma'am?"

"Does the name 'Sheepdog' mean anything to you?"

Uncle Tony shrugged. "Not sure."

"You might want to get sure," said Fedorov, but she didn't push it past that; instead, she added, "Don't make the mistake of thinking that you're the only person this organization has ever shit on."

"Understood, ma'am."

On Fedorov's way out the door, she glanced a last time at the two satellite photos leaning against the wall. "Really impressive," she remarked half under her breath, glancing back at Uncle Tony. "And another thing . . . polonium-210, it's a poison used by Russians. But it mostly comes from small radioactive batches enriched under the Soviet regime. Those came from reactors around Chernobyl, in Ukraine."

Uncle Tony took a shower, shaved, and then changed into the pile of clothes he'd thrown off his chair so that the White Russian had had a place to sit. After that, he got to work. First order of business: booking the next available flight to Marseille.

"OUR FATHER WHO ART IN HEAVEN, HALLOWED BE THY NAME . . ."

"Knock it off, Ephraim." Skwerl sat in the copilot seat next to Cheese, whose concentration was total as they flew below five hundred feet for a second pass at the single runway carved into the side of the mountain.

"Yea, though I walk through the valley of the shadow of death, I will fear no evil: for thou are . . . "

"Shut the fuck up, Ephraim!"

"He's making it hard to concentrate . . ." Veins were bulging out the side of Cheese's neck as he wrestled the yoke, desperately trying to keep the Challenger 600 from stalling and then plunging into the pine trees below in a fiery pinwheel as they turned from base to final approach.

"You're going in the back if you don't shut up!"

When Skwerl threatened this, Ephraim grabbed either side of his jump seat. He'd been in the back minutes before, on their first pass into the airstrip. Cheese had clipped some trees and waved off, sending Ephraim into a panic. Skwerl knew he should've insisted on keeping all the windows shut, so Ephraim couldn't see outside. Takeoff was technically the most dangerous part of flying; if you've got a faulty engine, you'll find out at takeoff without the speed or altitude to do much about it. But landings always seemed to frighten people the most. In fairness to Ephraim, this landing was particularly treacherous. The grass runway was only 1,762 feet long, nearly 1,000 feet shorter than the 2,775 feet landing requirement for a Challenger 600. The runway was built on an 18.6 percent gradient, allowing for the shorter distance. A jet could touch down on the uphill, rapidly decelerating, and it could take off on the downhill, like a ski jump. But the margins were tight.

Cheese started to hum as he brought their jet in, mumbling a tune to himself, "*You'll never know what you can do, Until you get it up as high as you can go* . . ." He flipped a switch, full flaps. "*Out along the edges, Always where I burn to be* . . ." He came back off the throttle, holding a few knots above stall speed. The plane shuddered; the wind passing up through the valley beat the fuselage from side to side at this lower speed. "*The further on the edge, The hotter the intensity* . . ." Treetops sped beneath their wings. This was the exact spot where they'd waved off before. Cheese kept pushing it, holding the jet right above stall speed, even as his controls shuddered, even as a jagged view of nothing but mountains filled their cockpit, a wall they were hurtling toward. Skwerl, to ease his own nerves, joined in, the two of them belting, "*Highway to* . . ." and then the edge of the runway came into view, a slim ribbon of grass swishing past. Cheese slammed his throttle forward, flaring the jet, "*. . . the Danger Zone* . . ." They lurched as their landing gear hit, tossing them forward on the uphill into their chest restraints. Cheese killed the engine and slammed on the brakes. In three seconds, they'd decelerated from over 100 knots to taxi speed. The blades on the turbofan engine whined as they powered down. In the silence of the cockpit, Cheese flipped switches on the avionics panel, delivering the last verse, "*. . . Gonna take it right into the Danger Zone.*"

Behind him, Ephraim began to dry heave.

A golf cart popped out from the trees, cutting them off as they taxied. It was Shane, waving for them to follow. He was swerving a bit, making this difficult. He drove like a drunk, which was the inevitable result of his mangled hand and missing eye. At first,

Cheese had no idea where Shane was guiding them. Then, on the far side of the runway, he deciphered a hangar bay. It was built right up against the pines and adorned with a mishmash of camouflage netting like something out of a low-budget, mid-century Lee Marvin or Charles Bronson flick. Cheese taxied the Challenger 600 into the bay. During the last hour of their flight, Skwerl had explained to Cheese and Ephraim his long, complicated history with Just Shane. Before stepping outside, Skwerl reminded them a final time that, from this moment forward, he was from Colorado. "You guys got it?"

"Got it," they answered.

Skwerl opened the hatch, unfolding the stairs. Just Shane was waiting at the bottom, his left arm (his good one) outstretched. "Welcome home!"

SINÉAD STILL HAD EPHRAIM'S PONY STABLED IN HER GARAGE when Mangrove showed up the next evening. When he asked, "Whose horse is that?" Sinéad had already slipped into character as Mistress S, and her response was a harsh "I ask the questions around here, pervert." But Mangrove was serious. He needed a place to stash his car, a BMW 3 Series from one of his dealerships painted a distinctive shade of aquamarine. Very recognizable. Sinéad glanced out her door, to where the BMW idled on the side of the road. She disappeared inside and returned with a black car cover. "Use that," she said, "and park around back."

An hour later, Sinéad's shoulder was a bit sore from working over Mangrove. When she undid his restraints from the leather spanking table (built by Ephraim), it was covered in fresh pools of Mangrove's sweat. "Thank you," he gasped, as she tossed him a robe. She then took off her red latex gloves and unzipped her boots. Swaddled in her robe, she walked barefoot across the barn's wood floor to a nearby minifridge. She tossed Mangrove a Gatorade.

"Christ," he said after taking a deep gulp. "Do you think we could ever do a double session?"

"It might kill you."

"I'd be okay with that."

Sinéad said, "It might kill me, too."

He laughed.

"Feel better now?"

"Much. But seriously, could we do a double session? Maybe get you that third tattoo?"

"I've got a no double sessions policy. You couldn't handle it, and I'm perfectly happy with the tattoos I have." Sinéad had taken out some Tiger Balm. She was working it into her sore shoulder as she glanced at Mangrove's back. A little red blotch was spreading through his robe. "You're bleeding." Sinead peeled the robe off his shoulders to reveal the deep crosshatch of welts she'd flogged into him. She took a moment to admire her work and then crossed the room again. A medical kit sat above the minifridge. She removed a tube of Neosporin and tossed it to Mangrove. "You don't want that to get infected." Clumsily, he reached over his shoulder, trying to daub the Neosporin on his back while Sinéad reminded him that they had other business to attend to.

"I asked my staff about Ali Safi."

"And . . . ?"

"Have you heard of DRCA? It seems Ali Safi is a security guard there. His brother was too. Turns out DRCA has quite a history. Our government funneled billions of dollars to them over the past two decades. Iraq, Somalia, Yemen, Afghanistan, Syria, you name it, DRCA was there; that is, until about three years ago. Then we cut all ties with them . . . What does the name Now Zad mean to you?"

Sinéad pulled her robe closed at the neck. "I'm asking the questions, okay?"

"Suit yourself." Mangrove was having a hard time getting the Neosporin on the center of his back. "Do you mind?" He held up the tube. Sinéad stepped behind him, applying little daubs while he continued, "My staff sent me the classified report on the Now Zad raid this morning. Parts of it are still redacted, but it reads like an epic fuckup. A team of CIA paramilitary guys had been tracking this big-shot Taliban commander for years, someone named Gul Bacha. They got word of a meeting that he was planning to attend. There was a team of Marine Raiders at a firebase nearby. The CIA guys showed up, explaining to the Raiders that they've got Gul Bacha in their sights and that at this meeting he's planning on recruiting some local fighters. What nobody told the Raiders was that Gul Bacha wasn't asking a group of militants to join his ranks. He was asking a group of Afghan contractors, who worked for DRCA, if he could quit the Taliban and start working for them. Turns out the Taliban's Quetta Shura hadn't paid Gul Bacha in months. He was pissed off and out of cash for his fighters. Gul Bacha was, basically, trying to defect, offering his services to the highest bidder. Did the CIA know all that and just want to kill Gul Bacha anyway? Maybe. The report isn't clear, though the Raiders definitely didn't know. When the Raiders and CIA rolled up on the objective, Gul Bacha's fighters opened fire, and so did the DRCA contractors, who weren't sure what was going on. They didn't capture or kill Gul Bacha—he slipped out the back, while the Raiders lost one of their own, a young sergeant. After the mission, one of the CIA guys . . . well, he sorta lost it. Acting as anonymous source, he leaked the details of what happened in Now Zad to the press."

"What does this have to do with Ali Safi, the name I gave you?"

"After Gul Bacha's fighters opened fire, the Americans killed dozens on that raid, Taliban and security contractors alike. The Taliban claimed they were mostly civilians and, given the mix-up with DRCA, the Americans didn't push back. A month or two after that, the U.S. government suspended all outstanding contracts with DRCA—they've got no business with the U.S. government anymore. DRCA is now owned by a privately held U.S. company, Cyberdyne Security. Its CEO was also a Raider, Ted McDermott.

This ownership transition happened about the time Ali Safi joined DRCA. But that's not all . . ." Mangrove paused, telling Sinéad that she'd missed a spot a little lower on his back. "Yeah, right there, thanks . . . where was I?"

"Ali Safi and DRCA."

"Okay, yeah, so you mentioned your friend's wife, that someone with a badge had come asking about him at an Esso station outside of Austin, right? Well, I had my staff reach out to the Bureau, to see if the field office in Austin had received any interagency requests. Internal records show a request filed by CIA only a couple of days ago for a joint apprehension of a woman named Fareeda Iqbal."

"Who exactly submitted the request?"

"It doesn't say. All we can see is that the request was made . . . Your husband was CIA, wasn't he?"

"He's not my husband."

"Sorry, Jay Manning." Sinéad set down the tube of Neosporin on hearing Mangrove utter his name. He was sitting with his back to Sinéad, so couldn't see how her expression suddenly turned to ice; otherwise, he might not have continued. "Even though Manning's name is redacted in the report on Now Zad, there's a FISA case against him where his name isn't redacted. He's the anonymous source who leaked the details of the raid to the press."

"What's your point?"

"If I was able to connect him to Now Zad, I'm sure someone else could."

Sinéad grew quiet.

Eventually, Mangrove asked, "How's my back looking?"

"Not great," she said. "But you'll live."

THE MOMENT FAREEDA FELT THE AIRCRAFT ENTER ITS DESCENT, Ali Safi apologized. He would need to put the hood back over her head and cuff her wrists.

They'd flown through the night and landed at daybreak. Their aircraft taxied for what seemed like an unusually long time. It eventually stopped and its engines powered down. Fareeda could hear people shuffling on and off, though no one spoke, and no one moved her around. She sat in her seat for what felt like hours. Then, blindfolded, she was escorted onto the tarmac and into the back of a van for a short ride. When she was led out of the van, her steps had an echo, and she could tell she was in a large, enclosed space. She assumed this was an aircraft hangar. A door creaked on its hinges as she was taken into a first room, and then another door opened, followed by a third, as she was taken deeper and deeper into whatever this place was. Inside a final room, she was guided to a chair.

Her wrists were uncuffed and she was allowed to remove her hood. The room had no windows. It was lit by two rows of halogen bulbs. Next to its door stood a man. He was slim, wearing a white shirt, black tie, and gray suit tapered at the wrists and ankles in the Parisian style. A couple of days' stubble coated his cheeks, and Fareeda wondered what part he had played in her abduction.

"Pour vous." He gestured to a brown paper sack on a table.

Then he left, shutting the door behind him. Several heavy locks shuttled into their casements.

Fareeda allowed a few minutes to pass, enough time so she felt confident no one would disturb her. She then crossed the room and stood beside the table. Carefully, she unfolded the brown paper sack. Inside was a takeout container with a plastic knife, fork, and napkin wrapped in cellophane. The smell of spices was familiar. When she opened the container, it was filled with Kabuli pulao—a rice dish mixed with dried fruits and carrots—and on top sat several skewers of marinated chopan kebab. It was the type of meal Fareeda might have served in her own home.

She sat down to eat. The food was delicious, and she couldn't help but think how kind it was of Ali Safi to have gone to such trouble.

"C'MON, SKWERL, DRAW." JUST SHANE STOOD ON THE AIRFIELD beside the jet, the fingers of his good hand fluttering at his side, ready to perform a quickdraw from an invisible holster.

"Man, I'm beat, and I can't do it left-handed."

"Don't tell me you forgot? Draw, motherfucker."

"Can we just head back to the—" But then Skwerl reached with his left hand to an invisible holster of his own. They drew their fingers like pistols on each other. They high-fived once. They pounded their forearms twice. They tilted forward, shaking the other's ankle, and then they faced off once more. Two slaps to the chest. Three snaps of the fingers, and, finally, they returned their imaginary pistols into their imaginary holsters.

Cheese watched, his mouth hanging slightly open. "What was that?"

"8233 handshake, baby," said Just Shane.

Skwerl glanced at Cheese. "Our old team," he said sheepishly.

"I should've guessed . . ." Cheese loaded into the golf cart.

"One of you is pretty ripe." Just Shane was holding his nose as they pulled off the airstrip and onto a single-lane dirt road. Skwerl regaled him with an account of their journey, including Ephraim's bout of airsickness. "That's alright," said Just Shane. "We'll get you cleaned up at the main house." Through a screen of pine trees, that house soon appeared. It was more of a deluxe log cabin than a house, all built by hand—or "one-handed," Just Shane bragged, gesturing to the dozens of nearby stumps he'd somehow cut himself.

A chimney sat at either end of the ample living room. Each was built of large, oblong stones. As Just Shane gave a tour, he proudly explained to Skwerl how he'd harvested most of these stones from Hopkins Creek, hauling them up one by one from the creek bed and then to his property in the back of his golf cart. He'd spent the morning fishing in the creek and had caught plenty of trout for that night. "They're really biting. Maybe tomorrow we could head down, just like—" Shane seemed about to say, *old times*. Then he paused and screwed his eyes up to the rafters for a moment, as if trying to recall the last time (if ever) the two of them had fished in Hopkins Creek.

Fortunately for Skwerl, the unrelenting reek of Ephraim's clothes prevented Just Shane from lingering too long on this question. "Christ almighty, we need to get you cleaned up." He brought Ephraim to a shower in the back. "The last few days have been cloudy," Just Shane explained. "The water's heated by solar power, so it might not be too warm." Just Shane had Ephraim leave his dirty clothes in a pile by the door, so they'd go in the next wash. Just Shane would get him something to wear in the meantime.

When Just Shane returned, Skwerl and Cheese were sitting around a plastic foldout table in the sparsely furnished living room. Although the house was finished, the interiors remained a work in progress. The kitchen was little more than a water spigot that poured into an aluminum basin. Just Shane had only a few plastic plates, cups, and metal camping utensils to eat off. A pile of them filled the basin and it was obvious he used everything until it ran out, then washed it all at once. "I plan on upgrading the interiors, but priority of work has gone to other projects around the property, like the airstrip. Lucky for you, I had that ready. It seems you all are in a bit of a jam? Maybe you're on the outs with

Big Brother?" He then shut his good eye, in what Skwerl could only assume was a nervous tic he'd picked up since the ambush where he had lost the other one. "I don't need and don't really want to know the details. Just tell me how long you think you'll be staying?"

"I'm not sure," said Skwerl. "How long do you think we'll be safe here?"

"How long? As long as you want," said Just Shane. "It's not as hard as you'd think to make a plane vanish, so long as you land in the right place."

"The last couple of days have made it seem otherwise."

"If you want Big Brother off your back, an airstrip like mine comes in handy. Take that pedophile Jeff Epstein, for instance. They still don't know who or what flew on that jet of his. If he figured out how to fly presidents and princes on and off his island and keep it a secret, I assure you that I've figured out how to do the same on my mountaintop, especially for American patriots like you all."

"I'm Afghan," said Cheese.

Just Shane clapped him on the shoulder. "Not to me you aren't!" He looked soulfully into Cheese's eyes, and then announced, "And another thing . . . Epstein did not hang himself in his jail cell." An accounting of Jeffrey Epstein's last days followed. Cheese's bewilderment only grew as he listened to Just Shane's host of conspiracy theories, which included an analysis of camera angles, visitor logs, and the varied intersecting interests of the Southern District of New York, the Clinton Global Initiative, the U.S. Virgin Islands, and the Bill and Melinda Gates Foundation. "Look it up," he kept saying, shutting his good eye in a nervous tic, and reminding them, "It's all there."

Skwerl didn't ask *where*. By now he was ignoring Just Shane. He had his phone out and was sweeping it in an arc overhead. "Do you get any service up here?"

Just Shane took a break from his diatribe and disappeared into a back room. He returned with an Iridium sat phone. "The best signal is out on the porch." When Skwerl stood to leave so did Cheese. Just Shane called after them, "Aren't either of you gonna help me get supper on?" Skwerl nodded at Cheese, who grudgingly turned around and stayed. "That's much appreciated," said Just Shane. He'd begun sharpening a set of knives and Cheese looked particularly reluctant to be left alone with him. "Don't worry," Just Shane added. "All we're gonna do is chop up some fish." He whacked down the blade on a cutting board, lopping off the head of one of the trout. "Nothing to it. See!" Once again, Just Shane turned toward Skwerl and shut his good eye, grinning like a lunatic.

It was only when Skwerl was out on the porch, dialing Sinéad, that he realized Just Shane closing his eye wasn't a tic at all; it was the way a one-eyed man winks.

SINÉAD DIDN'T RECOGNIZE THE INCOMING CALL. SHE WAS IN her Acura, speeding back to her barn from Mangrove's office. At first, she ignored her phone. When it rang a second time, same number, she answered with a hesitant "Hello?"

"Hello . . . ? Hello . . . ? Sinéad . . . ?"

The connection wasn't great.

"Who is this?"

"Toots, it's me."

"I've been trying you all day." Sinéad could hear the strain in her own voice, so took a breath. "Did you make it in okay?"

"Yeah, we made it."

"Listen, you need to come back."

"We just got here . . . ?"

"Have Aziz stay with the plane. You need to come back."

Skwerl didn't answer. He glanced through a window, into the kitchen, where Just Shane and Cheese were hard at work preparing dinner, chopping up the remaining fish, gutting them, and flinging the mess into compost bags. "What if you came out here instead?"

"That's not going to work," said Sinéad. "I can explain when I see you, but you need to get back. Does the name Ted McDermott mean anything to you?"

"Mac? Yeah, he was an old colleague. Why?"

"We need to pay your old colleague a visit."

IN UNCLE TONY'S OPINION THE INTERCONTINENTAL WAS THE finest hotel in Marseille. Even after what had happened to Henrik Hofstede in room 317, he didn't hesitate to stay there. He had booked himself a corner suite, making the reservation in alias not because this operation was particularly sensitive (after all, he was only in France) but because that alias had the most Hyatt rewards points to apply toward an upgrade. The hotel manager offered him a selection of floors at check-in (as well as a hundred-euro restaurant and spa credit) and Uncle Tony had chosen a suite on the third floor, only a few doors down from Hofstede's old room.

Uncle Tony would be staying in Marseille as a guest of his counterparts in French intelligence, though it was an invitation offered at his own suggestion. Since the death of Hendrik Hofstede, their two services had remained in close touch, particularly after the autopsy revealed traces of polonium-210. This is why the DGSE had readily agreed that Uncle Tony should take this trip, so they might consult on matters in person.

His flight from Dulles had arrived that morning at Charles de Gaulle. A connection had delivered him midday to Marseille. Uncle Tony hadn't slept well on the overnight flight, a rarity for him. His mind had remained continuously in motion, working over the meeting he would soon have with Colonel Christophe Grillot, who'd flown in from Paris for the occasion. Grillot commanded

Special Action, the DGSE's paramilitary wing, its equivalent of the Office. Uncle Tony envied the French system. He missed the red-blooded comradery of the SEAL Teams and resented a hierarchy that subordinated paramilitary officers like him to cake-eater bosses like the White Russian. The French granted their operatives the dignity of remaining in uniform, even though in Uncle Tony's estimation Grillot was not a man whose refined appearance suggested he was a serving military officer, let alone a long-serving commando with two decades' worth of experience on nearly every continent and in a dozen wars (albeit French wars).

In the late afternoon, as the descending sun reddened the terra-cotta-tiled rooftops that overlooked the Old Port, Uncle Tony waited for Grillot at a table on the InterContinental's veranda. He'd ordered a double espresso, to wake up, and would switch to whiskey when Grillot arrived. In the meantime, he was enjoying himself as he watched the daily sail charters return to the marina with their cargos of tourists, the sunburned women in their coverups and floppy hats, the men in T-shirts and damp swim bottoms. Chintzy *chansons françaises* played from Sonos speakers tucked discreetly around the veranda, a mix of Yves Montand, Serge Gainsbourg, and Édith Piaf—way too much "La Vie en rose." For a moment, Uncle Tony began to feel as if he was on vacation himself. Then he tried to remember the last time he'd had a vacation. He counted back the years, determining it'd been five . . . the trip to the Grand Canyon before his third wife had left him . . . that's when he'd thrown in the towel, on vacations, on wives, on anything where he'd proven himself an abject failure . . . which happened to be almost everything except for work.

He finished his coffee and asked his waiter for the cocktail menu. Before the waiter could return, Colonel Grillot stepped onto the veranda. Uncle Tony spotted him first. In that instant, he couldn't help but admire Grillot. His black tie perfectly knotted and worn with a crisp white shirt. His impeccably tailored grey suit with its narrow cut, elegantly tapered. It was a far cry from the Men's Warehouse 44L that Uncle Tony wore.

When Grillot caught sight of Uncle Tony from between the thicket of table umbrellas, he made a shoulders-back entrance. He stepped onto the veranda like a man stepping onstage to receive an award. His unshaved chin was raised high with the perfect amount of rakish stubble—not so little as to seem unkempt, and not so much as to seem like he was trying to grow a beard. One of Grillot's hands was stylishly slotted into the left pocket on his suit jacket (after Uncle Tony had left the SEALs, it'd taken two years of him complaining that his jacket pockets didn't work before he'd learned that they came sewn shut from the factory, and that to open them he simply had to remove the stitching).

What Uncle Tony admired (or even envied) about Grillot wasn't really sartorial—Uncle Tony couldn't have articulated the myriad stylistic flourishes deployed by his French counterpart. Fundamentally, what Uncle Tony admired was how Grillot was able to enter a room—any room—the way he seemed both visible and invisible to those around him, existing like a secret out in the open, whereas Uncle Tony, and those who worked in the Office, were distinctly invisible. In America, their job was to wear Men's Warehouse suits with the pockets sewn shut. They were blue-collar guys with white-collar masters. Not so in France.

"Quoi de neuf, Tony?" said Grillot as he settled into his chair.

"Neuf much, Christophe."

"Ah, I see you've learned French." Out of politeness, Grillot offered Uncle Tony a cigarette, which he declined, before Grillot lit his own. The waiter returned and the two of them ordered whiskies, a William Peel single malt selected by Grillot. "I'm glad you suggested this visit. Each day our director, he is asking me more questions, and each day I wonder if I'll have the answers." Grillot took a drag, exhaling a column of smoke. "What you've proposed works to everyone's benefit. But if this gets too noisy, the questions increase . . . and if I run out of answers, this deal of ours becomes impossible. You understand, of course?"

"Of course," said Uncle Tony.

"What happened on the third floor, this cannot happen again. This is what I mean by noisy."

"It won't happen again."

"The cutting on Hofstede's ribs, where his tattoo was, the Gendarmerie nationale took a great interest in that detail—though they tend to be grim fellows—and they took great interest in the polonium. Reading the case file, I felt sad for this Hofstede." A crumble of ash toppled from the tip of Grillot's cigarette and onto the table, missing the ashtray; Grillot brushed it aside. "A life spent entirely at war, most of them fought for bad reasons—Rhodesia, Mali, Syria. Some of them for good reasons—before his death, Ukraine. One like him deserves a soldier's death, not a poisoning in a hotel room."

"What difference does it make? He'd still be dead." Uncle Tony shut his eyes and massaged his temples, forming a brace with his middle finger and thumb.

"Ça va, Tony?"

"I'm fine . . . just a headache. Didn't sleep much on the plane." He turned behind him, to the speakers. "Also, this music isn't helping." He continued massaging his head as yet another Édith Piaf tune got going.

"Ah, but this song is special. You know it of course?" Grillot lifted a finger, waving it in sync with the warble of opening notes.

Uncle Tony returned a vacant stare.

Grillot began to sing softly, " '*Non, rien de rien, Non, je ne regrette rien* . . . ' You really don't know this one?"—Uncle Tony had heard it but didn't know what the words meant—"The lyrics, they translate as, 'No, no nothing at all, no I have no regrets.' This is a military song."

Uncle Tony raised an eyebrow.

"It is the marching song of the French Foreign Legion's 1st Parachute Regiment. Your friend Hofstede would've recognized it immediately."

"He wasn't my friend."

Grillot gazed up at the third floor of the InterContinental. "Whatever you want to call him, he was a legionnaire and would've sung it on parade." Grillot hummed a little more, ". . . 'C'est payé, balayé, oublié, Je me fous du passé . . . '" before adding, "When Édith Piaf first started performing this song, my country had been fighting its own bad war, in Algeria; it had been going on for six years, so a long war—maybe, not so long as some of your wars, but quite long. By this time, the public had turned against it. But the soldiers had not. No one wants to lose a war, especially a bad war—every soldier knows that the bad wars, these are the ones that are the most important of all to win, otherwise the people, they will never forgive you for losing. De Gaulle, he was president at the time. He understood that Algeria was lost long before his generals did. When he ordered French troops to withdraw, his generals viewed this as a betrayal, not only of them but also of their Algerian allies. They organized a putsch, backed by the Legion's 1st Parachute Regiment. It lasted five days, until French forces loyal to De Gaulle broke the resistance. The legionnaires were turned out of their barracks and marched through the streets of Algiers to prison. As they marched, they began to sing, 'Non, je ne regrette rien' . . . Piaf had only recently recorded this song. When she heard of this detail of the failed putsch, she dedicated the song's broadcast premiere to the defeated legionnaires. It has remained their marching song since. Even now, on quatorze Juillet, if you watch the parade down the Champs-Élysées, you can hear them sing in unison—no regrets."

"You think I have regrets?" Uncle Tony hunched his shoulders and came forward in his seat, the way he would in an interrogation.

"Every soldier has regrets. But it is just a story, Tony." Grillot took a final drag on his cigarette, slowly exhaling two tubes of smoke from his nostrils. "What you don't have is this jet you're looking for, and what you do have is a murder in this hotel"—again, Grillot glanced up toward the third floor—"as well as . . ."

Grillot paused a beat. "What are we calling her . . . a *captive*? . . . a *prisoner*? . . . You Americans like *detainee*, maybe we call her this, no?"

"Call her whatever you like."

"So you have a detainee locked in a hangar at the airport. She is quite comfortable, rest assured. This Ali Safi of yours, he demands it. Last night, he had me drive all the way to La Castellane, a banlieue on the outskirts of the city, simply to pick her up a container of food from this one restaurant. Ali Safi was insistent about displaying a certain type of hospitality. Perhaps you know this, but La Castellane, it is not so safe of a place. I went myself instead of sending one of my men. I must say, it's been years since I undertook so dangerous a mission for my country . . . it felt much like the old days." Grillot found his story quite amusing. He was laughing to himself as he fished a lighter from his suit pocket and slid out another cigarette from his paper pack. Before smoking it, he paused, tapping its filter against the table. His expression had, in a sudden reversal, turned rather dour. "Having spent some time with Ali Safi, it doesn't seem as though he likes you much."

"Can't say that I care." Uncle Tony rubbed his aching head. "But, given who I am, I don't suppose he would like me."

"My apologies, I didn't mean to offend." Grillot slotted the cigarette between his lips. "But it might be more than 'not liking you,' I think, perhaps, he hates you."

"I get your point."

"I'm not entirely sure that you do." Grillot took a drag, flicking off the ash. He pointed the cherry end up to the third floor of the hotel. "If he really hates you, it would mean he feels little obligation to follow instructions given by you. Maybe in certain situations, it could mean he would do the exact opposite of what you told him, out of spite."

Whatever Grillot was fishing for—perhaps a statement about Hofstede's murder, one that implicated Ali Safi—Uncle Tony wouldn't offer it. He answered with an unsatisfying, "Maybe so."

"Yes, maybe," said Grillot. "But because you are my friend"—and Uncle Tony arched an eyebrow, as if the prospect of their transatlantic friendship were enough of a novelty to warrant amusement—"I hope you'll excuse these observations. Be careful of Ali Safi, that's the only advice I'm trying to offer."

Their waiter arrived. Overburdened with a full tray of drinks, he delivered the two whiskies, clapping the glasses down unceremoniously as he shuffled to his next table. The veranda was filling with patrons who, after a day of sun, had put on their best resort wear for dinner. As Uncle Tony clutched his glass, he assured Colonel Grillot that their work together would remain on track, that there would be no more "noisy" episodes, despite the current situation with Fareeda, the missing Challenger 600, and Ali Safi's "erratic behavior" (this being the adjective he'd selected as if reaching into a grab bag of euphemisms).

Uncle Tony raised his glass, "What shall we drink to?"

"C'est payé, balayé, oublié, Je me fous du passé," said Grillot as they toasted.

Uncle Tony drank. "What does that mean?" He sat his glass back on the table.

"It's from the Édith Piaf . . . in English it translates as 'It is paid for . . . swept away . . . forgotten . . . I do not care about the past.' "

AS JUST SHANE AND CHEESE PREPARED DINNER, SKWERL HAD suggested they eat off some better plates than the ones that were stinking up the basin. They had a nice set aboard the Challenger 600 and Ephraim volunteered to grab them. When he returned ten minutes later, it was without the fancier plates and cutlery, but with urgent news. "An animal . . ." Ephraim said breathlessly as he stood in the doorway. He'd sprinted back and between gasps explained that some kind of animal had gotten inside the jet. Only moments ago, it was in the midst of trashing the interior.

It was difficult to take Ephraim seriously—he was wearing nothing but an old army poncho and boots. With his clothes in the wash, he'd needed to borrow a set from Just Shane. Most of the trousers had zip flies, so were out of the question, a zipper being a piece of technology forbidden by his religion. The few that had button flies were several sizes too large. When Just Shane had offered a belt, Ephraim had again refused on religious grounds, a buckle being considered immodest. Eventually, after exhausting all other options, they'd settled on the poncho, which Ephraim was wearing, tethered at the waist with a piece of twine, along with his boots.

The four piled into the golf cart and sped out to the jet, dust boiling up behind them on the trail. Just Shane had asked Skwerl to drive while, in the passenger seat, he loaded his grizzly bear defense gun, a Ruger with a 2.5-inch snub-nosed barrel, sliding six fat little .44 caliber shells into the revolver's open cylinder. Just Shane scanned the pines with his good eye, explaining that a certain grizzly had, for some time, been causing problems on his property. "This fella's given me trouble in the past," he mused as they rattled along toward the Challenger 600. "He's raided my trash . . . Dug through my compost bins . . . He even got in the house once . . . Door was shut, but he sprung the locks. I got a deadbolt now."

When they arrived at the jet, Just Shane held up his mangled right hand. He insisted the others stand back. Whatever it was might still be aboard. He approached with his pistol drawn, taking slow, deliberate heel-to-toe steps. It was as if he were again a bomb tech on some godforsaken battlefield and called to respond to an IED. Very slowly, Just Shane ducked behind the retractable stairs that led into the jet. When he stepped out from behind them, he nodded and mouthed the words *Claw marks* to the others who waited inside the golf cart, which Skwerl had combat-parked so it faced toward the woods for a speedy getaway. Just Shane climbed the ladder, his pistol at the ready. Then he disappeared inside the jet.

A moment later, Just Shane appeared in the door. "All clear!" He tucked his pistol in his waistband and pulled the collar of his T-shirt over his nose. "Man, it still stinks in there. The smell must've attracted that grizzly." He bounded down the stairs and invited Skwerl and Cheese to inspect the door latch, a recessed T-bar embedded into the fuselage. The pressurization hatch, a small side panel, was sprung open and the T-bar was extended a half-turn, in the unlocked position. Both were crosshatched with claw marks, as if the grizzly had simply banged on the hatch enough times to engage the dual mechanisms: a button in the T-bar to release the pressurization hatch and extend the T-bar; and then the T-bar itself, which needed a half-turn to open. Cheese seemed relieved by Just Shane's analysis. Shutting the door had been his responsibility, and it appeared he'd done nothing wrong. This was simply a case of a grizzly with a good nose who had gotten lucky.

After Skwerl climbed the stairs, Just Shane held out a restraining arm. "I'm telling you . . . it's bad in there." Skwerl nodded, but he ignored the warning and stepped inside. What followed was a string of expletives which not only seemed to startle Ephraim, who stood outside in his poncho, staring at his boots, flinching at every other word ("*Dumb-shit bear! . . . Fucking airstrip! . . . Cock-sucking jet! . . .* "), but also seemed to startle Cheese and even Just Shane. All three slowly shook their heads, piteous of Skwerl as he suffered this minor emotional breakdown.

When Cheese finally mustered the courage to follow Skwerl into the Challenger 600, he found him in one of the plush leather recliners, his head cradled in his hands. Deep claw marks slitted the cream-colored leather upholstery, the stuffing spilling out of each recliner, a disemboweled mess that Skwerl sat on like a deposed king upon his throne. He glanced up at Cheese. "What do we do? . . . The jet's trashed . . . No way we get our money now."

"Yeah," said Cheese, measurably calmer than Skwerl. "It's not good." He stepped into the cockpit. The narrow doorway had at least kept the grizzly out, though etched into the polished wood paneling on the bulkhead were more claw marks, and the ground was littered with coiled strips of mahogany, evidence of the grizzly's struggle to reach the cockpit, this being where the stench was strongest. Cheese tucked himself into the pilot's seat. He cycled a few switches, giving the avionics a quick once-over. Everything appeared in order.

When Cheese stepped out of the cockpit, he found Ephraim in the main cabin, gathering up the dishes and utensils he'd come for in the first place, as well as the fragments of two plates that the grizzly had knocked to the ground. Cheese announced that the damage to the jet seemed only cosmetic, but this did little to lighten Skwerl's mood. This rampage had knocked at least a million bucks off the value of the jet, which meant a hundred thousand dollars less from a bounty it seemed increasingly unlikely either him or Cheese would ever collect.

The four of them cleaned up the cabin as best they could, making certain to secure the hatch once they'd finished. Skwerl was scheduled to leave the next morning. Just Shane would give him a ride to Denver International and he'd fly back to Philadelphia, as Sinéad had insisted. Before they returned to the main house for the night, Shane had a final idea, a precaution so this wouldn't happen again. He would place a bear trap in front of the aircraft door. Just Shane zipped off in his golf cart. Within minutes, he'd returned with a rusted spring and C-clamp apparatus with mean metal teeth. Skwerl asked, "Where the hell did you get that?"

Shane pried apart its frying-pan-sized jaws and tittered like a little boy as he staked the anchor chain into the earth and removed the cotter pin, arming the steel trip plate—the trap was ready. "You never used one of these growing up?" And Skwerl, careful not to stray too far from his fictitious youth, suddenly recalled with remarkable clarity those rugged days spent with brother Jo, the two of them setting out before dawn, checking the traps around the family property, returning in time for breakfast and homeschool around the kitchen table. "Oh, we sure used 'em. I was just surprised to see you kept one up here."

"Oh, I keep all sorts of stuff up here."

THE FOUR OF THEM LOADED BACK INTO THE GOLF CART, AND it was dark when they arrived at the house. Just Shane placed a single Coleman lantern in the middle of a plastic table that Ephraim set for dinner. They ate mostly in silence, spitting out flimsy translucent bones from each bite of trout, which Just Shane had marinated in lemon juice, wrapped in foil, and baked in the oven with salt, pepper, and some herbs. Between bites, Skwerl explained that once he landed in Philadelphia and had a chance to speak with Sinéad, he'd call Just Shane on the Iridium to tell him the plan.

"And what are we supposed to do until then?" asked Cheese.

"Make sure the Challenger is ready to fly. Maybe you and Ephraim can clean up the interiors, get that stink out." This answer seemed unsatisfactory to Cheese, who cleared his plate from the table and stood hunched over the basin, facing away from Skwerl. "What else can I tell you?" Skwerl said to Cheese's back. "We're doing everything we can for Fareeda. You need to trust me on this one."

"Ha!" Cheese glowered over his shoulder at Skwerl. "Like you trusted Sheepdog? Like how I trusted you Americans to—"

"Fellas," Just Shane interjected. ". . . It's been a long day . . . Take it easy." He gestured to a projector and laptop on a shelf in the corner. "How about a movie?" Just Shane set the projector on a chair. He grabbed a sheet and hung it from the rafters on two pegs, forming a screen. He plugged the projector into a laptop that was then plugged into his Iridium sat phone. "I've got Netflix, Hulu, Apple TV, whatever you want." He glanced at Skwerl and then at Cheese. Neither said anything. "Ephraim, how about you? You want to pick?"

Ephraim gestured to his poncho. "I'm not one to watch movies, remember?" He began clearing the remaining dishes from the table.

Skwerl thought this was ridiculous. "You just flew on a jet, rode in a car, ate fast food, and you have a standing weekly session with my girlfriend . . . but you won't watch a movie? How do you figure that?"

Ephraim paused, a pile of dirty dishes balanced in his arms, as he faced Skwerl. "I am reform Amish."

"Reform Amish?" Skwerl crossed his arms over his chest. "I'm pretty sure that's not a thing."

"It is a thing."

"If you say so."

"And what about you? What are you? A spy–repo man? Is that a thing?"

Cheese laughed. "He's got you there."

"Someone just pick a movie . . ." said Skwerl.

Ephraim set the dishes beside the basin, where he took over from Cheese. "A ride on a jet . . . a drive in a car . . . fast food . . . that's the least of it. Before we met, I'd stolen to pay the wages of sin . . ." He was speaking wistfully into the basin as he continued the washing up; a religious man, it seemed he had picked this moment to confess himself.

"What does that mean?" Just Shane asked. "What did you steal?"

"Building supplies," said Ephraim. "To pay Mistress S, I stole from my community to build her a few pieces of furniture. If you must know, that's the truth of it. And my punishment was severe. Our elders voted to throw me out of the church. My mother and father told me never to return to our home. My siblings won't acknowledge me. If I had a wife, she would be considered a widow, though fortunately I never married—sinful perversion always stood in my way. The elders declared to our congregation that I was a case of hashtag MeToo."

"For Christ's sake," said Skwerl.

"Don't blaspheme."

"But you weren't MeToo-ed, Ephraim."

"This is what the elders said."

"They're Amish. They don't have zippers, let alone phones and social media accounts to MeToo you."

Cheese chimed in: "Maybe he was 'canceled'?"

Just Shane nodded, as if this sounded about right, while Ephraim shuttled his gaze between the two of them.

"He wasn't canceled, either," said Skwerl. "He's a little freaky and so they kicked him out the church—plain and simple, that's it."

"Whatever you call it, the church has left me. But I have not left my church. When I say I am 'reformed,' this is all that I mean."

"Understood," said Skwerl. ". . . So where have you been living?"

"My community of Amish—we're called Old Order—and we have been shrinking for years . . . *Whoever troubles his own household will inherit the wind, and the fool will be servant to the wise of heart.*' Many of the homes on the outskirts of our parish remain abandoned. I've lived in one of these for the past several months, allowed to work a small plot of land. I am in no rush to return to it and am quite happy to remain with you all so long as I'm useful. But I won't be watching your movie tonight."

"Fair enough," said Skwerl.

Ephraim dried the dishes with a cloth and then sat at a table where he'd spread fragments of the two broken Marie Antoinette plates like a jigsaw puzzle. His evening's entertainment would be trying to glue them back together.

"So, what's it gonna be?" Just Shane asked, scrolling through titles on his laptop. "Comedy . . . action . . . either of you got a favorite movie?"

"Whatever Cheese wants is fine."

"Do you have *Rambo*?"

Just Shane typed in a search. "Yeah, I got *Rambo*."

"Not the original. *Rambo III* . . . the one where he goes to Afghanistan."

As the movie began, Just Shane dimmed the Coleman lantern, leaving enough light so Ephraim could continue his project of trying to reassemble the plates. The opening sequence of the movie projected onto the bedsheet . . .

Ninety minutes later, John Rambo had helped the mujahedeen deal the Soviets a crushing defeat. He had single-handedly killed dozens if not hundreds of Russians, leading a cavalry charge and shooting a Hind helicopter gunship out of the sky with a bow and arrow. This orgy of violence ended with an onscreen caption: *This film is dedicated to the gallant people of Afghanistan*, and Bill Medley's lyrics, "*The road is long with many a winding turn . . .*" played over the credits.

Nothing was said, until Cheese offered, "Man, . . . I forgot how good that was."

"Are you kidding . . . ?" Skwerl turned in his chair. "It's garbage."

"*Rambo III* is the only lasting thing America has produced for Afghanistan?"

Neither Skwerl nor Just Shane debated the point.

"That movie was made when America knew how to win wars."

"And how was that, Cheese?" Skwerl leaned forward.

"It's like Reagan said, 'We win, they lose.' That's how you win a war."

"Sure, and Rambo leads the ground forces and Lieutenant Pete 'Maverick' Mitchell flies your close air support . . . You're living in the past." Skwerl crossed the room and turned up the light on the Coleman lantern. "Speaking of which, how's it coming, Ephraim?" He had managed to glue together one of the plates, which had broken into almost two dozen fragments. He was using a quick-drying glue, so had to hold the pieces against one another for a few seconds before they adhered. The second plate was giving Ephraim a harder time. It had broken into only a few pieces, but the glue wouldn't bond with the ceramic. He was about to give up.

"What's the problem?" Skwerl asked.

"This plate seems to be made of a different material." Ephraim held one of the fragments along its broken rim, which was banded with gold filigree and an embroidery of cornflowers and pearls. He ran his finger down the exposed side. "If you look closely, the porcelain is more porous. This is called *soft-frit*, a traditional ceramic, one that uses natural minerals and clays as raw materials. That makes it sturdier, less likely to shatter. But when it breaks, it is more difficult to mend. Manufacturers no longer produce ceramics of this composition. These older ceramics are less heat resistant. You can't microwave a plate like this. This other plate, the one that I've glued together, is a new type of ceramic made from inorganic compounds. These are harder, more heat resistant, and they glue back together if chipped or broken. Where did you get this plate?" Ephraim asked, holding up the one he'd successfully glued together, pointing out the precise *Bernardaud* painted in sans serif gold script on its back.

"At a boutique in Marseille."

"You see this other one"—and Ephraim turned over the fragments of the plate he'd failed to glue together, flipping each piece as if it were a card in a game of solitaire—"this plate has no markings on its back, but you can see this small print on the rim. It was made by someone else."

Cheese and Just Shane had also gathered around Ephraim's table. Each of them held up the glued-together plate while also examining the fragments, including the marking, the letters *LL*, but with the second *L* facing the first, interlocking to form a serifed triangle.

"How do you know all this stuff about plates?" Just Shane asked.

"We Amish," said Ephraim, "we don't use synthetic materials. What we use in our homes, we make in the traditional ways."

"You make plates like this?" Just Shane was admiring the

intricate patterning.

"No, nothing as immodest as this." Ephraim held up a fragment of the shattered Marie Antoinette plate. "It's probably been a hundred years, maybe even longer, since someone has used traditional ceramic compounds to manufacture pieces as extravagant as this." He turned to Skwerl. "These must be quite valuable. How exactly did you come across such plates?"

Chapter Four

MARIE ANTOINETTE

THREE TIMES EACH DAY, A TAKEOUT CONTAINER ARRIVED FOR Fareeda filled with delicious and familiar food. After that first night, it was Ali Safi who delivered her meals, and she didn't see the Frenchman in the grey suit, or anyone else for that matter. Aside from mealtime, she was left entirely alone. To stay active, she had taken to pacing the four corners of the conference room that now doubled as her cell. To pass the hours, she tried to sleep, but the foam pad placed in a corner for her was too thin. Given this uncomfortable pad and an increase in stress-induced Braxton-Hicks contractions, sleep only came in snatches. After a couple of days of this solitary confinement, Fareeda began to suffer. She craved human interaction. Which was why when Ali Safi arrived on the third night with her dinner, she asked if he would eat with her.

Politely, he declined.

Fareeda said, "It makes no sense we should both eat alone."

Ali Safi left the room, locking the door behind him. A few moments later, he returned, carrying a Styrofoam container identical to Fareeda's. He sat next to her at the table, unwrapping a plastic fork and knife. At first, they ate together in silence, neither knowing how to resume the conversation that had begun on the plane. Eventually, Fareeda tried. "So . . . do you like this work of yours?"

Ali Safi finished chewing a mouthful of rice. "Do I like it?" He seemed perplexed by the question.

"Yes, do you like it? . . . My husband loved being a pilot. He misses it. He tells me all the time how much he misses it. I don't know what to say back, or how to help him. I think a part of him took this jet, the one you want returned, not for the money. Of course, he says he took it because the money would help us." Fareeda placed her hands on her stomach. "But I think this is only partly true. I think he took the jet because he wanted to fly again."

"It doesn't sound like your husband is very happy in his new American life?" Ali Safi spooned up another mouthful of rice. "That must be difficult for you."

"I understand him." Fareeda leaned forward, fixing Ali Safi's gaze with her own. "To be an immigrant is one thing. You come to a new place, one that you have chosen, and you build a life. To be a refugee is something entirely different. You have not chosen your life. It has been forced on you. To live a life that you never wanted, this is a great burden."

"I think you complain too much."

"Is that so?"

"Yes," said Ali Safi with his mouth full of food. "You talk about the burden of one type of life versus another and which life is better. My brother worked for the Americans and then they killed him—he has no life at all. Of course, they said it was an accident. But only a fool believes there are accidents in war. Death, loss, destruction—the outcome is always the same. No accidents there. Since the fall of Kabul, DRCA has sent me all over the world, to Syria, to Africa, even to Europe . . . and there's little difference between them. In my work, I have witnessed unimaginable suffering . . . maybe you should try complaining less."

"Maybe . . ." Fareeda took another bite of her food and chewed slowly. "And you do this work because you enjoy it?"

"I do this work for the money."

"You're a mercenary then . . . you kill for money."

"You say that as if it should bother me." Ali Safi smiled, the same sharklike smile he'd shown Fareeda on the plane. "I've spent the last year in Ukraine," and he could hardly resist a final boast: "As an Afghan, killing Russians doesn't bother me one bit."

"So it's not about the money?"

Ali Safi stopped eating. He canted his head to the side like a curious bird. He considered Fareeda's question. "No . . ." he said, drawing out the word. "I do it for the money . . . Except in your case." He wagged his finger at Fareeda. "This operation, this one is special. This is one that I am *not* doing for the money."

"That's very generous of you," Fareeda said dryly.

Ali Safi shut his container of food. Before standing from the table, he said, "I'm glad that you think so," and then he left and double locked her door.

SKWERL LANDED LATE MORNING FROM DENVER INTO Philadelphia International. When he stepped out of the airport, Sinéad was idling curbside at arrivals. She picked him up and they sped south in her Acura down I-95 to Cyberdyne Security's corporate headquarters, situated in a drab northern Virginia office park. The drive took a little over three hours, which gave Sinéad plenty of time to explain what she'd learned from Mangrove, not only about Cyberdyne but also about its relationship with DRCA.

"After the Now Zad raid," Sinéad explained, "the U.S. government pulled the plug on DRCA."

"So where does Cyberdyne fit in?"

"Cyberdyne took up the slack, funding DRCA programs. It started with Afghanistan, but they're now funding DRCA programs in Syria, Libya, Taiwan. They picked up nearly every contract that the U.S. government dropped. Without government funding, DRCA would have had to fire thousands of indig soldiers."

"So Cyberdyne kept those paramilitary programs intact?"

"Some have even expanded," said Sinéad. "DRCA is now

unconstrained by the U.S. government. They've grown their operations and client base. Today, their biggest contract is with Ukraine's International Legion. They've underwritten the pay of thousands of American-trained foreign fighters serving in its ranks."

"That's all interesting," said Skwerl. "But what's it got to do with the jet I've got parked on a mountainside in Colorado?"

"Your point of contact in Kampala, he was working for DRCA when he was murdered."

"H worked for DRCA . . ." Skwerl was putting the pieces together. "That means he worked for Cyberdyne."

"Correct."

"Which means we need to talk to Mac."

"We'll be there in another hour."

Sinéad parked the Acura around the back of Cyberdyne's headquarters. She and Skwerl entered a set of double doors that led them into an unimpressive linoleum-tiled reception area. Inside was empty except for a security guard who sat barricaded behind a chest-high desk, eating his lunch from a Tupperware container. "May I help you?" He brushed a few crumbs from his shirtfront.

Sinéad took the lead, explaining that they were here to see the CEO of Cyberdyne Security.

"IDs, please."

Both Sinéad and Skwerl slid over their driver's licenses, registered to the same Pennsylvania address. The guard shined a UV light on the surface of each to check its infrared watermark for authenticity. Reluctantly, he picked up the phone, dialing another office. "I've got a Jay and Sinéad Manning at the front desk"— Skwerl grabbed Sinéad by the arm, so she wouldn't correct the security guard on their marital status. "They're here to see Mr. McDermott . . ." On the other end of the line, Skwerl could hear a voice dictating a long set of muffled instructions, not a good sign. "Yep . . . yep . . . got it . . . yes, understood." The security guard hung up the phone. "I'm sorry, Mr. McDermott isn't here. If you call his office, you can see about scheduling a meeting."

"That seemed like a lot of back-and-forth just to tell us he's not here."

The security guard had returned to his lunch. "Sorry," he said, stabbing together a bite of what appeared to be last night's tuna casserole. "He's not here." The security guard handed them back their IDs. "Have a nice day."

Skwerl and Sinéad exited the building. "Now what do we do?"

"Let's schedule a meeting," said Sinéad, trying to remain upbeat.

"No," said Skwerl. "If what you're saying about DRCA and Cyberdyne is true, Mac's never going to take a meeting with us." Skwerl stepped backward, glancing up the front of the building. He pointed to one of the corner offices. "Mac's up there. I'm sure of it."

Skwerl wandered out into the parking lot.

"What do you want to do?"

"His car," said Skwerl. "It's got to be parked out here somewhere."

"You know what he drives?"

"No, but I've got a feeling that I'll know it when I see it."

Skwerl and Sinéad wandered around the lot, but not for long. Parked in a far, inconvenient corner, where no one might scratch it, was a newly restored Ford Bronco. Black paint job. Black interiors. Shiny as an eight-ball. Mint condition. Skwerl gave a low whistle when he saw it. "Beautiful . . . looks like a '72 . . . maybe a '73 . . ."

"How can you be sure that's his car?"

"No one else in that building can afford a car like this." Skwerl stepped toward it gingerly, as if the car were a large animal that might spook. He placed his hands on the side of the Bronco, almost petting it as he peeked inside, searching for any items left out on the seat or dashboard that would conclusively identify this as Mac's car. Because the Bronco was backed into its parking space, it took Skwerl a moment to notice that essential detail: a Ventum

One road bike, built especially for triathletes, locked on a rack over the spare tire.

"Bingo." Skwerl glanced side to side, to make sure no one was observing him. He came down into a crouch examining the car door. "Nothing fancy here," he said like a diagnostician. "Standard key entry. If it's an early '70s model, that means it's probably a six-cut sidebar system." He placed his cheek against the door, staring at the mechanism from the side. "Likely a single cylinder." He leaned back and considered the door handle a little while longer. "Doesn't seem to have an exterior retaining clip. But I can get in through that poke hole in the face cap."

"You want us to steal Mac's car . . . ?"

Skwerl sprung back onto his feet, brushing off his hands on the back of his pants. "No," he said. "We're gonna hide in the backseat, wait for him to get off work. When he pulls onto the street, we'll have our little talk with him."

Skwerl returned to the Acura, where he scrounged around for lockpicking materials. He found one of Sinéad's leather bodices sheathed in plastic from the dry cleaner. He neatly folded the bodice and left it on the backseat, taking the wire hanger. Wedged between a seat cushion he also found a few hairpins. Sinéad used these to fix her tightly drawn ponytail into place when she worked. Skwerl tucked the hairpins into his pocket. Equipped with these items, as well as a large navy blanket they'd hide beneath in the backseat, Skwerl returned to the Bronco. He showed Sinéad where to repark her Acura, so it'd have a better view of Cyberdyne's entrance. If Mac or anyone else approached, Sinéad was supposed to honk her horn twice. But Skwerl told her not to worry, a lock like this should take him no time.

He got to work.

After reparking the Acura, Sinéad could see the entrance to Cyberdyne Security through her front windshield while through her rearview mirror she could watch Skwerl, crouched into a squat, poking the lock with so many hairpins he might as well have been an acupuncturist. Five minutes passed. Then fifteen. It was closing in on half an hour when Sinéad noticed that no one had entered or left Cyberdyne. If it weren't for the cars parked out front, she might have thought the entire office was deserted, that no one even worked there.

The sun was dipping below the horizon, casting a glare, and so she adjusted her rearview mirror for a better angle on Skwerl. He had come out of his crouch and was now standing, jimmying the entirety of the unfolded wire hanger into the gap between the window and doorframe. Skwerl was too far away for Sinéad to hear him, but he was mouthing curses as he wiped sweat from his forehead. He shimmied and tugged on the bent end of the wire hanger—it was stuck. Skwerl kept pulling, his attempts to free the hanger growing increasingly desperate as he came up on tiptoes, struggling for leverage; clearly, he needed help.

Sinéad might have let Skwerl continue to struggle, but then through her peripheral vision she glimpsed the double doors at Cyberdyne's front entrance swing open. Mac strode out into the parking lot, clutching a leather briefcase, his navy sports coat slung over his shoulder and his tie loosened after a day at the office. Sinéad honked the horn, but Skwerl didn't stop working—maybe he didn't hear, or maybe he was determined not to leave the wire hanger jammed in the door, tipping off Mac that someone had tried to break into his car.

Sinéad leapt out of her Acura and sprinted across the parking lot. They had a minute, likely less, before Mac would see them. Arriving beside Skwerl, she didn't tell him that they had to go, that there were worse things than Mac knowing someone had tried to break into his car. She didn't say any of this because she knew it wouldn't have mattered—Skwerl was determined to unlock the door. "Put your hands above mine." She followed Skwerl's instructions. "Ready?"

"Ready," she said.

"Pull . . . c'mon, pull . . ."

They collapsed in a heap on top of each other. Sinéad glanced across the lot, toward the building's front entrance. Mac had slipped out of view. They had only seconds. As they stood, Skwerl was muttering about the lock, how picking it shouldn't be so difficult. That the hanger shouldn't have gotten stuck. That a quarter turn clockwise should defeat the single-cylinder system and pop the door open. Sinéad took a final glance at the elaborate system of hairpins Skwerl had slotted into the door handle as well as the wire hanger he'd jammed into the window frame. That's when she noticed the old-fashioned lock knob through the window, on the top of the door's interior panel. Skwerl hadn't bothered to check it. The knob was in the up, unlocked position—it had been the whole time.

The hairpins and wire hanger clattered to the ground the moment Sinéad popped open the door. Across the parking lot, they could now hear the echo of Mac's footfalls. "Get in," whispered Skwerl. He grabbed the wire hanger and navy blanket and leapt inside the Bronco, tumbling into the backseat. Sinéad followed, slamming the door shut behind her. They flung the blanket over their heads. "You couldn't pick the lock," Sinéad whispered, "because the door wasn't even locked."

"Shhh . . ." Skwerl nudged her in the ribs with the wire hanger. Mac's footfalls were coming close. His dark silhouette loomed next to the driver's side door. Before Mac climbed inside, he crouched low, picking up a couple of the hairpins. He inspected them between his fingers and Sinéad could feel Skwerl reposition the wire hanger as if he'd decided to now brandish it as a weapon in case the heavily bent hairpins provoked Mac's curiosity and he noticed them both in the backseat.

But Mac dismissed the hairpins, flicking the one he'd inspected onto the ground like how a person flicks away a cigarette butt. He climbed into his Bronco, fastening his seatbelt with a metallic click. When he turned on the ignition, the radio started. It was tuned to a classic rock station. As they pulled out of Cyberdyne's headquarters, Skwerl couldn't seem to help himself. Delighted (and amazed) as he was to have pulled this off, he made little noises beside Sinéad; she had no way to shut him up, no way to stop him from humming along to some tune she didn't know as they sped out into the night.

WHEN UNCLE TONY RETURNED TO HIS ROOM AFTER DRINKS with Grillot, he began to scroll through messages on his phone. He then swapped out his SIM card (the one registered to his alias with the Hyatt rewards points) to one registered in his true name, so he could check his encrypted email as well as his Signal and WhatsApp. The incoming traffic was mostly routine, status updates on the myriad programs run by the Office, all handled by his support staff. Few of these messages required any action by him. He might have been in charge at the Office, but nearly all the correspondence he received either had him on the "cc" or "to" line along with one of his several deputies.

For a person who ran a global network of covert armies, correspondence took up a surprisingly small part of Uncle Tony's day. He hated email and was, admittedly, a bit of a Luddite. He believed that technology was the sworn enemy of secrecy and he worshipped at the church of compartmentalization, in which cryptonyms were his scripture and the reports officers who managed them his high priests. Like any dogma pursued to extremes, it placed Uncle Tony out of step with the world around him. He had once sent a developmental asset an email in which he had asked for the same email address to which he'd just sent the message. The most common Uncle Tony response on correspondence was "Call me." When he returned to his room, in a role reversal, this was the message that was waiting for him from his boss, the White Russian.

It was late afternoon on the East Coast, and so Uncle Tony rang her office line figuring he might catch her at her desk at Langley, on the seventh floor of the New Headquarters Building. Like Uncle Tony, Alejandra Fedorov believed in compartmentalization and picking up the phone. Unlike Uncle Tony, she handled most matters herself. She discouraged emails with heavily populated "cc" and "to" lines. She would say that she believed it was important to keep circles of information tight. Only those with the need to know should know. She answered her own calls by practice, despite the robust administrative staff barricaded in cubicles outside her corner office.

After dialing a long sequence of numbers, Uncle Tony found himself on the line with her. "What do you know about a joint apprehension request made in Austin?" Fedorov had offered no exchange of pleasantries, no small talk. She had answered the phone, heard Uncle Tony's voice, and fired off her question. "The Bureau's field office has received inquiries from a new HPSCI member, a Congressman Mangrove. His staffers have been sniffing around."

Uncle Tony needed to play for time. "Let me look into it."

"Please do. Otherwise, I'm going to start making inquiries of my own."

Immediately after getting off the line, Uncle Tony swapped out SIM cards. He placed a local call, to Ali Safi at the airport. They would meet the next morning over breakfast at the InterContinental. This game with Fareeda had gone on long enough.

CHEESE COULD HARDLY STAND THE WAITING. HIS WIFE HAD been taken, as had his unborn child, and he was half a world away, marooned with this jet on the side of a mountain. To pass the time, he'd enlisted Just Shane and Ephraim to help with some cosmetic repairs, the hope being that when he and Skwerl delivered the jet they might still recoup most of their commission. This ordeal might not have been worth five hundred thousand dollars, but the thought of getting less—or even getting nothing—was too depressing to entertain.

Where the grizzly had clawed the side of the fuselage, they'd unfastened the rivets and Ephraim had spent a day banging out the dents with a hammer before repainting and lacquering the panels. These were now drying in a shed off the airstrip. The three of them had also disassembled the damaged seats, restuffing the plush cushions and armrests, and then stitching the upholstery back together with fishing line and a large-gauge needle. The result was a Challenger 600 whose interiors were intact, but with a distinct Frankenstein look about them.

When the jet had first arrived, Just Shane hadn't wanted to know any of the details, where it'd come from, where it was going. But the plates had piqued his curiosity. They were installing the last of the reassembled chairs, tightening down the retaining bolts, when Just Shane asked Cheese what he planned to do with his share of the money. "My wife's expecting," said Cheese. "We need a bigger place, a condo or house with two bedrooms. I'll use half for a down payment. I'll save the rest."

"I guess that makes sense."

In the silence that followed, Cheese detected an air of disapproval. "You don't think that's smart?"

"I didn't say that."

"But it's not what you would do."

With his good hand, Just Shane was cranking down a last bolt at the base of the chair. "No . . . that's not what I'd do."

"So what, then, would you do?"

"For starters," said Just Shane, tossing the wrench into an open tool chest, "I wouldn't hand my money to some bank. You buy a house, you'll put down what . . . twenty percent of the value? That means the bank owns eighty percent. Even if you get a fifteen-year or thirty-year fixed mortgage at a good rate, that still means the bank owns four-fifths of your house, which means you don't really own your house, which means the bank can take it away. Do you trust the banks?" The question wasn't rhetorical. Just Shane was pointing his mangled right hand at Cheese, demanding his answer.

"No," he said. "I don't suppose I do trust them."

"Then why would you hand them your hard-earned money?" Just Shane took a little leap in the air, plopping onto the chair. He bounced up and down on the cushion a few times to test it. The restitched leather squeaked under his weight. "Five hundred grand is a nice chunk of change, don't get me wrong, but it's not going to last you forever. Those antique plates Ephraim thinks are worth something, they might extend your payday, but with a new baby, a mortgage, give it a couple years and you'll be out of cash. Then what'll you do . . . ?"

"Get a job."

"Back at the Esso station?"

Cheese grew silent.

"No offense meant," said Just Shane. "I'm just asking." He

pointed out the nearest window, to his vast property. He explained to Cheese that in addition to inheriting a healthy 401(k) from his aunt ("God rest her soul"), for the past five years he'd invested one-third of his monthly VA check into crypto, a mix of early valuation Bitcoin, Dogecoin, and Ethereum. "I got in on the ground floor, grew my portfolio, and got out at the right time." Most of his money was now in precious metals (copper and gold) and a few pieces of high-end art (he favored Old Masters). ". . . These are all assets that I hold myself in a secure location," though, rather coyly, he didn't offer details. "How do you think I could afford this place?" Just Shane grew quiet, before adding, "My point, Aziz"— and he placed his hand on Cheese's arm as he dispensed with his nickname—"is that you need a plan for yourself and your family, one that's better than a single heist and job prospects at an Esso station. What about Sheepdog? Do you think he could offer you more work?"

"Maybe," said Cheese. "He's Skwerl's contact. But I don't think Skwerl even knows who he really is."

"Shame about Skwerl . . ." Just Shane was crouched next to the tool kit, slotting the many screwdrivers, wrenches, and ratchets into their correct places.

"What do you mean by that?"

Just Shane didn't answer right away. His mouth was moving silently as he counted the sockets in his set, making sure none were missing. "Now Zad," he said. "They never should've been on that raid . . . and then the way the Office hung Skwerl out to dry for blowing the whistle . . . after he had to watch Dickhead Mike bleed out, of course it all got to him . . . I'm amazed Skwerl's not in the psych ward . . . Sheepdog probably saved his life . . . Gave him a chance to make money, a reason to get up in the morning, a way to stick it to Big Brother, who, after that FISA case, has proven more than happy to take every dime that Skwerl makes . . . You want some advice? More important than whether you get your full commission on this jet is that you and Skwerl figure out who this

Sheepdog character is."

"Given how shitty this operation has gone," said Cheese. "I'm not sure I want to know who Sheepdog is."

"That's understandable," Just Shane replied. "But whether you like it or not, Sheepdog might be the only future the two of you have got."

Before Cheese could say more, their conversation was interrupted. Outside, the Iridium had begun to ring.

SKWERL WAS WAITING FOR THE RIGHT MOMENT. HE COULDN'T do anything so long as they were speeding down the highway. Under the blanket, Sinéad lay very still beside him. Mac—believing he was alone in his Bronco—had begun humming along to the classic rock station on the radio. Peeking out from the corner of the blanket, Skwerl watched the road signs shuttle past. Left onto Chain Bridge (Mac was humming "Sweet Caroline"). Merge onto the GW Parkway (it was the B-52s and "Love Shack"). Take the Key Bridge exit into Georgetown (Abba and "Dancing Queen"). Mac was headed toward the C&O Canal towpath, most likely to log some after-work miles on his road bike. Once Mac crossed the Key Bridge, when he turned onto K Street, Skwerl became sure of it. Slowly, he bent the wire hanger so it formed a garotte, one he could use to strangle Mac—or at least to hold at Mac's neck and threaten to strangle him—as soon as he parked the Bronco.

Sinéad squeezed Skwerl's arm under the blanket. It was the only way she could communicate what Skwerl surely knew she was thinking: *Don't do anything stupid, Jay.* And Skwerl wasn't dismissive of this warning. Over a lifetime, he'd engaged in ample stupid behavior. Depending on how the next ten minutes went, this plan might prove to be the apotheosis of his stupidity. Skwerl had, however, learned to pause in the moments before committing himself to a course of action with irrevocable consequences (like breaking into the car of the CEO of Cyberdyne Security and threatening to strangle/kidnap/do god-knows-what to him). But if Mac was going to reveal who had taken Fareeda, who had killed H, and who Sheepdog was, then Skwerl knew he needed to scare him—and Mac wasn't so easy to scare. Hence the wire hanger to his throat; it was, Skwerl thought, a good plan—or at least not a stupid plan.

As Mac parked at the entrance to the C&O Canal, the inside of the Bronco grew darker. His parking spot was below an overpass onto the Whitehurst Freeway. The sound of traffic above formed a steady cadence. Mac was mumbling the lyrics to "A Whiter Shade of Pale" as he prepared for his bike ride. "*One of sixteen vestal virgins, Who was leaving for the coast . . .*" He unbuttoned his work shirt and pulled on his Lycra cycling jersey . . . "*And although my eyes were open, They might have just as well've been closed . . .*"

Skwerl flung back the blanket and reached the wire hanger over Mac's head, throttling it against his neck. Mac gasped, grasping for the hanger. But as he did Skwerl applied more and more pressure. "Put your fucking arms down . . ." he said as Mac continued to struggle, bucking against his seat, kicking at the dash, digging his thumbs between the wire hanger and his airway. With every attempt to resist, Skwerl pulled harder and harder against Mac's throat, causing him to make little squeaking noises like air escaping the pinched end of a balloon. "Put your arms down, Mac."

"Skwerl . . . ?" he gasped.

"Put 'em on your lap."

Mac, hacking and wheezing, followed his instructions. Skwerl glanced over his shoulder at Sinéad. When he'd pounced from under the blanket, he'd inadvertently tossed it in her face, so she had only just untangled herself. Her eyes widened and she held up her hands, giving Skwerl a look that asked, *What the hell do you want me to do?* "The seatbelt," he said. "Secure his arms with it." One transferable skill from Sinéad's other job was her expert ability to tie a person up, so they couldn't escape—Sinéad could boast a perfect record in that regard.

Glancing at Mac, Sinéad mouthed the word *sorry*, and then leaned over him and began her work. She coiled the lap belt around his wrists and legs. She rigged the chest belt over the headrest and then lashed it down, fastening the buckle. Within seconds, she had Mac tied up, as constricted in his own seatbelt as if he'd fallen into a python's clutches. Skwerl removed the wire hanger from his neck. This allowed the interrogation to begin.

"What the fuck, Skwerl . . ."

"I'm the one asking the questions."

"That wasn't a question, you asshole."

"Who is Sheepdog? Why don't we start there."

Mac rested his chin on his chest. He began shaking his head. "I have no idea."

"Does he work for DRCA . . . or for Cyberdyne . . . ?"

"If he worked for me, Skwerl, don't you think I'd know who he was? You stole a Challenger 600 that belongs to DRCA. Why'd you steal one of my jets?"

Skwerl whapped him on the leg with the wire hanger. "I'm asking the questions."

"Quit it . . . that hurt."

"Who is Sheepdog!" Skwerl whapped him again but this time got too close.

Mac headbutted Skwerl. "Why'd you steal my jet!"

Skwerl blinked a few times to regain his bearings. He noticed Sinéad roll her eyes. She was right to be annoyed. This was going nowhere, so Skwerl tried a different tack. "First of all, I didn't steal your jet. I *repossessed* it, and I was only responding to the email Sheepdog sent to the network—a network that *you* suggested I join. I didn't know the jet belonged to DRCA, or that Cyberdyne owned DRCA, or that you were connected to any of this."

"What email are you even talking about?"

"The one Sheepdog sent out, looking for a pilot . . ."

"I'm a network member and I never saw any email."

Skwerl fished out his phone, scrolled through his inbox, and then held the screen in front of Mac so he could read it: *Sheepdogs, A member of the network is searching for a commercial pilot with special operations experience for a short-term project, good pay. Inquire direct.—Sheepdog.* Mac studied the email for a moment and then turned to Skwerl, shook his head disappointedly, and announced, "Sheepdog didn't write that."

"And how would you know?"

"Pull out my phone . . . it's in my right pocket." Skwerl knifed his hand into Mac's pocket. He removed the phone and, holding it up to Mac's face, swiped up to unlock it. "Now go into my email and search *Sheepdog*." Dozens of messages popped up, averaging one every two or three weeks and going back several years, to around the time Mac joined the QX program at Uncle Tony's behest. "Open any of those emails," said Mac. "Now, look at that one you just showed me and then look at the ones on my phone . . . see the difference?"

Skwerl didn't see, at least not at first. The text in the email's body was identical, not only in font but also in layout. Same with the subject line. It was Sinéad who noticed the difference; it was in the addresses. "The one on your phone has the recipients in the 'bcc' line," she explained. "That other email, it's got only Jay's name in the 'cc' line."

"Which means . . ." said Mac, guiding Jay to his conclusion.

"Which means I'm the only one who got this email . . . that the recipients always go in the 'bcc' line, never the 'cc' line . . . that it didn't go out to the entire network . . . that Ali Safi set me up."

"Ali who?"

Skwerl explained to Mac that Ali Safi was a security guard who worked for DRCA. He had appeared unexpectedly in the hangar in Kampala, and then at the InterContinental in Marseille, where he'd murdered H. Mac had never heard of H either. "H was the contact Sheepdog—or whoever was posing as Sheepdog—gave me when I landed in Kampala."

"And what about this Ali Safi?"

"Ali Safi . . ." Skwerl added, "He's relentless. He won't stop until he has this jet. He's the one who kidnapped my partner's wife."

"Wait a second," said Mac. "Ali Safi murdered one man and kidnapped someone else, all for a Challenger 600? DRCA has at least a dozen of those in our inventory . . . they're not difficult to come by. And your million bucks for a commission, that represents . . . what . . . twenty percent of the value? So the entire jet is worth what? Five million?"

Skwerl felt compelled to mention the incident with the grizzly—the jet might be worth a little less than five million now. Skwerl was going on about the interiors, how he had a handy Amish guy who was helping repair them at this very moment, when Mac interrupted, "With all due respect to your Amish guy who does interiors, whoever set you up is going through a huge amount of trouble for, relatively speaking, not a huge amount of money . . . Can you think of another reason someone might want that jet?"

Skwerl grew silent.

He could think of one reason, but he wasn't going to tell Mac.

"Listen," said Mac. "It's not right how the Office has treated you. Uncle Tony came by a few days ago asking about you and Sheepdog, saying that you'd stolen something . . . I don't know what Uncle Tony wants, but it sounds like he's the one who duped you. Maybe it's time you gave him a call and tried to clear this up. Just a word of advice."

Skwerl thanked him for the advice, and along with Sinéad began to untie him from his seat. They would allow Mac to commence with his bike ride on one condition, that he leave his phone behind. Skwerl assured Mac that when he returned, he wouldn't find him or Sinéad crouched in the backseat of his Bronco. Mac had little choice, so agreed. Freed from his seat, he finished changing into his cycling gear. He hoisted his road bike off the Bronco's back tire, clipped into his pedals, and rode down the towpath. Beneath the canopy of trees, his single headlight burrowed its way into the darkness, a little wobblier than usual.

Skwerl snatched Mac's unlocked phone off the driver's seat. He searched the contacts, finding the number he wanted, and then called.

Uncle Tony answered as if he'd been asleep. "Hey Mac, any news?"

"Yeah, this ain't Mac, it's Skwerl. News is I've got your plates."

WHEN CHEESE HEARD THE IRIDIUM RING, HE LEFT JUST SHANE working in the cabin of the Challenger 600 and stepped outside to answer the call. It was Skwerl, and Cheese was eager to tell him about the progress they'd made on the jet. Ephraim had managed to bang out most of the dents from the side paneling. Although the interiors still had some problems, the stench in the cockpit was mostly gone and they'd managed to stitch back together the leather upholstery on the chairs. "In any negotiation," Cheese explained, "we'll likely have to accept a discounted commission, but the jet is in better condition than when you left, and this should be enough to get back Fareeda . . ."

"Cheese, listen to me . . ."

But he wouldn't stop. "When she gets back, I'm getting her a puppy. She's always watching those ads for the ASPCA, and I've always said we can't afford a dog, but this has gone on too long, and when she gets home the first thing that I'm going to do is . . ."

"Cheese . . . listen!"

The line went silent.

After releasing Mac and placing the phone call to Uncle Tony, Skwerl and Sinéad had picked up her Acura from the lot where they'd parked it, returned to Tysons Corner, and checked into a nearby hotel. This was where they were placing this call from. "Those plates you have," Skwerl explained, "the ones we ate off . . . Those are real—" But he was still struggling to get a word in.

"Uh, yes Jay, . . . of course they're real . . . are you alright? Is Sinéad with you?"

Clearly, Cheese was failing to comprehend. "No, they're the *actual* plates. They're the originals, the ones from Versailles, commissioned by Marie Antoinette. When that plate broke, Ephraim was right. He couldn't glue it back together because it was old—*really old*. No one makes plates like those anymore because they're the originals."

"So you think we can get a good price for them after we deliver the jet?"

Sinéad was sitting next to Skwerl on the hotel bed. She had brought out her business laptop, the one she managed accounts with at Knotty Pleasures. She was clacking on the keyboard, pulling up the findings from a bit of cursory research. These types of items rarely came onto the open market. In 1837, the year that Louis Philippe, the last king of France, designated Versailles a public museum, he also created the Versailles Acquisitions Policy, which still exists. This policy allowed the French authorities to aggressively bid for and acquire artifacts original to Versailles while keeping the sums they paid a state secret, hidden from the public. Occasionally, they would miss an artifact and it would fall into a private collection. Sinéad found one, an auction summary from Sotheby's, a decade old. Skwerl read the details to Cheese, specifically how a similar four-dish tea set commissioned in 1785 by Louis XVI had sold to an unnamed Qatari buyer for $6.12 million. The price seemed unfathomable to Cheese. "Who drops that kind of money?"

"Someone who likes tea . . . Cheese, how many plates did you say we had?"

"Around three dozen—" He choked on the words.

Skwerl did the math. "We're sitting on about $60 million."

"Including or not including the plate you broke?" On the other end of the line, Cheese took a deep breath. He collected himself, so that when he spoke again his voice was calm and measured as if initiating some procedure in the cockpit. "What do you need me to do?"

"Fly back out here tomorrow. I've got a plan."

When Skwerl explained to Cheese that he should land at Aero Services Aviation in Chester County, where they'd departed from, Cheese made all the predictable objections: that they'd blown their cover at that airfield; that their tail number would no doubt wind up in the flight logs again; that they should try a different FBO or figure a way to fly out of the country direct, maybe stopping in the Caribbean to refuel before crossing the Atlantic. Skwerl cut him off, asking, "Do you trust me?" Cheese answered, "You? . . . No, not at all. Look at the mess you landed us in." Skwerl reframed the question and asked, "Do you trust Sinéad?" The line again went silent, until Cheese asked, "Landing at that FBO again is her idea?"

"Yeah." Skwerl glanced at her, and she nodded.

"Alright then. For her."

They arranged for Cheese to depart first thing the next morning, placing him at Aero Services Aviation by early afternoon. When they hung up, Skwerl turned to Sinéad and asked her if she was sure about Chester County, that they could stop there with no problems. "You don't need to worry," she said. "I got you guys out of there, didn't I? I'll be able to get you guys in."

Skwerl hadn't, until now, had the chance to ask Sinéad about that evening. How had she gotten them out of there? What was it that she had said to the security guard and to whoever was working in the tower? How had she convinced them to let the Challenger take off without any of the requisite paperwork and with what was so obviously a phony tail number?

Sinéad shut her laptop. "You really don't know?"

"No, I don't."

Sinéad placed the laptop on the bedside table, so it would be out of their way, and then she fit her body against Skwerl's, placing one long leg seductively over his. Her hand rested on his chest, and she drummed her fingertips against it. "Too bad," she said. "I would've thought you could figure it out." Then she rolled away from him, switching off the side lamp and dismissing him with a "Goodnight."

Skwerl switched the side lamp back on. "Wait a second . . . don't I get a clue?"

"A clue?"

"Yeah, a clue."

"Hmm . . ." She rolled back toward him, though not all the way. "Your clue is the motto of where you used to work."

"Semper Fidelis . . . ?"

"Not quite," she said. "The other place you worked."

"Have It Your Way . . . ?" One glorious high school summer Skwerl had done nothing but attend raging parties, smoke a lot of pot, and work shifts at Burger King.

"No, jackass."

Sinéad shut off the light again. She pulled the blanket over her shoulders and turned onto her side. Through the darkness, Skwerl said, *"And ye shall know the truth and the truth shall make you free."* He could feel Sinéad face toward him. "You told the guys at the FBO the truth?"

"Is that so crazy? When I was standing out on the tarmac, I asked that guard for help—people will surprise you when you ask them directly for help. Then I told him a little bit about who you were. That was enough to convince him to drive back to the tower. After that, I told him about Now Zad and showed him the article written about you. When I explained to him and his colleagues in the tower how you couldn't work, and how the Office had screwed you over, they weren't only willing to turn a blind eye, they wanted to help. Don't you get it . . . these are guys working the graveyard shift at an FBO. All day long they're watching rich assholes fly in and out on their planes. And you're stealing one of these planes. By the time I left that morning, they were the ones thanking me.

They loved being able to help."

"But I'm not stealing planes now," said Skwerl. "I'm stealing plates. It's a lot more money."

"It is," she said. "And a lot more dangerous."

"What if I told you that I'd figured out a way to get Fareeda back and also make sure that Ali Safi and Uncle Tony don't run off with the $60 million."

Sinéad pulled herself close to Skwerl, once again slinging her leg over his. She rested her palm on his chest, tapping her finger against his bare skin like she was composing a message in Morse code. "I'd tell you that I was interested."

Chapter Five

ALI SAFI'S REVENGE

NIGHTMARES PLAGUED ALI SAFI. IN THE YEARS SINCE HIS brother's death, his subconscious would reconstruct the Now Zad raid, projecting it from the dark recesses of his mind like archival footage. Hundreds if not thousands of times, he was forced to live events that he hadn't experienced. He had been in Kabul the night his brother was killed, working toward his mathematics degree. His ambition had been to leverage that degree into a career with one of his country's fledgling financial institutions. He would become a banker and live his life ensconced in the relative safety that wealth afforded. But his dreams of the raid had come to feel more real to him than his memories of Kabul. A life dedicated to vengeance takes a toll. Some men go crazy, some burn out. Some, like Ali Safi, live in their darkest dreams.

The raid always began with a sound in the darkness, the low rhythmic thumping of helicopter blades. Later, U.N. and Government of Afghanistan investigators would conclude that his brother had been sleeping on the roof along with a mix of DRCA security guards and Gul Bacha's fighters. This group would have been the first to see the dark, oblong form of the helicopters as they reared backward on their final approach.

In Ali Safi's dream, the next sound is the first shot. Some nights, Gul Bacha's fighters—most of whom are veteran Taliban—take this shot from the roof; the Americans are coming for them, how could they not resist . . . On other nights, it's the Americans who shoot first; they've disembarked their helicopters and are ducking between mud-walled compounds, firing upward at the dark silhouettes they glimpse on the rooftops . . . No matter who takes the first shot, the air becomes thick with rifle fire, and when these rounds pass close the snapping sound is like a string plucked next to the ear. Ali Safi is then left to endure the exchange that follows. He watches as the men on the roof fire on the Americans. He listens as his brother begs Gul Bacha's fighters to lay down their weapons: don't they know the Americans will kill those who resist; don't they know their choice is to surrender or die.

An eerie silence: the Americans have stopped shooting.

Overhead, there's a droning sound. A gunship, an AC-130; it's flying an oval racetrack attack pattern. Three guns poke from its left side as it enters this counterclockwise maneuver designed to bank the gun barrels downward. Largest among them, menacing as a lightning bolt, is a 105mm cannon. The shell it fires is the size of a can of Pringles, those American chips his brother loved so much that Ali Safi would bring them home on his return trips from Kabul. The gun has begun its grim work, chugging away. The impacts fall in quick succession, the sound like a soda can crushed underfoot, and each chomping off whole sections of mudbrick homes—an exterior wall, a roof, a corner bedroom—the entirety of Now Zad is being devoured.

This is the part of each night where Ali Safi relives the instant of his brother's death. Gul Bacha's fighters have finally stopped shooting at the Americans. Like passengers on a sinking ship, they rush to the single point of escape, a stairwell off the roof. Some still carry weapons. Others have dropped them, clattering, to the floor. They trample over their sleeping mats. This scramble plays out in a matter of seconds. But time assumes strange proportions in Ali Safi's dream, and this episode is agonizingly drawn out. Each of his brother's steps toward the exit becomes a possibility unto itself, an alternate life, one in which he still survives, a hope that tonight it ends differently, that he makes it off the roof.

But no one does.

He sees his brother, his consternation, the strain in his face like a runner near the finish line who has already lost his race. A flash of light. Darkness.

And then daybreak, the Americans linger in the diffuse grey morning light, sorting through rubble. They are searching. When they find the dead, they leave them, the bodies tangled within their own homes, their faces dusted with what remains. When they find weapons, they pull them from the rubble, making great efforts to excavate every rifle, machine gun, or rocket-propelled grenade, like archaeologists pulling a lost civilization from the earth. They stack these weapons in a heap in the center of town. Each addition to the heap is a line in a story that these men will construct to some hidden tribunal, explaining what they did and justifying why. Ali Safi won't sit on that tribunal—he knows no such privilege will ever be afforded to him.

Years later, Ali Safi learned the identity of one of these men. All it'd taken was a Freedom of Information Act request to identify Jay Manning, whose friend had died on the raid, as the anonymous whistleblower in a news article about Now Zad. This makes Manning the only person that Ali Safi could ever hope to hold accountable for his brother's death. Ali Safi's fathers and uncles, traditional Pashtuns all, might have called this accountability *badal*, the right of retribution under the dictates of *Pashtunwali*, the law of the Pashtuns. But Ali Safi considers himself a modern man, a cosmopolitan (more Kabul than Now Zad) who doesn't fall back on anachronistic tribal customs. When, in his dreams, he sees Jay Manning—his rifle slung across his chest, his helmet's chin strap unfastened, his eyes sunken from lack of sleep—standing over his dead brother, the desire Ali Safi feels is universal (not tribal), it is the accounting one person owes another, regardless of culture and custom. What Ali Safi demands—what he knows he needs if he is ever to stop having these dreams—is something far simpler: *revenge*.

Until he met Uncle Tony, Ali Safi had never spoken of these dreams—he didn't see the point. After his brother's death, the U.S. government offered him a solatia payment of 200,000 afghani (about $5,000) to support his family. DRCA, by way of compensation, offered him his brother's old job. He accepted both, telling himself that after three or four years' work, he would have earned enough to return to university and resume his studies. Then Kabul fell, and the conquering Talibs shuttered his university, deeming it an institution of the old apostate regime. He had no other prospect than to continue his work with DRCA. This is how, not even a year after the fall of Kabul, Ali Safi found himself in Ukraine, a serving soldier in its International Legion paid by DRCA.

This is when he met Uncle Tony.

DRIVEN IN A BLACK MERCEDES, COURTESY OF SPECIAL ACTION and Grillot, Uncle Tony raced north on the Boulevard Jacques Saadé, toward the airport. Outside his window, along an esplanade that fronted the Mediterranean, the proprietors of the cafés hosed down their allocation of sidewalk, each lashing water side to side as they cleared detritus from the night before into the gutters. With doglegged hand cranks, they opened their shuttered facades, allowing the eastern sun to reflect in the floor-to-ceiling windows that faced the quay. The first rush of early-morning commuters would soon arrive, either taking a table to eat or, if they were in a rush like Uncle Tony, grabbing something to go.

Originally, Uncle Tony had planned to host Ali Safi for a leisurely breakfast on the terrace of the InterContinental, in which they would discuss the orderly exchange of Fareeda for the Challenger 600. Uncle Tony had believed a resolution was within his grasp. Under the protection of Grillot and the French intelligence service, he felt quite at ease, happy to conduct business in the open. But the call he'd received from Mac's cellphone in the early hours of that morning had disabused him of any notion that this crisis would swiftly resolve itself. Simply put, Skwerl knew about the plates. This significantly complicated a plan Uncle Tony had begun developing months earlier, on the night that Ali Safi had walked up to him in the Grand Hotel in Lviv and, beneath the crystal pendants of the lobby chandelier, said, "I work for DRCA and we need to talk."

A lesser intelligence officer, one without Uncle Tony's acumen, might have balked at so forward an approach. But Uncle Tony had the experience to know that a direct approach demanded a direct response, so he'd answered, "Do you have a business card?" Which, of course, Ali Safi didn't. But he did have a pencil stub, and when he reached into the pocket of his military parka, which smelled sourly of the cold and was stained with patches of grease, he removed a matchbook to scribble his number on. Uncle Tony recognized the type of matchbook immediately, it came from inside the cellophane-wrapped accessory pack of an MRE. This was enough for Uncle Tony to honor the appointment they set for the next day. They'd agreed to meet across from the Taras Shevchenko Memorial, at the Vienna Coffee House, which was so close Uncle Tony had pointed to it from the lobby before returning that evening to his suite.

The next morning, Uncle Tony had a desk officer at headquarters run traces on Ali Safi. Little came up. Like most Afghans, he had no birth certificate. A 2006 census sponsored by USAID had recorded his name alongside a birth year of 1996, which seemed propitious, the Taliban having seized Kabul a first time that September. This was also the year that Uncle Tony, as a much younger paramilitary officer, had first traveled to Afghanistan. In those days, a spirit of post–Cold War optimism pervaded every corner of America's foreign policy apparatus. History had ended and the long march of progress had come to feel like a parade. Religious dogma and tribalism stood little chance against Levi's jeans and cable television. Certain colleagues of Uncle Tony's believed they could make common cause with the new Taliban leadership in Kabul against certain shared enemies. A small delegation that included Uncle Tony had traveled to the war-ravaged capital to deliver this message, emissaries from a post-historic world to the newly formed Islamic Emirate, for whom history was everything, committed as their regime was to restoring to the present an ancient and brutal version of Islam from the past.

Upon reviewing the scant details of Ali Safi's early life, Uncle Tony found that the years following his birth proved mostly a blank, until he appeared at Kabul University, listed in 2018 as a student enrolled in its math department. In 2019, he coauthored a paper with an adjunct on the faculty; its title, "Figural Patterning of Algebraic Expressions," read like a foreign language to Uncle Tony, who at his own university had majored in sports medicine and minored in women's studies (an ill-conceived plan to meet girls). In the paper's précis, which was written in Dari and translated to English, the authors had referenced the original Arabic definition of algebra: ". . . the reunion of broken parts." Uncle Tony had liked this and, as he first sat down with Ali Safi, felt predisposed to like him as well.

Hunched over his coffee that afternoon at the Vienna Coffee House, Ali Safi had the look of a cornered animal. When Uncle Tony asked how he'd managed to leave Afghanistan, Ali Safi began with his work for DRCA, which had already taken him to Syria and North Africa. He had watched the fall of Kabul on television in Tripoli. Six months later, after Russian tanks rolled across the border into Ukraine, his supervisor had announced that DRCA was looking for volunteers "to work in Europe," where they'd earn double their usual pay. Ali Safi had known without being told what this "work" would entail. He and a few dozen others had boarded a plane, which landed in Warsaw. DRCA had driven them to the border on tour buses, as if they were a sports team; after crossing the border, they had transferred to Ukrainian military transports, where they were driven to the zero line like cattle. For the last nine months, they had fought in and around Mariupol, Zaporizhzhia, Mykolaiv, staying mostly in these southeastern oblasts, their ranks thinning. At this point, Uncle Tony asked the obvious question, "How did you make it back to Lviv?"

"I deserted." Ali Safi could read the disappointment on Uncle Tony's face and immediately added, "Don't worry. I'm going back. And after you hear what I have to say, I believe you'll want to come with me."

Uncle Tony ordered a second cup of coffee as well as a piece of apple strudel served with a dollop of whipped cream for Ali Safi, who ate it in three enormous bites before settling back into his story. During the Russian occupation of Kherson, his brigade had held a line of trenches north of the Dnipro River, which fed into the Black Sea to the south. "Beautiful country," Ali Safi explained. "As an Afghan, I had never seen the sea until leaving home, and it felt tragic to fight in such a place. I felt as if I should be on holiday instead. But here we were, us and the orcs, hunting one another among the wreckage of people's homes. A few of these were quite spectacular, dachas abandoned by the wealthy Ukrainian elite. The Russians had looted these several times over, hauling out the appliances, the washers and dryers, the stereo systems and flat-screen TVs. The Russians weren't alone in their looting. Given the opportunity, my Ukrainian comrades had done the same. And why shouldn't they? For years, too many of their elites had sold Ukrainian interests to the highest Russian bidder. The average soldier blamed these elites for the war as much as Putin. By the time I arrived along the Dnipro, these dachas had been looted and re-looted, picked to the bones like a meal eaten many times over. Soldiers of both armies had torn the interiors to the studs, even stripping the copper wiring. There is a saying, do you know it? . . . 'War is moments of terror punctuated by long periods of boredom.'"

Uncle Tony had finished his coffee. He'd waved down their

waiter, who refilled his cup before he answered that, yes, he was quite familiar with the saying.

"Well, I've learned otherwise," said Ali Safi. "I believe it is more accurate to say that war is moments of terror punctuated by long periods of looting . . . If we assaulted a Russian position, maybe a series of buildings they had reinforced, or a trench line occupied for some weeks, the instant the assault was over and the smoke had cleared and we had evacuated our wounded, we would spend the long hours afterward searching for anything we could steal. Obviously, the longer the war goes on, the less there is to take . . . this is basic arithmetic. But the longer the war goes on the greater its privations become, so something small, like a can of tinned peaches, an unopened pack of cigarettes, or a good metal spoon—items a soldier would think little of in the early days of a war—become objects of great value. There is less, but whatever little remains is coveted all the more. And so, the impulse to loot remains constant."

"What's your point?" Uncle Tony had by now decided that if this booger-eating Afghan didn't tell him something truly compelling by the time he'd finished this latest cup of coffee, their meeting was over.

"Our commanders largely permitted such behavior," continued Ali Safi, though speaking more quickly, as if driving toward a point. "They accepted that this was part of how a soldier survives on the battlefield. On occasion, as we sat in our fighting positions, there would be a large detonation somewhere in the distance. The commanders, fearing that this might signal a fresh Russian assault, would get on their radios and too often it would be revealed that a group of soldiers had found a hidden safe or secure room inside one of the dachas and they were trying to blow it open. With limited stockpiles of C-4 and PLASTEX, our commanders couldn't have us wasting our stores of demolitions this way. A protocol was put in place: so long as we weren't in positions on the zero line, all demolitions would be kept under key in a storage locker.

As an Afghan soldier, it was assumed I had no home to send stolen valuables back to, so I was entrusted with the locker as a collateral duty. I suspected that before long one of my comrades would come asking for the keys, but it had surprised me when the person who asked was my squad leader, a Latvian who went by the self-appointed nom de guerre 'Ice Man.' But no one called him 'Ice Man.' Behind his back, we called him 'Victory Tooth' because he only had one of his two front teeth. Before the war he had played minor league hockey, and during his last game in Riga, the other team had punched the tooth out in a three-on-one brawl. This was only days before the invasion. Like many who lived in the Baltic states, he'd rushed across the border to kill Russians. He'd been at the front ever since, killed plenty of Russians, but hadn't yet had the chance to fix his missing tooth. He said he would take care of this when the war was over, at the Victory."

"Victory Tooth . . ." said Uncle Tony. "That's good." He drained his cup of coffee, choosing to remain in his seat.

Ali Safi continued, explaining how Victory Tooth (or the Tooth for short) had approached him with a proposition. A week before, while out on a reconnaissance, one of the Tooth's two vehicles, a BTR, had broken down. His other vehicle had been a British-made Husky, a mix between a dune buggy and a Humvee, which was too light to tow the armored BTR. This was outside the village of Dar'ivka, along Route M14, where the Dnipro bends to the north before hooking south, near a particularly beautiful tract of land with several stately homes. The Tooth had volunteered to stay behind with the BTR while the others drove ahead for help. While he waited, it started to rain. The Tooth left the BTR roadside and sheltered in a nearby dacha, one he'd stayed in the summer before. Though he'd had no need of it back then, he remembered it had a large fireplace in the living room. Having escaped the rain, the Tooth collected a few scraps of wood and lit them in the fireplace. Smoke gathered quickly, filling the living room. He kicked out the fire, but on closer inspection, when he tried to open the flue, he could see that the chimney was a fake. Not only was it bricked shut, but its back was made of flimsy drywall.

Uncle Tony asked the obvious question, "What was behind the drywall?"

"A hidden room," said Ali Safi, leaning across the table. A gleam had appeared in his eye. "The Tooth knocked out the drywall with the butt of his rifle. When he peered in from the outside, the room at first seemed empty, its floor covered in dust. But when the Tooth ducked inside, his footprints revealed a panel, about as large as this"—and Ali Safi leaned back, framing the table with his hands—"and in the panel's center was a recessed combination lock. Well, there aren't many locksmiths on the front. But there are plenty of explosives, which is why the Tooth sought me out. His proposition was simple: if I agreed to quietly supply him with a half satchel charge of C-4, say twelve pounds' worth, he would give me a twenty-five percent cut of whatever he found."

"Twenty-five percent," Uncle Tony had said. "Why not negotiate a better deal?"

"I'm not a greedy man," answered Ali Safi, though he sounded rather unconvincing. "I used to be a university student, and although I once thought that I would re-enroll with the money I earned at DRCA, I was coming to think of my future differently, so I agreed to the proposal. The first step came two days later, when I met the Tooth in our motor pool at a little after midnight. He had one of the Huskys gassed up, and I'd brought the promised half satchel charge. We exited our lines without announcing it to anyone, and as we drove the twenty minutes toward Dar'ivka, we were just as likely to be killed by our own forces as we were the Russians. We spoke little, each of us trying to listen for the low humming that might signal a drone overhead or for the distant report of incoming artillery. More than once, the Tooth muttered, 'This better be worth it.' Like him, I also wondered what—if anything—might be in the floor safe. When we arrived at the dacha, it was exactly as the Tooth had described. We ducked into the chimney and passed through the hole broken into the drywall. Sure enough, inside the hidden room was the safe recessed into the floor. Beneath the light of our headlamps, we molded a donut-shaped charge of C-4. We rested it on the safe's locking mechanism, popped the fuse ignitor, and scrambled outside the house in case we brought its roof down on our own heads. We had to wait a couple of minutes after the detonation for the smoke and dust to clear, but when we climbed back through the chimney, we found our calculations had proven correct. The C-4 had blown the locking mechanism out of its casement and the safe door was flopped open."

"What was inside?"

"A wooden crate," said Ali Safi. "Using our bayonets, we levered it open. Packed in straw were dishes. They were beautiful, but it seemed odd to keep them in a safe. We had been expecting gold, or jewels, or cash. Not dishes. The Tooth was equally confused. But with the dishes he noticed an inventory slip."

Ali Safi had then reached into his parka and removed a transparent plastic sleeve. Inside were a few sheets of paper, which he placed on the table, so Uncle Tony might make a closer inspection. The sheets were yellowed with age and bound with a rusted staple in the top left corner. Uncle Tony read the first page, which listed each of the plates and any discrepancies in their condition, a chip here or a blemish there. The inventory was handwritten in an elegant, looping cursive, all in French. He flipped to the second and third pages; they were much the same. But what he saw on the fourth page gave him pause; here, the text was in German, and not handwritten but done on a typewriter. It seemed to confirm the inventory taken on the preceding three pages. This last sheet was signed in a type of blue ink that over time had faded to a shade of red, and it was stamped with an official seal, a winged eagle perched on a garland. In the center of the garland was a swastika.

"Looks like you found some Nazi dishes," said Uncle Tony,

sliding the pages back across the table.

Ali Safi carefully reinserted the pages into the plastic sheath, which he left sitting on the table between them. "That's what we thought at first," he said. "We couldn't move the plates that night, so we decided to leave them. The Tooth wanted to sell them to our brigade's supply sergeant for a few thousand hryvnia, but then I showed him this—" Ali Safi pointed to a line on the inventory's first page that listed Royal Sèvres Manufactory as the company that had made the plates, and he explained that these were artisans who'd served the royal court at Versailles, fulfilling its most extravagant requests, to include those of Marie Antoinette, who had commissioned this particular service. Ali Safi pulled out his phone. A person could buy replicas from a very high-end French manufacturer, a place setting of ten costing nearly 3,000 euros. On their website was a note that they were produced from the original sketches made by Royal Sèvres Manufactory, while the plates themselves had been lost long ago. "The Germans must've stolen them during the war," said Ali Safi, "and the Soviets must've stolen them from the Germans after that, and somewhere along the way an enterprising Ukrainian stole them and placed them in this safe."

"And now you and your friend are the latest to steal them, congratulations."

"*Steal* isn't the word I would use," said Ali Safi. "Unfortunately, the Tooth never saw the plates again. He was killed before we could recover them."

"The Russians?"

"Sadly, no. His death was quite unfortunate. The Tooth had already spoken to me about his plans for after we recovered the plates. His dream was to return home, back to Riga, to buy the minor league hockey team he had once played for. A bit of research showed we could demand an enormous sum for the plates, tens of millions of dollars. The French government had a history of repatriating lost artifacts with few questions asked, and they would surely accept these. The money would be more than enough to fund the Tooth's plan. The night before we would recover the plates he had decided to celebrate. He drank himself into a stupor along with my squad mates. He had soon declared himself the best ice skater not only in the squad but in the entire International Legion—no small boast among a group of drunk Latvians. The others demanded he prove it. They challenged him to cross a frozen segment of the Dnipro with a pair of figure skates they'd found in a looted home earlier that week. The skates were a couple of sizes too small, and as the Tooth stutter-stepped halfway across the ice, it collapsed beneath him. He might have been a great skater, but he was a terrible swimmer."

"That's a pretty dumb way to die."

"Most of the ways people die in war are dumb."

Uncle Tony couldn't argue with this. "So now you're the only one who knows where these plates are?"

Ali Safi nodded.

"How are you planning on spending that money?" asked Uncle Tony. "That's assuming you can transport them off the zero line safely, and find a buyer, and not get yourself killed in the process. You gonna buy an ice hockey team, too?"

"Not exactly," said Ali Safi. "I was hoping to make a trade with you."

"My organization isn't in the flatware business."

"This isn't an offer that I'm making to your organization . . . This is an offer that I'm making to *you*. I'll help you recover the plates—that's tens of millions of dollars directly into your pocket, enough for you to retire on many times over—if you agree to help me with something."

"That all depends . . ." Uncle Tony had begun thumbing through the inventory sheet again, trying to decipher its columns of French and German. "What could I help you with that's worth so much money?"

"Jay Manning."

Uncle Tony's eyes shot up from the inventory sheet. "How do you know Jay Manning?"

"He killed my brother. If you help me kill him, the plates are yours."

THREE MONTHS HAD PASSED SINCE THAT CONVERSATION. AS Uncle Tony finished his drive from the InterContinental, beyond the port of Marseille, and out toward the airport, he could hardly believe the string of bad luck he and Ali Safi had endured since then.

At first, everything had gone according to plan. Ukrainian airspace was closed to commercial flights, so they had driven the plates across the border into Moldova where a modest bribe to a pliant customs agent had allowed the single crate to enter without inspection. No problems there. French customs would prove trickier. Uncle Tony thought it unwise to fly the crate directly to Marseille. Instead, he'd had the plates shipped to a DRCA facility in Kampala where one of their Challenger 600s was undergoing maintenance. The contents of the crate were then unpacked into that aircraft's galley kitchen. When flying into Marseille, the plates would now appear like part of the meal service, hardly warranting closer inspection by a customs agent. But the stopover in Kampala served an essential double purpose. It would give Ali Safi his chance for revenge . . . Ali Safi's revenge was the price Uncle Tony had to pay for the plates.

This is where their luck had turned. Ali Safi, posing as a low-level security guard, was supposed to stumble across Skwerl in the act of stealing a jet and kill him. To aid the operation, Uncle Tony had brought in an unwitting accomplice, Henrik Hofstede, a soldier with a reputation of unquestioning obedience to any and all orders who'd fought on the wrong side of several wars. But H had proven incompetent. He was supposed to ensure that he and Cheese escaped on the jet, transporting Uncle Tony's plates safely into Marseille after Ali Safi had killed Skwerl. Then Uncle Tony would hand the plates off to Grillot, who would pay the agreed-upon price of $62.7 million, no questions asked.

But this wasn't what happened.

Uncle Tony had been cleaning up that mess ever since. And now, in another setback, he had received a call, only hours ago, from Mac's phone, in which Skwerl had announced, "I've got your plates." As Uncle Tony pulled up to the hangar at Marseille International, it was to tell Ali Safi that their leisurely breakfast at the InterContinental would have to wait. If he was to get his revenge, they would need a new plan.

WHEN SKWERL ANNOUNCED TO SINÉAD THAT HE HAD A PLAN TO recover Fareeda and ensure that Uncle Tony and Ali Safi didn't run off with the Marie Antoinette plates, this hadn't been an empty boast. The first step of that plan involved Skwerl setting his alarm for 4 a.m., which was 10 a.m. in Marseille. He had checked online, and this was when the boutique where he'd bought the single Bernardaud plate would open. He and Sinéad had stayed up late, until well after midnight, occupied both with their scheming and recurrent bouts of lovemaking, so that when the alarm went off in their hotel room, it took all of Skwerl's willpower not to roll over, pull her close to him, and sleep until late morning. Instead, he woke up and, sitting naked in his bed, with the sheets scalloped around his waist and a single lamp casting a honeyed glow across the room, dialed the number.

Although Skwerl didn't speak French, he recognized the shop manager's voice immediately. "We met about a week ago," said Skwerl. "I'm the American who bought the single plate from you."

"Oui, monsieur. The Bernardaud plate, the one from Versailles."

"Oui," Skwerl said self-consciously. "That's the one. Um, listen, I'd like to purchase the full set."

"Very good. We have them in stock. You will come to the store?"

"That's the thing . . . I need you to ship them to me, overnight express delivery to the U.S. Is that possible? I'll pay whatever it costs."

"This is possible," said the shop manager, "but it will be quite expensive." On the other end of the line, Skwerl could hear him tapping at what sounded like a calculator. "For a full set, so this is three dozen pieces, your price comes to 11,876 euros." The line fell silent. Skwerl could again hear the tapping sound. "Overnight delivery to include shipping and VAT, this will cost you another 4,000 euros or so. I won't have the exact amount until I pack the plates and deliver them to the post office to be weighed. Your total will be close to 15,000 euros. I will need to place a hold on your card in that amount immediately. Is this permitted?"

"Yes, that's fine."

Sinéad, who was lying on her side behind Skwerl in the bed, had been listening passively to the entire call. When Skwerl agreed to this sum, she shot up. Her expression had turned wide-eyed, and she began to shake her head violently. When the shop manager asked about method of payment, Skwerl had gestured to Sinéad's jeans, which were flung across a chair on the other side of the room. He wanted the AmEx business card she carried; it was tied to the account that held their recent windfall from Knotty Pleasures.

"No way," she said, hissing the words. "I worked my ass off for that money."

Skwerl placed his hand over the phone's receiver. "I need you to trust me."

Reluctantly, she stood from the bed and returned with the card. She flung it at him, so he had to retrieve it from the floor. He shot her a look, but then went through the task of slowly reading off the card number and CVN. An extended beat of silence ensued as the shop manager ran the AmEx. When his voice came back on the line, saying that the charge had cleared and asking the details of where he should ship the plates, Skwerl could feel Sinéad's gaze sinking into him. Skwerl arranged for the shop manager to ship the plates to Aero Services Aviation, arriving the next night and requiring his signature.

"Very well, monsieur," said the shop manager as he took down the last of these details. "I'll handle the matter now. This has been a pleasure."

Skwerl hung up.

Sinéad had dressed and was sitting on the chair in the corner of their hotel room. "You're a real asshole, Jay."

"C'mon . . ." Skwerl walked naked across the room and handed Sinéad the AmEx. "That's not fair."

"You're right, calling you an asshole isn't fair to regular garden variety assholes. You're not an asshole, you're delusional, and a narcissistic sociopath . . . with PTSD . . ."

"I love it when you talk dirty to me." Skwerl was putting on his pants.

"What if you don't get our money back?"

"I told you last night we were going to swap out the original plates with a set of decoy plates. Where did you think we'd get the decoys? Sam's Club?" Skwerl sat on the edge of the bed, across from Sinéad. She'd turned her head away and he caught their reflection in the darkness of the hotel room window.

"The more I think about this plan, the less I like it. You're playing games with our future, Jay."

"Those plates are worth $60 million . . ." Skwerl leaned forward on the edge of the bed, taking Sinéad's hands in his own. "Toots, c'mon, we can't give that up."

Sinéad faced him now. "You're playing games with Fareeda's life, too. Have you thought about that? Sure, if your plan works, we all get rich. But what if it doesn't? This Ali Safi has already killed one person. He'll kill her."

"That's not going to happen."

"How do you know?"

Skwerl dropped her hands. "Because I'm not going to let it happen."

He crossed the room, searching for his shirt, which he'd flung off the night before as the two of them dove into bed, flush with what he'd believed was their imminent success. They had already discovered the truth about the plates, about Uncle Tony posing as Sheepdog, and the connection that existed between DRCA, Cyberdyne, and the Office. It stung that Sinéad would doubt him now, particularly as she wasn't offering a better plan. Did she really expect him to live off a sinecure she provided through the profits of Knotty Pleasures? Skwerl found his shirt under the bed. He pulled it on and stepped toward the hotel room door.

"Where are you going?"

"Breakfast." Skwerl pointed out the window, to the flashing neon Denny's sign two blocks away. The Grand Slam cost $8.99— two eggs, two pancakes, two sausages, with coffee included. He had a ten-dollar bill in his pocket, enough for that. He was soon installed in a red vinyl booth, the only customer in the restaurant, his whole plate drenched in maple syrup, eating heartily.

Sinéad wasn't wrong about the risks in his plan. He was taking a big one with Fareeda's life. He simply saw the nature of that risk differently. If he and Cheese returned to their old lives, in which he was supported by Sinéad and Cheese was scraping by at the Esso station, the two of them were already dead, and they would drag down and bury the two women they loved with them. Did this make Skwerl a *delusional narcissistic sociopath with PTSD*? No, at least he didn't think so. But he knew that after speaking out publicly against the Office and after losing the FISA case (which he never had a chance at winning), his life options had dwindled to near zero. He felt like a fool for believing that work for Sheepdog held any long-term prospects. That idea had blown up in his face; but if he and Cheese had a chance to restart their lives with this money, they had an obligation to take that chance, particularly when Uncle Tony would line his pockets with that money if they let him. After everything Uncle Tony had done to Skwerl—from Now Zad to FISA to posing as Sheepdog—the idea that Uncle Tony would walk away with $60 million was more than Skwerl could stomach. What would he even do with that kind of money? Uncle Tony had no wife, having run through a string of them decades before. The word *refined* did not apply to his tastes; in fact, if Skwerl hadn't known that Uncle Tony was already in Marseille, he might have expected him to appear in this very same Denny's for a Grand Slam.

The door swung open and the little chime above it rung as Sinéad stepped inside, searching for Skwerl. Instead of sitting across from him, she slid beside him in the booth and looped her arm around his, placing her head on his shoulder so his cheek rested alongside a curtain of her fragrant hair. "I'm sorry," she said. "You're not a narcissistic sociopath . . . You might be delusional, but that all depends on whether or not this plan of yours works."

"And the PTSD?"

"C'mon, Jay . . . you see as many 'dead people' as that kid in *The Sixth Sense*."

He pulled her close. "I love that movie."

"I know you do."

The waiter came over, asking Sinéad if she wanted anything. She ordered the same as Jay, but with tea instead of coffee, which was $.75 extra. Her breakfast soon arrived, and she asked Jay to go over the plan one last time.

Skwerl explained that after eating they would check out of their hotel and drive north, to Aero Services Aviation. That afternoon, Cheese would land with the Challenger 600, bringing Ephraim, who they needed to get home. Even if the Old Order Amish had excommunicated him, Skwerl worried that someone might notice he'd gone missing and start asking questions. As for the original Marie Antoinette plates, Cheese would leave them with Just Shane, for safekeeping. When Sinéad asked whether they could trust Just Shane (she described him as sounding "unhinged") and if, perhaps, it didn't make more sense to store the plates at their house, Skwerl wouldn't hear of it. "*Paranoid* is the word that I'd use to describe Shane, not *unhinged* . . . There's a big difference, and his paranoia is why he's the right person to watch over $60 million of ultra-expensive dinnerware."

All that would be left to handle were the Bernardaud plates. On arrival, Skwerl would supervise their transfer to the Challenger 600 and placement into the galley, where they would appear indistinguishable from the originals. Then they'd fly to Marseille. Sinéad had insisted on making the trip over Skwerl's protests about her safety and objections that her presence might upset Uncle Tony, who wouldn't be expecting an unknown woman to arrive. "Just tell him that I've come for Fareeda. She's pregnant and she'll need another woman on hand in case of a medical issue."

"But you're not a doctor?"

"That's hardly the point."

Skwerl understood the point—too much was riding on this exchange for Sinéad to be left out. He wasn't going to convince her to stay behind; and so she would land in Marseille along with him and Cheese. Skwerl still had to negotiate with Uncle Tony the exact mechanics of Fareeda's transfer. Everything would hinge on speed. The longer they remained on the ground, the higher the likelihood that something might go wrong. Skwerl felt confident that he could negotiate for Uncle Tony to have a second jet ready with Fareeda already aboard. They'd park their Challenger 600, load into this second jet, and be down the runway in minutes.

"Do you really think it'll be that easy?"

"No, Toots, I don't."

The waiter brought over their check. The two Grand Slams, plus the tea, plus a tip, was a sum larger than Skwerl possessed. Sinéad said not to worry. She had enough to cover them both.

Chapter Six

THE SWAP

EPHRAIM WAS SUPPOSED TO FLY TO CHESTER COUNTY WITH Cheese, but at the last minute Just Shane suggested he stay behind in Colorado. Ephraim had reservations about returning home as he'd come to believe that Just Shane's off-the-grid lifestyle had much to commend it; also, his clothes had dried, which might have contributed to him feeling a bit more at ease in his surroundings as he had at last unburdened himself of the rope-belted poncho. As Ephraim considered his next move, he felt in no hurry to resume his meager existence as an excommunicate in the Pennsylvania countryside. He was enamored by the idea of an extended stay with Just Shane, who was coming to feel like a benefactor of sorts as he inducted him into the varied intricacies of managing a survivalist compound. Just Shane also liked the idea of having Ephraim around. "An extra set of hands," was how he'd put it, "just in case," And so the three of them agreed, Ephraim would stay behind.

Alone in the cockpit of the Challenger 600, Cheese reached into the avionics panel, manually shutting off his transponder. He dropped his flaps, halved his throttle, and began his descent toward Chester County; here, neatly partitioned farm fields yielded to the more complex and suburban geometries that banded the Philadelphia outskirts. Cheese raised air traffic control over the radio as he entered the upwind leg of the traffic pattern.

He wondered whether the crackling voice issuing him landing instructions had been at the airfield several nights before when he had slunk away with Ephraim and Skwerl; and if the person in the tower had been there, he wondered why they'd now authorized his same phony tail number to land.

Cheese couldn't quite figure it out. If for other people clear thoughts arrived in the shower or on a run, for Cheese they arrived in the cockpit. As he turned from base to final in the traffic pattern, the thought ringing loudest in his mind was that it didn't really matter why he was being cleared to land—maybe Skwerl had arranged it or Sinéad, who knew? His job now was to stop asking questions and to play his part.

His part was to get to his wife and fly her safely home.

AS FAR AS UNCLE TONY WAS CONCERNED, IT DIDN'T MATTER that Skwerl had figured out the plates were real. He'd arrived earlier that morning at JetEx in Marseille and had taken up with Ali Safi in a vacant office. This was across the corridor from the locked conference room where they had kept Fareeda. Containers of half-eaten Afghan takeout were scattered across the desk, leftovers from meals Ali Safi had shared with her. Uncle Tony was picking through them—his version of breakfast—as he described the rather upsetting call he'd received from Mac's cellphone, which had somehow fallen into Skwerl's hands.

"The thing is," said Uncle Tony as he sniffed and then deliberated over one of the open containers, "that even with them knowing the plates are real we still make out the same."

"How so?" Ali Safi sat at the table behind a cup of unsweetened chai with his arms folded. He appeared tired, but not as if he hadn't slept enough—he'd gotten plenty of rest while waiting at the airport—rather, he appeared sunken into himself, eyes sunk into their sockets, chin sunk onto his chest, body sunk into his chair. What Ali Safi wanted—revenge—was taking too long, and Uncle

Tony was trying to sell him on waiting a little longer.

"I know Jay Manning well," said Uncle Tony, "and he thinks he's discovered what we've been hiding, which is the value of those plates. He thinks now that he's revealed this secret, he's got the upper hand. We need to let him keep thinking that. But the plates don't change anything. That's not our real secret." When Ali Safi asked what this mysterious *real secret* was, Uncle Tony clapped him on the shoulder. "You," he said to Ali Safi. "What you want. Your revenge. That's what Skwerl doesn't understand. He thinks this thing has been about the plates and me. But it's never really been about either."

"No," said Ali Safi firmly. "I suppose it hasn't."

"This is about you, and your brother. Your family was wronged, and you've wanted to make that wrong into a right. I've got a lot of respect for that." Uncle Tony casually excluded his $60 million compensatory package paid in fine eighteenth-century porcelains from his disquisition on *wrong versus right,* as if perhaps Ali Safi might have forgotten about that detail. Uncle Tony kept holding on to Ali Safi's shoulder, and when he gave it a too enthusiastic atta-boy tussle, Ali Safi shrugged him away. Hardly noticing this (or much else for that matter), Uncle Tony continued, "We'll make the trade, Fareeda for the plates, and once we've done that, you'll be able to move against Skwerl."

"What happens to her?"

"That's very chivalrous of you," quipped Uncle Tony, who seemed genuinely amused that Ali Safi would care what happened to Fareeda. "She'll go home, flown back by her husband. You know him, don't you?"

Ali Safi took a sip of his chai, set it on its saucer, and gazed into its surface before nodding. "I briefly worked perimeter security at Eagle Base for DRCA. Everyone knew him."

"That was then. What's important now," Uncle Tony announced, "is that you get your chance with Skwerl. I get those plates. Everyone gets what they want . . . even Fareeda, she's getting released."

"Almost everyone." Ali Safi took another sip of his chai.

Uncle Tony glanced up from the container of food he was picking through, not quite understanding what Ali Safi meant.

"Jay Manning," said Ali Safi. "He does not get what he wants."

"No . . ." Uncle Tony went back to his food. "He most certainly doesn't." Then he glanced up, and added, "But he was never supposed to."

UNCLE TONY SPENT THE REMAINDER OF THAT MORNING AT THE airport meticulously planning. He identified an empty hangar at the far end of the runway that could accommodate both the Challenger 600 and an older model Gulfstream VI that he'd rented from a Moldovan aircraft broker at a below market rate. The Moldovans, like the Ukrainians, had found themselves in Moscow's crosshairs of late, and so were eager to grant favors to operatives like Uncle Tony who at some later date could grant a favor in return—say, if Russian tanks ever crossed their border.

Even with the good rate, the deposit for the Gulfstream was exorbitant, yet the latest bloated charge Uncle Tony would place on an overheated DRCA expense account. Post-IPO tech wunderkinds and hip-hop moguls had long favored the Gulfstream, with its beaked nose and dart-shaped fuselage. So did minor heads of state, which gave Uncle Tony a high degree of confidence that Cheese could ably pilot this second aircraft back to the U.S. Uncle Tony had brought Ali Safi to the hangar so they could choreograph and rehearse the swap.

The two jets would be parked on either side of the hangar with the Gulfstream's nose pointed toward the exit. Cheese would simply have to ease forward on the throttle and he'd roll right out onto the taxiway. Ali Safi was happy for him and Fareeda— two fellow Afghans—to make their escape. All that mattered to him was the moment he would confront Skwerl. He and Uncle

Tony had decided this would occur after he loaded Fareeda into the Gulfstream. At this moment, Ali Safi would be walking back toward Skwerl, who would be exiting the Challenger after having passed off the plates to Uncle Tony.

"Where are you going to carry your pistol?" Uncle Tony was standing with Ali Safi in the middle of the hangar, beneath a dozen rows of halogen bulbs.

"Under my suit jacket." Ali Safi unsheathed a palm-sized Sig Sauer P938 from a concealed chest holster. He dropped the extended ten-round magazine and locked the slide to the rear, ejecting a single round from the chamber. He handed the pistol over to Uncle Tony, who'd long been a fan of the P938. It was the smaller version of the P226, which Uncle Tony had used in the SEAL Teams. The first person he had ever shot at close range had been with a P226. This had been at a checkpoint in Mogadishu, in the '90s, when Uncle Tony was thirty years younger and forty pounds lighter, back when life allowed him to think less and eat more, unlike now, where every year he was stuck thinking more and eating less. Uncle Tony peered into the P226's empty chamber. The hangar's overhead lights shone surgically clear; under them, the pistol gleamed, its perfectly machined parts catching the light, so they seemed to wink back at him. Had there been a speck of carbon on any surface, Uncle Tony would have spotted it. He imagined Ali Safi oiling and cleaning the pistol—its upper receiver, lower receiver, and barrel—over and over, until the scent of solvent, sweet as a magic marker, permeated his fingertips, a constant reminder of the clean pistol and the possibility that one day he'd have the chance to use it.

Uncle Tony didn't want Ali Safi to fuck up his chance. "Don't keep it in the holster," he said. "Jay's quick and he's good and if he sees you reach for it you might lose that contest. Keep it in your pocket." Uncle Tony placed the pistol into Ali Safi's suit jacket. "When you walk toward him, you don't look him in the eyes. Stare at his chest. Then you lift your pistol and fire through your jacket."

Uncle Tony demonstrated once, walking toward Ali Safi at speed, staring at the ground in front of him. At the last moment, Uncle Tony fixed his eyes center mass on Ali Safi's chest. He raised a hand that was already tucked into his jacket pocket and, pointing his finger at Ali Safi, said, "Bang."

"But I'll shoot out my jacket pocket . . . it'll ruin my suit."

"I been doing this almost thirty years," said Uncle Tony. "Trust me. It'll work. I've got a closet filled with ruined suits to prove it."

Uncle Tony left Ali Safi in the hangar beneath the artificial lights rehearsing this maneuver like an actor abandoned on a stage. If the swap was going to occur in the next day or so, Uncle Tony would need Grillot's help with another sensitive matter. That afternoon, they met for lunch at the InterContinental. A light rain had begun to fall, which prevented them from sitting on the veranda; instead, they found themselves tucked into a dimly lit booth in the restaurant's back corner. When Grillot arrived, he seemed agitated. He wouldn't have time to eat. The French ambassador in Kyiv had summoned him for an audience. His flight to the Polish border left in two hours. He'd catch a train from there.

"What's in Kyiv?"

"The International Legion." Grillot uttered the name contemptuously as only the French could do, as if certain words taking up residence in one's mouth was an offense unto itself. "Their finances are a disaster. Nearly half of the fighters—the decidedly good half—are mercenaries of one stripe or another. They haven't been paid in months. The Ukrainians don't have the funds and you Americans have shredded their budget. If we can't figure a way to pay them, the ambassador fears they will abandon their positions, or mutiny, or worse—go over to the Russians. So, they're sending me to solve this problem. Before you ask 'how?,' don't. Because I have no idea."

None of this was news to Uncle Tony, so he said little. Front of his mind was the favor he needed. Relative to Grillot's current predicament, it was a small ask. "I'm going to need your help with a body."

"A body?"

"Oui."

"Don't fucking 'oui' me, Tony. Who are you planning to kill?"

"I'm not planning to kill anyone. I just need your help. Can you or can't you?"

"Putain de merde! . . . Where and when do you need this help?"

"Tomorrow, in the early evening, that's when emergency services will receive a phone call about a break-in at the airport. There's a jet, a Gulfstream VI, someone is going to try to steal it. One of the culprits will be killed in an exchange of gunfire with an off-duty security guard from DRCA. When the gendarmes arrive, I need them to take the body—no questions."

"I already had to clean up one of your messes." Grillot peered above them, pointing to the hotel ceiling as if to an invisible stain. "Why would I agree to this?"

"Because if you do, when you return from your trip, your plates will be waiting for you . . . I imagine that would please everyone at DGSE, including *le directeur*."

Grillot stared at Uncle Tony. He eventually removed a pen and pad from his suit jacket. "You call this number," he said, scribbling it down. "These aren't the gendarmes . . . these are my guys. They'll come and clean up the mess." Grillot held out the slip of paper, pinching it between his index and middle finger like one of those thin lady cigarettes Uncle Tony scorned French men for smoking. When he reached for the slip, Grillot tucked it back into the palm of his hand with the dexterity of a magician. "Why do they call you Uncle Tony?"

"Just give me the paper."

Grillot shook his head, made a sour face, and stood to leave.

"Every family has a crazy uncle, right . . . ?"

Grillot sat back in his seat.

"In my family—my work family—that's me." Uncle Tony flashed a toothy grin, smiling like a lunatic as if to underscore the point.

Grillot laughed, holding out the slip of paper again. "Okay, Tony. But every family also has a favorite uncle. Maybe you are him too?"

"Maybe."

"Please, no more messes."

Uncle Tony snatched the slip of paper from Grillot, tucking it into his pocket. "That's where you've got me wrong. To you, it looks like I'm making a mess. When really, I'm just cleaning up."

AFTER LANDING AT AERO SERVICES AVIATION, CHEESE HAD found an empty corner office in the hangar, drawn the accordion blinds, pulled two chairs together, and slept with his jacket thrown over his shoulders. When he awoke, it was early evening. Stepping out of the dim office, into the gleaming lights of the hangar, he was pleasantly surprised at the progress Skwerl and Sinéad had made in the intervening hours. Like a man leaving his seat at a restaurant only to return and find his dinner lavishly set before him, Cheese awoke to find the Challenger 600 fully fueled, his flight clearances registered with an accommodating air traffic control, and, most importantly, as he boarded the jet, the Bernardaud plates slotted snugly into the galley's mahogany display case. They were indistinguishable from the originals.

The three of them—Cheese, Skwerl, and Sinéad—took off at a little after sundown. As soon as they left U.S. airspace and set their course across the Atlantic, Skwerl and Sinéad climbed into the back of the jet where they fell soundly asleep, each reclined in one of the chairs whose upholstery had been so grotesquely mauled and then restitched. The two were racked, dead to the world, utterly smoked, a condition of fatigue Cheese understood given the extent of their preparations. He knew all that they'd endured the past several days, from driving down to northern Virginia to confront Skwerl's old colleague, Mac, whose dealings at Cyberdyne made him sound like a war opportunist of the first degree, to arranging shipment of the Bernardaud plates from Marseille at an exorbitant cost; though, admittedly, a trifle when compared to the $60 million windfall Skwerl anticipated.

A low moon hung at mid-sky in the east, casting a pathway of silvery light across the black ocean below. As Cheese followed this pathway, which coincided with the heading inputted on his flight computer, he tried to comprehend what he, or Skwerl, or any of them would do with such an obscene sum of money. Cheese had raised this briefly as they'd loaded the plane, but Skwerl had turned defensive, saying there was nothing "obscene" about it, and that from Uncle Tony to Marie Antoinette, these plates had never belonged to any legitimate authority, and so they might as well belong to them. "We're not stealing from anyone," Skwerl insisted. Cheese heard Skwerl out. All he really wanted was not to have to work at the Esso station, to be able to keep flying, and to keep a roof over his young family's head and food on their table. "With your half," Skwerl said, "you'll be able to do all that."

"But I don't need $30 million for that."

To this, Skwerl had offered a decidedly clear response. "Cheese . . ." he said, planting his hands on his hips and shaking his head, ". . . shut up and get your ass in the plane."

And here he was, ass in the plane, less than an hour out from Marseille. Cheese supposed Skwerl was right. Such questions could wait. They could worry about the $60 million, what to do with it, and the morality of such a sum after Fareeda was safely returned home. Before takeoff, Skwerl had explained that there would be a second jet, a Gulfstream VI; of course, Cheese knew how to fly it—he could fly anything with wings, as he was fond of reminding those who asked—but Skwerl had seemed quite relieved when Cheese confirmed this. Tonight, everything would hinge on speed. Uncle Tony had assured Skwerl that Fareeda would be in this second jet. All Cheese had to do was park the Challenger 600 in its hangar, board the Gulfstream, and then Skwerl would board behind him once Uncle Tony had taken possession of the plates.

In minutes, they would begin their descent. Cheese climbed into the back cabin and woke up Skwerl and Sinéad. Returning to the cockpit, he disengaged the autopilot. The coastline twinkled on the horizon as Cheese continued to head east, bleeding altitude, while beneath him, the silvery pathway of moonlight that had guided his passage these many hours vanished, consumed by the port city below.

SINÉAD SAT IN THE JUMP SEAT, SANDWICHED BETWEEN SKWERL and Cheese. They had landed without incident and were taxiing down the runway. Skwerl read from a set of handwritten directions that, the afternoon before, Uncle Tony had dictated over the phone. "Turn left off runway 31 . . . now a right on taxiway D . . ."

"Okay . . ." said Cheese, taking the turn.

"Now left on taxiway B . . ."

They lurched forward as Cheese hit the brakes.

"Why are you holding short?" Skwerl double-checked his notes: *left tw B*.

"I'm not seeing taxiway B."

Skwerl glanced out the cockpit. On a sign staked to the ground was the black letter *E* framed in an iridescent yellow. "Take a left here."

"But you said 'taxiway B.'"

"*B* sounds close enough to *E* . . . I must've heard Tony wrong over the phone."

Sinéad shot Skwerl a nervous glance and shifted in her seat. "Didn't they teach you the phonetic alphabet in the military . . . *Bravo* . . . *Echo* . . . ?"

"We weren't on a walkie-talkie . . . I thought I heard him right." Skwerl could hardly blame her for being on edge. This was too much of a close-run enterprise for sloppy mistakes. Experience had taught Skwerl that the difference between a successful operation and a failure often hinged on matters as trifling as hearing *B* when someone said *E*. Fortunately for the three of them, the turn onto taxiway E led to a turn onto taxiway C, followed by the outlying taxiways on the far, western end of the airfield whose letters . . . G . . . F . . . H . . . matched the directions in Skwerl's notes. "Can I buy a vowel?" Skwerl joked as they pulled up to the isolated hangar, but no one laughed.

The bay door was open. The Gulfstream VI was parked inside, the light reflecting off its white, toneless skin, its nose pointed toward the taxiway for a quick departure, just as Uncle Tony had promised. Cheese held short, his engines idling, uncertain whether he should pull into the vacant parking space beside the Gulfstream. "What do you think?"

Before Skwerl could answer, Uncle Tony climbed out of the Gulfstream and descended its stairs onto the hangar floor. He stepped in front of the Challenger 600, pacing backward and waving his hands as he mimed taxiing instructions—*a little to the left . . . now a bit to the right . . . pull it in . . . pull it in*—and then he made an X with both arms. Cheese cut the engines and they parked. He sat motionless inside the cockpit, the newfound silence ringing in their ears, until Skwerl finally placed a hand on his arm. "You ready?"

He nodded.

Skwerl glanced at Sinéad, who nodded as well.

Cheese opened the door to the Challenger 600. He stepped out first, followed by Sinéad, while Skwerl remained in the entrance. He and Uncle Tony had agreed on a precisely choreographed swap. Ali Safi would stay in the Gulfstream with Fareeda while Skwerl would stay in the Challenger with the plates. When Cheese saw that Fareeda was safe and sound, he and Sinéad would give a thumbs-up to Skwerl. Conversely, when Uncle Tony saw the plates were safe and sound, he would give Ali Safi the thumbs-up. Ali Safi would then leave the Gulfstream and Skwerl would leave the Challenger, the swap complete.

However, as soon as Sinéad descended from the Challenger 600, it became clear that Skwerl had already gone off script. "What the hell?" Uncle Tony was standing at the bottom of the Challenger's steps, staring incredulously at Sinéad, who kept her eyes fixed straight ahead as she followed Cheese toward the Gulfstream. "You never said anything about bringing your wife."

"She's not my wife." Sinéad and Cheese had only a few more steps to take until they reached the Gulfstream. "What does it matter to you?"

Uncle Tony seemed to think about it for a second. He shrugged. "I suppose it doesn't." Then, seeing that Sinéad and Cheese were now climbing into the Gulfstream, he climbed aboard the Challenger 600.

Skwerl remained standing in the door, keeping one eye on Uncle Tony and another on the opposite side of the hangar. Cheese and Sinéad needed to be quick. Once they gave the thumbs-up, Skwerl could hurry Uncle Tony to give the same to Ali Safi. But Uncle Tony had gotten distracted. "Sweet Jesus," he said as he stepped into the main cabin. "What the hell happened in here?" He was running his fingers over the roughly repaired upholstery and the jagged claw marks on the interior mahogany paneling.

"A grizzly," said Skwerl.

"As in a *grizzly* bear? Are you kidding me?"

Across the hangar, Sinéad stepped out of the Gulfstream. She reached her arm out like she was flagging a cab and gave a thumbs-up. Skwerl should've felt enormous relief that the plan was proceeding apace, except Tony was growing fixated on questions about the grizzly. "Where were you that a bear got in the jet?"

"We had to park at a pretty remote airfield," said Skwerl. "Someone got sick in the jet and the bear must've smelt it."

"Who got sick?"

"C'mon, Tony . . ." Skwerl shot back. "We're thumbs-up on the Gulfstream."

"Alright . . . relax." He stepped into the galley. Running his fingers over the tops of the plates, he began to count, moving his lips silently. Skwerl couldn't tell if he was counting the number of dishes or counting the millions that he'd soon pocket. He imagined that Uncle Tony would give Ali Safi a cut, though definitely not fifty percent. Uncle Tony was too wily for that. He'd likely promised this Afghan the commission originally meant for him and Cheese, a measly million out of $60 million, not even two percent. Whatever Uncle Tony had negotiated with Ali Safi, Skwerl felt certain it was a raw deal. Across continents and decades, from Laos and Cambodia to Afghanistan and Iraq and Syria, from the Montagnards and Contras to the Kurdish Peshmerga and Ukrainian International Legion, guys like Uncle Tony—the centurions of America's secret wars—always wound up screwing over the indig. That was their legacy. Maybe they didn't mean for it to be, but good intentions counted for little. When Skwerl had mentioned the dynamic once to Sinéad, she had casually diagnosed it as a case of "organizational schizophrenic sociopathy."

"My count's good," announced Uncle Tony. "That's all of 'em."

As Uncle Tony marched from the galley kitchen toward the door, Skwerl couldn't help but ask what he planned on doing in retirement. "I just have a hard time imagining you sitting on a beach somewhere or playing golf."

Uncle Tony stood in the door with his arm thrust out, giving the thumbs-up signal. "Who says I'm retiring?"

Before Skwerl could ask another question, Ali Safi appeared in the door of the Gulfstream. He was climbing down the steps. Skwerl did the same, so that the two were walking straight at one another.

ALI SAFI HAD MADE CERTAIN THAT THE GULFSTREAM WAS WELL provisioned. Earlier that day, he'd gotten Uncle Tony to swing by his favorite restaurant so that when Fareeda's husband boarded the jet several containers of food would be waiting. He couldn't quite bring himself to apologize for having put Fareeda through this ordeal. He hoped that the food would show he harbored no animus against her or her husband, who he still remembered fondly as Aziz "The Big Cheese" Iqbal, one of the finest—if not the single finest—fighter pilots ever produced by his country's air force.

When it came to animus, Ali Safi reserved his for Skwerl. After wishing Fareeda and Cheese (and this other American woman who Uncle Tony hadn't mentioned) goodbye, he descended the steps of the Gulfstream and, with a determined gait, strode toward the Challenger 600. Behind him, the Gulfstream's engines were idling, the noise so loud it seemed to crowd out all thought, which Ali Safi appreciated; he didn't want to think too much about what he was about to do.

His hand was in the right pocket of his suit jacket, gripping the P938. Uncle Tony had told Ali Safi to avoid eye contact with Skwerl, to look only at his chest, and then only at the last moment, as he was about to take his shot.

Skwerl was walking straight at him . . .

Ali Safi laced his finger through the trigger guard, taking a step . . .

He lifted his gaze, fixing it on Skwerl's chest, taking another step . . .

He began to raise his arm, his hand in his pocket, feeling the weight of the pistol cradled in his palm . . .

But before Ali Safi could finish the movement, Uncle Tony appeared in the door of the Challenger 600. "Skwerl, you motherfucker!" He carried a plate in each hand. In a single violent movement, he reached across his body and flung the first like a frisbee. With remarkable, aerodynamic precision—as if the craftsmen at Bernardaud might have designed the plate for this purpose alone—it careened toward the back of Skwerl's head. In an equally remarkable display of agility, Skwerl ducked at the last moment, so the plate whipped above him. Ali Safi, who until a fraction of a second before had been concentrating every ounce of his attention on Skwerl's chest and the pistol in his jacket pocket and the revenge he would soon exact, couldn't reorient quickly enough to avoid the dinner plate striking him center chest, knocking the wind out of him, leaving him laid out on the hangar floor.

"You piece of shit!" Uncle Tony leapt down the stairs of the Challenger 600, vaulting over the handrail so he was positioned behind Skwerl, who'd managed to run a few steps both toward the Gulfstream but also in the direction of Ali Safi, who, gasping for air, held one hand to his chest and used the other to prop himself up from the floor. Uncle Tony wielded a second plate. He planted both his feet, bent his legs a little, and, instead of throwing the plate like a frisbee, flung it in a single overhead motion like a hatchet. It hit Skwerl between the shoulder blades. He let out a gasp and collapsed onto his knees, only an arm's length from Ali Safi.

They must have been able to hear the breaking plates inside the Gulfstream because Cheese revved the engines, trundling them onto the taxiway, while Sinéad poked her head outside, desperate to see what, if anything, could be done to help. When Skwerl saw her, he waved toward the runway, gesturing for her to leave him behind. He had no chance of escape now, no chance of outrunning Uncle Tony, who at that very moment was covering the dozen or so steps between them.

Skwerl braced as Uncle Tony charged across the hangar. But instead of pummeling Skwerl, Uncle Tony leapt into the air, throwing his body with reckless abandon past Skwerl, tackling Ali Safi, who had managed to get to his feet unnoticed and was standing menacingly behind Skwerl with his hand in his jacket pocket.

Uncle Tony was now wrestling with Ali Safi. "Not yet!" Uncle Tony kept saying, pinning Ali Safi's arm to his side, restraining him. "Not until I get my plates." Uncle Tony and Ali Safi continued their struggle. Suddenly, Skwerl saw it, a flash of black metal. It was a pistol, which he recognized as a Sig Sauer P938—a peashooter favored by SEALs. Small as the pistol was, they wrestled over it like two kids having a thumb war. Their scuffle lasted only a few seconds—long enough for Skwerl to watch, frozen in place—and ending when the pistol accidently discharged.

Uncle Tony howled. "You fucking shot me!" He glanced down at his foot. The heel was blown out as if a firecracker had gone off inside his boot. Even though he was the one who'd gotten shot, Uncle Tony came away from the struggle in control of the pistol. He aimed it at the Gulfstream, which was out on the taxiway, more than a hundred yards off and headed for runway 31. Firing at the jet wouldn't accomplish anything, except to attract unwanted attention. Uncle Tony turned to Skwerl and Ali Safi, leveling the pistol on them both. He lifted a piece of shattered ceramic from the ground. "These plates are fakes," Uncle Tony said to Ali Safi. "If you kill him"—and now he gestured at Skwerl with the muzzle of the pistol—"we'll never get the real ones."

Ali Safi slit his eyes at Skwerl.

"I'm sorry," said Skwerl. "But *what* is your deal?"

Ali Safi was slightly bent over at the waist and struggling to breathe. With great determination, he now managed to stand fully erect. He placed his hands on his hips, and, fixing Skwerl's gaze with his own, said, "You owe me a debt."

Skwerl turned to Uncle Tony. "Is this guy serious?"

Uncle Tony was balanced on one foot. Blood dripped from the toe of his boot and pooled on the pristine hangar floor. Through a grimace, he said, "You killed his brother," and then he directed Ali Safi to zip-tie Skwerl's wrists behind his back, a task he was only too happy to perform, while Uncle Tony continued, explaining how Ali Safi's brother had worked as a security guard in Now Zad.

"Now Zad . . ." Skwerl turned over his shoulder, toward Ali Safi, who was threading his wrists through the zip ties. He pulled them unnecessarily tight. "This life," said Skwerl, as he gazed morosely at Uncle Tony, "it follows you."

"It most certainly does."

Across Marseille International, in the middle distance, a private jet tore down runway 31, lifting into the air. Skwerl watched the ascent of its blinkering taillights but couldn't see whether it was the Gulfstream—the jet was too far off and the night too dark. Skwerl faced back toward Uncle Tony. "So what happens now?" He gestured toward Ali Safi. "You going to let your buddy get even for Now Zad?"

Ali Safi dipped his chin to his chest and set his nostrils wide, hunching his shoulders forward like an animal who had at last cornered his prey.

"He's not going to do anything . . ."

Ali Safi shot Uncle Tony a glance.

"You're not touching him, not until I say so. Where are my plates, Skwerl?"

"Loosen my wrists first."

Uncle Tony nodded at Ali Safi. Reluctantly, he adjusted the zip ties, making them a bit more comfortable. When he stepped behind Skwerl, he muttered something in Dari, which Skwerl could only assume was a curse on him, his family, his dog, his cat, and a promise of the horrible and painful death that Ali Safi would, in due time, inflict. Skwerl, whose Dari was rudimentary at best, couldn't quite make the whole thing out; it was a lot of words.

"Okay," said Uncle Tony. "Now . . . where are my plates?"

"I need to make a call." Skwerl glanced at his front left pants pocket, where his phone was—with his wrists bound, he couldn't get it out himself.

Uncle Tony, who'd been bleeding from his foot this whole time, began to feel a bit woozy. His complexion turned suddenly pale and beads of sweat broke out across his upper lip and forehead. Clumsily, he plopped onto the ground.

"We should call an ambulance," said Skwerl.

Ali Safi took off his jacket, the one he'd been carrying the pistol in. He bundled it into a ball that Uncle Tony could use to elevate his leg. Slowly, in this reclined position, Uncle Tony's color began to return. He removed his phone and dialed a number. Skwerl could hear the voice that answered, it was French. Uncle Tony said, "It's time to come to the airport," and then he hung up.

"Is that an ambulance?"

"What the fuck do you care, Skwerl?"

Lying down had stanched the bleeding, though Uncle Tony already had made quite a mess. Piece by piece, he was considering the pile of shattered and bloodstained plates surrounding him. He picked up a fragment with *Bernardaud* etched in sans serif gold script on the back. He held it up, so Skwerl could see. "Did you really think I wouldn't notice?"

"I was just playing for time."

"Well, you're out of it."

Skwerl again asked if an ambulance was coming.

"It's not an ambulance," said Uncle Tony. "It's a cleanup crew. Had everything gone according to plan that crew would have had to clean up a body. Understand?"

Skwerl glanced down at the broken plates. He understood.

SINÉAD WASN'T THE TYPE TO GET ANXIOUS. HAD SHE BEEN SHE would've been in hysterics as they lifted off from Marseille. Given that emotional regulation, self-possession, centeredness were attributes she embodied (even under the direst of circumstances), the outburst that might have been expected from anyone else was, in her, subdued to a single utterance, "We're kinda fucked."

Neither Cheese nor Fareeda, who were packed next to her in the tight cockpit, would disagree. They'd all heard the plates crashing, so knew Skwerl's gamble had only partially paid off. Sinéad thought this might not prove too disastrous: Uncle Tony wanted his plates back, while she wanted Skwerl back. A straight swap would settle the matter. The only reason they'd found themselves in this position was because Skwerl had had the bright idea of trying to keep the plates. He hadn't been willing to let that $60 million go. Who could blame him after Uncle Tony and the Office had made it impossible for him to earn a normal livelihood? But a sum of money—no matter the size—wasn't worth dying for.

"This shouldn't be too complicated," said Sinéad. "We trade Skwerl for the plates. Everyone gets what they want."

Cheese had invited Sinéad to sit in the copilot seat, Skwerl's usual spot. Fareeda was perched on a small jump seat between them. Cheese had flown one-handed for most of the flight, seemingly unwilling to release Fareeda's hand now that they had finally been reunited. With the roles reversed, and Sinéad and Skwerl suddenly separated, Cheese could understand what Sinéad was feeling, no matter how *centered* or *emotionally regulated* her outward appearance. She needed some assurance, from anyone, that Skwerl would be okay, that the situation would resolve itself; except Cheese wasn't certain it would, and instead asked, "Did you get a look at Ali Safi?"

Sinéad nodded, though she had only glimpsed him as he charged at Skwerl.

"And how did he seem to you?"

"How did he seem?"

"Yes," Cheese said, leading Sinéad along. "How would you describe him?"

"He seemed totally unhinged." Sinéad swallowed, and, for the first time, lost her bearing. "Like he was going to kill Jay. What's your point?"

"I think you're right . . . he wanted to kill him."

"Then why didn't he?"

"The plates," said Cheese. "Uncle Tony isn't going let Ali Safi lay a finger on Jay so long as we have the plates."

Sinéad was confused. "That's what I already said . . . this isn't too complicated. We hand over the plates to Uncle Tony and he gives us Jay. It's a straight swap."

Fareeda, who'd been sitting quietly between them, understood the point her husband was driving at. "But you're forgetting Ali Safi," she said in just above a whisper. "Where does that swap leave him?" Fareeda had spent the past several days holed up with Ali Safi. She knew about his brother, about Now Zad, and his single-minded determination to exact revenge. Fareeda had the unenviable task of explaining this to Sinéad, disabusing her of the idea that a straight swap—Skwerl for the plates—was realistic. "Ali Safi won't accept that," Fareeda insisted. "He won't stop until he gets revenge for Now Zad."

"Where does that leave us?"

Neither Cheese nor Fareeda had an answer. For the time being, all they could do was fly west. When they landed late the next morning at Aero Services Aviation, Cheese had several missed calls and a voicemail, all from Just Shane. He had heard from Skwerl and needed to speak with Cheese; it was urgent.

BEFORE LEAVING COLORADO, SKWERL HAD SPOKEN WITH JUST Shane about the plates; specifically, what might happen if Uncle Tony discovered the fakes. Skwerl had used the word "hostage" several times as he and Just Shane ran through this contingency. Not only would Skwerl be taken hostage by Uncle Tony, but Just Shane would have to treat the authentic Marie Antoinette plates like the hostage he'd exchange for Skwerl. The two of them had established communication protocols. The first of these was that if Skwerl ever called, it would be to the Iridium and he would call twice, hanging up after the first ring each time before allowing the call to ring through on the third try.

After Skwerl and Cheese had left for Marseille, Just Shane had turned his attention to some projects around his property, enlisting Ephraim's help. They had spent a morning putting the final touches on a chicken coop, an afternoon reframing and installing a warped trellis on the main house, and the better part of a day trying to retain solar-heated water for the shower—they were ultimately unsuccessful. It was after this failed effort, while Just Shane was taking a bracing shower in the evening, that Skwerl finally called.

Just Shane flung open the vinyl curtain, his head foaming with shampoo as he reached for the phone that he kept on his folded towel. "Hello?"

"You're supposed to wait for me to call three times."

"Sorry."

"I need proof of life," said Skwerl. "I'm calling you on video."

Skwerl hung up. There'd been no time for Just Shane to tell him that he was in the shower or that he needed a couple of minutes;

also, there was something in Skwerl's voice—an edge that sounded almost desperate. Just Shane knew this call needed to happen now. As for "proof of life," this was another protocol he and Skwerl had arranged. To confirm the authenticity of the Marie Antoinette plates to Skwerl's captors, Just Shane and Ephraim would don ski masks, hiding their identities, and allow an inspection over a video call. When Skwerl had explained this to Just Shane, it had all sounded pretty standard like any other hostage negotiation, or at least the ones he'd seen in the movies and on TV.

Just Shane stood in a puddle outside the shower, wrapped in a towel, with his head a foaming mass of shampoo. He put on his eyepatch (which he only took off to shower and sleep) and ran into the main house. He grabbed a pair of full-face ski masks from the closet and then attached the Iridium to his laptop, so it'd be ready to receive the incoming video call. Ephraim, who had been in the kitchen preparing dinner, knew what to do. He ran over to a closet by the front door, rolling out a large hardcover aluminum suitcase they'd carefully repacked with the Marie Antoinette plates. Just Shane was about to run back into the shower to rinse off and dress when the laptop began to ring with the incoming call.

Just Shane froze. Nearly naked, he was uncertain what to do.

He told Ephraim to put on his ski mask. He did the same, and though he was wearing only a towel and his eyepatch, he answered the call.

An older man appeared, holding the phone at arm's length as if he were about to take a selfie. He was in his mid-fifties, still in good shape, if a little heavy, like a weightlifter who refused to debase himself with cardio. Although Just Shane had never met him, he figured this must be Uncle Tony.

"What's with the fuckin' ski masks?"

Just Shane and Ephraim glanced at one another; neither answered.

"Where are my plates?"

Just Shane nodded. Ephraim laid the aluminum suitcase flat

on the floor. Carefully, he opened it. One by one, he removed the plates, which they'd wrapped in an assortment of bedding and towels and every other available linen in the house. Uncle Tony asked to see the back of the plates, paying special attention to the discreet interlocking L markings that distinguished these as being produced at the Royal Sèvres Manufactory. After having been duped once by Skwerl, Uncle Tony insisted on examining every piece. This took some time, so that Ephraim and Just Shane eased into a rhythm, in which one would unwrap the plate while the other rewrapped it and then repacked it in the suitcase. As they worked, the sudsy shampoo in Just Shane's hair began to saturate his ski mask and stream quite painfully into his good eye.

Once they packed away the last plate, Just Shane asked to speak with Skwerl. Uncle Tony, satisfied that everything was in order, passed him the phone. On glimpsing Just Shane, Skwerl blurted, "What's with the towel?"

"I was in the shower when you called."

Skwerl peered at the screen. "Are you crying?"

Off camera, Uncle Tony asked, "Is this guy for real? He's crying?"

"I got shampoo in my eye." Just Shane winced and wiped his eye again. "I'm not crying!"

Uncle Tony snatched the phone back. "Why don't you put some clothes on. Rinse out your eye. Maybe grab a new mask. We can wait."

"I'm good." Just Shane wasn't going to be bossed around, not by Uncle Tony or anyone. He would sit here, as a point of pride, in his towel and ski mask, for as long as it took to negotiate the terms of Skwerl's release. Fortunately for Just Shane, it wouldn't take much longer. The terms were simple: Uncle Tony would happily hand over Skwerl. The price was the plates.

"Where do you imagine this swap taking place?" asked Just Shane. "Have you got an airport in mind?"

"No more airports," Uncle Tony snapped back. "No more

Challengers or Gulfstreams . . . none of that. We're going to make this swap on my turf, a warzone, where I control things, where you can't fly in or out, not unless you want to meet the business end of a surface-to-air missile. There's an overnight train that leaves Chelm, in Poland, each afternoon. It heads east across the border, to Kyiv, arriving a little after 6 a.m. If you want to see Skwerl alive again, I'd suggest that one of your colleagues—and the plates—be on that train in three days. It's already booked."

"And on arrival?" asked Just Shane. "What then?"

"They'll be met at the station," said Uncle Tony.

"And taken where?"

But Uncle Tony didn't answer; instead, he glanced at his watch, a Panerai Submersible with a dial the size of a desk clock. "You all don't have a lot of time," and, speaking directly to Just Shane, he added, "I'd also suggest you put some clothes on."

Uncle Tony hung up.

Just Shane tore off his ski mask and tossed it to the ground. With the heel of his good palm, he gave his throbbing eye a hard rub. Ephraim was carefully rolling the aluminum suitcase across the room, toward the closet. Just Shane had to remind him to take off his ski mask. "What do we do now?" asked Ephraim.

"It doesn't seem like we've got much of a choice . . . We need to do what Uncle Tony says," and then, as if following that advice, Just Shane rinsed off in the shower and put on some clothes.

GRILLOT'S MEN ARRIVED IN THE HANGAR EXPECTING TO FIND A body; instead, they found Uncle Tony in one of the adjacent conference rooms—the one where they'd kept Fareeda penned up. His bloody foot was propped on the desk. Fortunately for him, the P938 fired a relatively small-caliber 9mm round as opposed to a larger .45 or .357. Although the wound was deep—white striations of bone appeared through the flesh when Grillot's men irrigated and sutured Uncle Tony's heel—the bullet hadn't broken or fractured anything. One hour and three Vicodin later, Uncle Tony had his foot in a plastic boot. With a pair of crutches, he was already moving around.

The entire time Grillot's men had worked on him, Uncle Tony was setting plans in motion over the phone. Experience had taught him that, in these moments—when events go awry, when both sides are scrambling—a good plan delivered on time is better than a perfect plan delivered too late. This is what fighter pilots called the OODA loop, the ability to *observe, orient, decide, act*. In a dogfight, whoever could get inside the other's OODA loop would win the engagement. The call that Uncle Tony had placed to Skwerl's two dufus buddies in Colorado had clearly gotten deep inside their OODA loop.

Uncle Tony had a second call he needed to make, and it was nearly as important as the first. He needed to inform Grillot—as calmly as he could—that the handoff of the plates hadn't gone as planned. Grillot would hear this news soon enough, if not while on his trip to Kyiv then from the two fastidious men who, at this moment, were tidying up the mess of bloody rags, clippings of suture wire, and gauze scattered across the floor. It was better, Uncle Tony knew, that Grillot hear the bad news directly from him. He placed the call.

"Bonne soirée, Tony."

"You got a minute?"

"Oh, Christ," said Grillot. "What is it?"

"A complication . . ." Uncle Tony described the events of the last couple of hours, providing highlights like how "Skwerl double-crossed me," and assurances such as "Ali Safi won't do anything rash." When Grillot asked about the original plates, and where exactly they were, Uncle Tony was forced to produce an answer, one he had hoped to withhold. In a quiet, almost meek voice, he said, "Colorado."

The line filled with a string of expletives, all unintelligible, yet spoken in a guttural and irrefutably melodic French. A silence followed, which did little to dissuade Uncle Tony from launching into a description of his grand plan. The transfer of plates would occur in Kyiv, where no one could fashion a quick getaway on a private jet or otherwise surprise him. Also, given the large DRCA footprint in Ukraine, this was an environment Uncle Tony thought he could better control. Grillot was already there and, if he wanted, Uncle Tony could pass him off the plates in three days. Grillot could simply take them back to France via diplomatic pouch, the deal completed, the previous complications forgotten. The more Uncle Tony explained this plan, the more he became convinced of it himself. There was even an InterContinental Hotel in Kyiv, built among the onion-domed cathedrals surrounding Mykhailivska Square, where Uncle Tony could use his Hyatt reward points to reserve a pair of rooms.

"So, what do you think?"

"Let me talk to my men," said Grillot. Uncle Tony handed the nearest of the two operatives from Special Action his phone. He could hear the short, choppy rhythm of Grillot's voice issuing orders on the other end of the line. The operative nodded in cadence with these orders, his head bobbing along as he obediently muttered, "Oui, mon Colonel," over and over before returning the phone to Uncle Tony, allowing Grillot to explain, "These two will escort you and your associates across the airport, to the main terminal. You will board a flight to Warsaw. From there, I will arrange your transfer by armored sedan to Kyiv. Let me know when you're ready for me to collect the plates and I'll come by the InterContinental."

Uncle Tony thanked Grillot, assuring him that he would deliver the plates without any further complications.

Grillot listened patiently, before observing, "There might be one complication, but I'm sure it's nothing you can't handle . . ."

"What would that be?"

Grillot reminded Uncle Tony that the entire reason he'd traveled to Kyiv was to meet with his ambassador and discuss the dismal state of the war. They needed to see what more, if anything, could be done to shore up Ukraine's defenses. "This isn't a conversation we are having simply among ourselves," Grillot said. "One of your colleagues is here, too. This woman, I believe she is your boss. She introduced herself to me as Alejandra Fedorov, but she has a nickname"—and Grillot laughed—"which is not so good a nickname in Ukraine."

"You mean the White Russian."

"Yes, she is here. Only a minor complication, I am sure."

CHEESE HAD THREE DAYS TO GET TO CHELM. SINÉAD DIDN'T want him to go. She was worried it was a setup, a trap of some kind. "Why should he fly halfway across the world to bring them the plates?" she had argued. "Why don't they come to us?" Fareeda hadn't wanted him to go either, though her objections were different. She had spent time with Ali Safi and didn't think Cheese would be in any imminent danger (Skwerl was another matter); rather, she simply didn't want to be separated from her husband again and wondered if someone else might take his place. Cheese, of course, wouldn't hear of this. If someone was going to go, it should be him. But he wasn't certain of any plan where Uncle Tony set the conditions.

Ephraim and Just Shane had flown the plates back east, on Southwest Airlines. If flying Southwest wasn't nerve-racking enough, the airline had forced them to place the large aluminum suitcase in checked baggage. They landed at Philadelphia International only hours after the Gulfstream touched down. By now everyone had congregated at Sinéad's farm and, having gathered in the kitchen, Just Shane had lent his voice to the debate. He argued that someone needed to get Skwerl, immediately, and he even volunteered to go himself if Cheese refused. Just Shane believed that Skwerl's life was in too much danger, that his career at the Office had proven nothing but trouble, a tangle of intrigues and lies. "If I have to go all the way to Chelm or Kyiv or wherever to drag Skwerl back home, to Colorado, then that's what I'll do." Ephraim tended to agree with Just Shane, nodding along. Though he made no real argument of his own, he simply quoted a passage of scripture. "Proverbs 20:22: '*Wait for the Lord and he will avenge you.*'"

Cheese despaired, averting his eyes to his phone—they'd never rescue Skwerl—and there, as surely as if Ephraim had conjured it through prayer, was an email, the sender as impactful as if it were the Lord Himself . . . *Sheepdogs*, the message began, *I am aware that a network member in bad standing provided the two of you with an unsanctioned tasking. Rest assured that measures have and will be taken to ensure a resolution to this breach. To that end, depart on schedule from Chelm to Kyiv. Make no delay.—Sheepdog* . . . Beneath the signature line was written . . . *cc: Skwerl, Cheese.* Evidently, they were the only two recipients.

When Cheese showed the email to Sinéad, she said, "It could be real, but it could also be another fake," and when Cheese showed it to his wife, she said she had changed her mind. The message was good enough. He should go. Ultimately, what other choice did they have?

Chapter Seven

THE PAYROLL AND
THE PAYBACK

AFTER CHECKING INTO A TWIN ROOM AT THE INTERCONTINENTAL in Kyiv, Skwerl had spent a day and a night handcuffed to one of the bedposts. He'd been forced to share the room with Ali Safi, who snored, while in a connecting junior suite Uncle Tony stayed up watching movies with the volume set too loud, like an old man might, a career's worth of gunfights and explosions having degraded his hearing. He started with *Platoon,* followed by *When Harry Met Sally,* and ended with *Pulp Fiction.* Skwerl listened in. These were three of his favorites. Like Uncle Tony, he also couldn't sleep and found himself mouthing choice lines as he waited for morning. *"The only thing that can kill Barnes is Barnes . . ."* followed by *"Waiter, there is too much pepper on my paprikash . . . but I would be proud to partake of your pecan pie . . ."* and, lastly, as the sun rose, revealing the gray, humorless city through a window flecked with misty rain, *"That's when you know you've found somebody special. When you can just shut the fuck up for a minute and comfortably enjoy the silence . . ."*

As Tarantino's Mia Wallace—wife of notorious gangster Marsellus Wallace—uttered this line, Ali Safi ripped a snore so loud it jolted him awake. With a groan, he rolled out of bed, glared at Skwerl, and disappeared into the bathroom. The shower turned on and, still cuffed to the bedpost, Skwerl listened to Chuck Berry croon, *"It was a teenage wedding and the old folks wished them well . . .*" as he imagined Mia Wallace and Vincent Vega at the Jack Rabbit Slim's dance contest, twisting in the movie. His imagination soon diverted, taking a dark turn. What were Uncle Tony and Ali Safi's plans for him?

The song finished and Uncle Tony turned off the TV. He appeared in the adjoining doorway, balanced on crutches, his foot in a plastic boot, his eyes finding Skwerl on the bed and then settling on the shut bathroom. "He in there showering?"

Skwerl nodded. "Would you get me a drink from the minibar?"

Uncle Tony opened a bottle of Diet Coke and placed it in Skwerl's cuffed hands. Skwerl flipped onto his belly so he could bring the bottle to his mouth.

"Tell him I'll be back in an hour."

"Where should I tell him you went?"

Uncle Tony offered a sly grin. "Nice try. Just tell him an hour, okay?"

No sooner had Uncle Tony hobbled out into the hallway than Ali Safi swung open the bathroom door, emerging from his shower in a cloud of steam and swaddled in towels. "Where'd you get the Diet Coke?"

Skwerl delivered Uncle Tony's message and faced away from Ali Safi, toward the window, offering him a little privacy while he changed. Having dressed, Ali Safi flopped down on the twin bed next to Skwerl's. He switched on the TV, but instead of tuning in to a movie, he settled on a local news channel, *1+1*, which was broadcasting its morning show in Ukrainian. Lying flat on his back, with his hands folded over his chest and legs crossed at the ankles in front of him, Ali Safi appeared as if he were reclined on a therapist's couch. He stared at the ceiling, largely ignoring the parade of grim images flashing on the screen and the urgent tone of the news anchors, who Skwerl couldn't understand but Ali Safi seemingly could from his months at the front.

"What are they saying?"

Ali Safi glanced at the screen. "Nothing good. We're losing

ground in the Donbas and the southeast, there are worries about the Russians opening a new front in the north, near Kharkiv." The story shifted to Kyiv, to a press conference of Allied dignitaries gathered at the presidential palace. "The Europeans and Americans are announcing a new aid package," Ali Safi said. "The Defense Ministry is thanking them but also discussing shortages . . . of weapons . . . of equipment . . . of ammunition . . . of personnel . . ." And as Ali Safi translated this last of their complaints, he went on at some length about how DRCA hadn't made payroll for months. "If the Allies don't provide more support for Ukraine, foreign volunteers won't stay, not if we aren't paid."

"It's tough to rally international support for mercenaries."

"Why use such a nasty word?"

"I've been to a lot of wars," said Skwerl. "They attract three types, the three *M*s: mercenaries, misfits, and missionaries."

Ali Safi laughed. "A good theory. But I am not a mercenary—you should know better. I am a missionary."

"A missionary needs a mission." But as the words escaped Skwerl's mouth, it was obvious what that mission was. From the moment Ali Safi had found the plates, he had stopped being a mercenary (or even a misfit). As soon as Uncle Tony would allow it, Ali Safi would execute his mission. Skwerl recognized this. He knew it was why they'd brought him here, to Ukraine, a place where life was cheap and his could be snuffed out with few, if any, repercussions. No authorities would come poking around—no White Russian, no HPSCI staffers, nobody. He would be just another casualty in this long-running war.

"Which are you, Jay?" Ali Safi seemed genuinely amused by his own question. "Maybe you were a missionary once, but no longer . . . If you are a mercenary, it doesn't seem you are very good at it . . . This leaves only a last, unfortunate option."

Skwerl rolled onto his side. He didn't answer. Though Ali Safi was right about one thing: he was out of options.

UNCLE TONY HAD A BREAKFAST MEETING SCHEDULED WITH THE White Russian. He had requested the meeting, not because he particularly wanted to see her, but because it would have seemed suspicious had he taken this trip and not acknowledged they were both in Kyiv. Typically, Uncle Tony would have suggested they meet at Comme Il Faut, on the second floor of the InterContinental, a restaurant that was aggressively French, foie gras with every course and brie on everything, as if determined (like Ukraine itself) to prove its Europeanness. He was fond of holding court at whatever hotel he stayed in, as this cost him the least amount of time traveling between meetings, particularly now that he was on crutches. However, he would have to make an exception on this trip. Four floors above, he was holding an American hostage, a man who had proven himself unpredictable. Ali Safi, his partner in this enterprise, was a man hollowed out and made equally unpredictable in his thirst for revenge. Given these liabilities, Uncle Tony thought it best to meet offsite. The White Russian had suggested an Italian restaurant, Veterano Pizza, a ten-minute walk from the hotel, on Sofiivs'ka Street, where they wouldn't be bothered. That sounded fine, though Uncle Tony would have to Uber.

He arrived five minutes early and Alejandra Fedorov was already there, waiting at a table in the back. As he sat down, she asked about his foot, and he made up a story about dropping a weight on it during one of his workouts. Hung above her on the wall was a shadow box with a map; except it wasn't your typical map, it was a collage of spent 5.56 shell casings gathered from various battlefields, these formed the original borders of Ukraine, before the Russian invasion. Set onto a camouflage backing and surrounding the map were embroidered shoulder patches, each from a different Ukrainian Ground Forces unit. Most of their mottos were in Cyrillic, but a few were in English: "The Black Zaporizhzhians," "Border of Steel," "Hammer and Anvil," and nearly all of them featured a skull, or crossed rifles, or daggers, an iconography of death that needed no translation.

The waiter who brought their menu had only one usable arm; a sutured flap of skin covered the stump of the other below the elbow. His face was ghostly pale. On his right cheek, it appeared that he was having an acne breakout, but on closer inspection, Uncle Tony could see that the slightly raised black bumps beneath his skin weren't a dermatological condition—part of an adolescence this young man had only recently put behind him—rather, these were pieces of fragmentation, as fine as sand, pushing their way out of his face. When he returned a moment later with their two waters balanced on a tray, he asked for their orders. Neither Uncle Tony nor Fedorov had much appetite. They both asked for coffee and returned their menus.

"The owner only hires veterans," said Fedorov. "Hence, 'Veterano' Pizza. Most are disabled." She had heard of this place from her counterpart, the chief of SBU, the Sluzhba bezpeky Ukrainy, or Ukrainian Secret Service. His son had come to work here, a Marine with the 36th Brigade who, two years before, had survived the three-month siege of Mariupol. She pointed out that unit's shoulder patch, a Sea Dragon on a blue shield, among the others in the frame.

"And how's his son doing?" asked Uncle Tony.

"I don't ask. There aren't enough pizza parlors in the world to deal with the problems this country's veterans will face once the war is over."

The waiter returned with their coffees. In a maneuver he hadn't quite yet mastered, he hoisted his tray one-handed from his shoulder and onto the table, spilling some of the coffee. He apologized, wiping up the mess with a fistful of paper napkins before returning to the kitchen.

"What's brought you here, Tony?"

"Just checking on the situation," he said. "Same as you."

"And what would you say the situation is?"

"We're giving them enough to fight but not enough to win."

"Like we always do."

"Yeah, like we always do." Uncle Tony stared ponderously into his cup. A beat of silence passed before he added, "Wouldn't you like to win, just once?"

"Win?" She blurted out the word as if it had never occurred to her.

"Yeah, win. Kick some ass. Give the indig everything they want . . . and more."

"Sounds fun," and she smiled as if Uncle Tony had said something truly charming. "But that's not my job, and it's not your job either. We're not here for *their* country, but for *ours*. Right now, on certain programs, our interests no longer converge."

"Like payroll for our guys."

"Is that why you're here?"

Uncle Tony unhinged his jaw to speak, but at the last moment he decided against it. He didn't need to explain to her what she already knew, which was that if payroll wasn't met for select units of the International Legion their sectors along the front might collapse.

"Like I said, just checking on the situation."

"This war, Tony, is much bigger than your nostalgia for some program we can no longer afford to underwrite."

He took another sip of his coffee and studied the shadow box a little more closely, making a careful examination of the shoulder patches around the map. Fedorov noticed him doing this. She understood what he was looking for and asked if he had found patches for any of the units whose ranks contained his old indig, the Afghans, Kurds, and Iraqis that he and his colleagues at the Office had trained over the years and who had quietly filtered across the border to fight. Uncle Tony continued his search. The patches in the shadow box represented only a fraction of those units on the front, that ceaseless muster of regular army divisions, territorial defense brigades, separate battalions, and volunteer companies. Eventually, Uncle Tony gave up. He couldn't find any patches of units with his old guys in them.

Fedorov shrugged. "It's probably for the best," and then, after considering the map herself for a moment, she added, "It'll be like they were never here."

THE TRAIN DEPARTED CHELM AT A LITTLE AFTER 6 P.M. FOR Cheese's twelve-hour journey, Uncle Tony had booked him into a sleeper car, which held two facing rows of seats that could comfortably pull out into four bunks. Cheese rolled the aluminum suitcase packed with the Marie Antoinette plates into his cabin and then stowed it under his seat. He hoped he would have the sleeper car to himself.

He would not.

In the moments before the train lurched out of the station, the sound of cursing (understandable in most any language) approached from down the corridor. Cheese's door slid open. A man built thick and wide as an ancient column and dressed in camouflage, who had at least six inches on Cheese, growled at him in an unrecognizable, consonant-filled language. Cheese pushed his heels against the suitcase, to make sure it was as far under his seat as possible. The man jabbed his thumb at his chest, introduced himself as "Tomas," and extended his hand. His head was shaved. His black beard hung to his chest. Slung over each shoulder was an enormous bag. They were made of the same type of cheap yet renewable material used in the eco-friendly shopping bags that Cheese sold for a quarter at the Esso station—bags nobody ever bought.

Tomas gestured around the cabin. He was asking animated questions. Cheese returned a blank stare. Tomas sighed, allowing his bags to thud onto the floor. Then he reached into his shirt and took out his phone, an enormous Samsung which he wore on a cord around his neck. He repeated himself into it. Google translated his words into English, revealing the mystery of what he wanted in a robotic, Phrasealator voice: "These bags are . . . fuck-ing . . . heavy . . . give me . . . some help."

Tomas pulled down one of the bunks. Cheese helped him heave up his bags, one of which was filled with his helmet and body armor. Velcroed beside a Ukrainian flag on his plate-carrier was a red flag bisected by a white stripe. Tomas noticed Cheese noticing his flag and asked him, "Where from?" When Cheese said, "Afghanistan," this caused Tomas to dip into a long, irritated monologue. Then he stopped himself, realizing Cheese couldn't understand him. Again, he pulled out his Samsung. "I watched . . . the evacuation . . ." He shook his head mournfully. "Abbey's door was such a . . ." When he heard the translation, Tomas cut himself off. He repeated the words, but the translation came out the same.

"You mean the Abbey Gate?"

Tomas nodded, speaking again into his phone. "Abbey's door what a . . . cluster fuck . . . pieces of bodies . . . arms . . . legs . . . heads . . . picking them up for days . . . like here."

As the train left the station, their conversation through Google Translate continued. Tomas explained that he had spent the past year fighting in the southeast. When Cheese asked why he'd volunteered, Tomas gave him a look, as if it was the dumbest question he had ever heard. "Because that . . . fuck . . . Putin isn't going to stop . . . those Russian orc invader assholes . . . look what they've . . . done." He reached up into his bag and tore off the red-and-white flag Velcroed to his body armor. Then, as if to rest his case, he added, "I'm Latvian."

Tomas wasn't the first foreign fighter Cheese had come across. The day before, after he'd taken the bus from Warsaw to Chelm, he had been waiting in one of the town's cafés for his train. A man and woman, both in their twenties, sat at one of a dozen tables. "You sure you don't want anything to eat?" the man had asked in English. His steel-toed boots fell heavily on the floorboards. He was American, with a beard, but to Cheese his beard read less *American Sniper* and more *Gandalf*. He was pale, doughy, and wore a flannel with a vintage black *1993 Metallica Nowhere Else to Roam* T-shirt underneath. He vanished for a few moments and brought back two coffees and a meat pie for himself.

The woman he was with had removed a pack of cigarettes from her handbag. She fidgeted with its top, opening and closing it, precisely ordering the movement of her hands as if weighing whether to excuse herself for a smoke and vanish out the back of the café. But her date had started talking, which kept her in her seat. His words crowded the small café. He began by saying that he couldn't believe that he would soon return to Ukraine, to fight (and possibly die) in a war, when only a year before he was living a boring life in the States, working a retail job he hated.

She had stopped fiddling with her pack of cigarettes and left it open.

Then he blurted, "I've always been attracted to redheads, but I had to go to war to meet a redhead as beautiful as you."

She removed one of her cigarettes.

"I know about fear," he added nervously. "I've felt it in combat and overcome it. But when I'm around you, I feel nervous in a way that I can't overcome."

She tapped her cigarette's filter on the table and said something about not feeling well.

"Wait a second," he said, rummaging through his pockets. "If you need a Midol, I've got some. I would always carry them for the female soldiers . . . they were my comrades, too . . ."

Her lighter was out now.

Then, forlorn, he added, "It's also for me." He began to explain, at great length, that he suffered from a recurrent bladder infection. The most effective treatment, he'd found, was medicinal marijuana, but he couldn't use that on the zero line without endangering his comrades, hence the Midol, and the inference that his discomfort was yet another gallant sacrifice he'd made for the Victory— *Slava Ukraini! Glory to the heroes!* And, if she ever came to the States with him, she would see how he could get her all the legal marijuana she wanted.

The young woman hadn't gone outside for a cigarette, but instead excused herself to the ladies' room. The erstwhile foreign fighter sat by himself and finished his meat pie. He was still waiting for her to return when Cheese's phone had rung. It was Uncle Tony, wanting to confirm that he would be on that night's train. When Cheese answered, and when the young man heard his voice, in English, he gave Cheese a look—the same one a dog makes when it's caught peeing on the rug.

Although Cheese himself was sympathetic to Ukraine's cause, a person would have to place their life on hold to fight. This meant a person typically couldn't have much of a life to begin with. A foreigner with a job, or a family, or myriad other adult commitments, couldn't drop everything to enlist "until the Victory." If a person didn't have these commitments, it might be for a reason, and perhaps these folks—like Midol-man and even Tomas—hadn't been the best raw material from which to forge an international legion to fend off the Russian invader. But they were all there was, and it seemed to Cheese that it was this way in every war.

As Cheese trundled along toward Kyiv in his sleeper car, he couldn't help but notice that Tomas was missing the index finger on his right hand. As unobtrusively as he could, Cheese asked him through the Samsung what he did in Latvia before the war. "I was a . . . truck driver . . . shit job and fucking hated it . . . before that I robbed banks . . . sold drugs . . . did drugs . . . prison . . . then came war . . . one month ago, my . . . brother was fighting . . . he drown in a frozen river . . . dumbass . . . now I return . . . for payback . . . war is shit . . . but it is still better . . . than driving a truck . . ."

Tomas listed at length everything he despised about trucking: sleeping on roadsides, not being paid for time he had to wait offloading goods, the monotony and boredom of hours spent behind the wheel. As he talked, he became increasingly animated and soon reached into one of the bags that Cheese had helped him hoist onto the bunk. His whole face lit up conspiratorially as he rummaged through its contents. Then, as if he were exhibiting some ancient and illicit relic, he removed a two-liter bottle filled with ochre liquid that looked like jet fuel. "Polish whiskey," he said, presenting the bottle to Cheese. Black particles, like pepper grounds, floated around in the whiskey—which Tomas noticed Cheese noticing. He shook the bottle vigorously and they seemed to vanish. He set out a pair of paper cups he must've gathered from the restroom. Cheese politely declined, saying, "I am Muslim." Tomas shrugged, yet filled both cups nevertheless. He lifted the first, said, "Fuck . . ." and shot the whiskey. He lifted the second, said, ". . . Putin," and shot it as well. He then leaned his head against the window. He began to swig directly from the bottle, brooding at the view outside. Within an hour, Tomas was drunk, and Cheese was lying in his bunk, peacefully asleep.

The next morning, a steward knocked on the cabin door. In fifteen minutes, they would arrive at the train station in Kyiv. Cheese sat up, flinging aside a scratchy train blanket. Tomas must have thrown it over him in the night. Except Tomas was gone, as were his bags. All that remained were the two paper cups crushed on his seat. Cheese felt a jolt of panic. He imagined for a moment that Tomas had stolen the aluminum suitcase. He leapt out of his bunk, landing in a crouch, to find that his suitcase was exactly where he'd left it. The train made no stops in the night so perhaps Tomas had simply found another cabin to sleep in.

Cheese brushed his teeth and washed his face. By the time he finished, they were pulling into the station. He glanced out the window. On the platform, waiting, was Uncle Tony on crutches.

IT WAS AGONY, ALL THIS WAITING.

Fareeda had agreed to stay with Sinéad instead of returning to Austin. Ephraim and Just Shane had decided to stay on as well.

The four kept vigil by the phone, anticipating the call that would tell them the swap was complete, that Skwerl was safe and on his way home with Cheese.

Sinéad would have preferred to wait in silence. She suspected that Fareeda would've preferred the same. But Ephraim and Just Shane seemed determined to chatter for hour after hour, moving room to room in the house. To pass the time, they discussed the specifications of Ephraim's modest property—floor plans, soil composition, rainfall dispersal—and the renovations Just Shane suggested he make to remove himself entirely "from the grid" and become completely self-sufficient. "King of your own castle" was a term Just Shane deployed repeatedly, and every time Sinéad heard it, it grated a bit more. On and on they went, debating the merits of one septic system over another and the relative efficiencies of different water filtration techniques. There was also composting to discuss—oh, how they loved to talk about composting. By the second day, Sinéad couldn't take it.

That morning, Fareeda had caught her at the door, putting on her jacket. "Where are you going?"

"Out." Sinéad paused, glanced at her Acura parked in the driveway. "You want to come?" Fareeda shouldered past, sliding through the door, determined not to miss her chance at escape.

It wasn't until they had pulled onto I-76 that Fareeda finally asked where they were headed. Sinéad didn't have a destination in mind, she had simply wanted to get away. Fareeda suggested a drive into Philadelphia. She had never been and wanted to visit the birthplace of her adoptive nation. Given her rough landing in the United States, Fareeda harbored mixed feelings about that nation; but, if nothing else, her child would be American, so this was reason enough to spend that morning visiting a landmark or two.

They started at Independence Hall. After picking up coffees nearby, the two women strode onto a square whose red bricks matched the main building's facade. Two smaller, arcaded wings jutted from either end of Independence Hall, while at its center a limewashed bell tower rose into a steeple. Built into the tower was a clock. Its hands, painted gold, read a little before 9 a.m.

The streets were filling with morning commuters as Sinéad played tour guide. She did her best to recall snippets of eighth-grade history, how both the Declaration of Independence and the Constitution were debated in the hall, and how on the last day of the Constitutional Convention, when a lady spotted Benjamin Franklin leaving, she asked, "Well, Doctor, what have we got, a republic or a monarchy?" and Franklin had replied, "A republic, if you can keep it." She remembered her teacher saying how after the Constitution was ratified, bells rang out across the city.

Fareeda pointed to the other side of the square, to the Liberty Bell housed in glass, and asked that they pay it a visit. After gazing at the bell, she said, "The crack seems very large, like the whole bell might split in half." A nearby placard recounted the history of the bell and how after arriving from Britain in 1752 it had cracked on its very first ringing. Fareeda liked the idea that the bell, this symbol of America's Liberty, was broken from the start. "I like that they didn't care," she said, "that they kept ringing it, making the crack bigger and bigger. It's a very American thing to do, all that ringing, don't you think?"

"I guess," said Sinéad, though given how the country had treated Jay, sentimentality about it no longer came so easily to her.

Fareeda winced and reached to the base of her spine.

"You alright?" Sinéad asked.

"My back," said Fareeda. "It hurts sometimes, because of the baby."

Sinéad reached into her pocket and offered up her own meds. "They're nothing strong, just anti-inflammatories I take for work," she said. "They take the edge off." Fareeda swallowed one dry while Sinéad asked what she planned to do once her husband returned—assuming everything in Kyiv went to plan.

"I thought you might ask me that."

"You did?"

"Yes, because we are both confronted with the same problem: our men. They are each a little broken, wouldn't you say?" Sinéad didn't disagree, so Fareeda continued: "My husband and I could return to Austin. He could go back to his job. Our baby will be born, but Aziz, working all day and into the night at the Esso station, he will hardly see us . . . Jay, he can't really earn money, can he? He owes a debt to the government, so they take every penny he makes, correct? That's why he came to my husband in the first place. What will he do when this is over? Will you support him? And if you support him with your . . . work" (and Sinéad didn't like how Fareeda said *work*, but let it go) "is Jay the type of man who won't resent you for it?" Fareeda pointed to the bell. "If you strike the bell, the crack gets bigger, no?"

"What are you suggesting?"

"Nothing yet. But if they come back, this Sheepdog, whoever that is, will ask them to do more work."

Sinéad agreed it was likely.

"And they will want to do that work."

Again, Sinéad agreed.

"They will want to go, and we will have to let them. Because we love them."

"I'm not willing to go through this again, not for any amount of money," said Sinéad, "so I hope there's a 'but' here."

"*But* . . ." and Fareeda turned away from the bell, taking a step nearer Sinéad and leaning in conspiratorially ". . . there are some people who must be protected from themselves. My husband and Jay are two such people. It is important that you and I have our own relationship, not only for our sake but for theirs too."

"So what does that relationship look like?"

Fareeda crossed her arms over her chest. She took in their surroundings, the Liberty Bell, Independence Hall, the jagged skyline whose high-rises towered above this oldest corner of the city; the idea that so foreign a place might someday feel like home seemed as improbable as the idea that she and Sinéad would someday become confidants and that their two very different families would become braided together. "I guess," said Fareeda, "that what I am proposing simply looks like this, what we are doing now, that no matter what work Sheepdog assigns Jay and Aziz that a separate understanding exists between the two of us. That we help them, but we also help each other. What do you think?"

"Agreed," said Sinéad. "But there's something else: Sheepdog. If Jay and Aziz can't figure out who he is, we need to."

Fareeda agreed to this, too, though neither of them knew exactly how they'd go about uncovering Sheepdog's identity. For a moment, Sinéad felt as though she should offer some gesture to commemorate their deal. A handshake felt too formal. A hug too sentimental. This brief, awkward moment was mercifully interrupted when, above them, the clock struck the hour—9 a.m.— and its bell began to toll.

ON THE DRIVE FROM THE TRAIN STATION TO THE InterContinental, Uncle Tony explained to Cheese how the transfer would work. They sat in the back of an Uber, the aluminum suitcase in the trunk. "I've gotten you a room," he said. "When we arrive at the hotel, you aren't under any circumstance to leave it. I will inspect the plates with you in that room. Assuming they are authentic and in good condition, I will bring Skwerl to you. After that, I will take the plates and the two of you will depart tonight back to Chelm on the same train you arrived on. Agreed?"

Cheese agreed, though what other choice did he have? The drive to the InterContinental was short, only fifteen minutes. This was a good thing, as with every sudden stop, or every bump in the road, Cheese feared that no matter how securely they had packed the plates one might shatter. He wondered what would happen if Uncle Tony opened the aluminum suitcase and found only fragments.

When they pulled up to the hotel, their driver popped the trunk. Strangely, the doorman didn't offer to help with their luggage even as Uncle Tony hobbled around to the back of the Uber. Cheese heaved the aluminum suitcase onto the sidewalk while Uncle Tony looked on. As they passed the doorman, who stood at his post in his livery, Uncle Tony peeled a few hundred hryvnia from a large roll in his pocket. He slid the cash into the doorman's palm, seeming to tip him for nothing. Or, as Cheese now realized, not for nothing. But for looking the other way. As they stepped inside the marble foyer, Cheese also noticed how from the concierge to the receptionists, everyone seemed studiously to ignore them. They rolled the aluminum suitcase to a bank of elevators and ascended to the sixth floor, room 636.

BY THE TIME UNCLE TONY DEPARTED FOR THE TRAIN STATION that morning, Ali Safi had spent two days cooped up with Skwerl in the one hotel room. The day before, when Uncle Tony had gone to a meeting with one of his work colleagues, Ali Safi had considered killing Skwerl. He still had a quantity of the polonium-210. He could've poisoned Skwerl, dissolving a dose in one of the many Diet Cokes Skwerl demanded from the minibar. But Ali Safi's honor wouldn't allow it. He had given Uncle Tony his word. He would wait until the exchange of plates had occurred. Ali Safi wouldn't cheat Uncle Tony out of his money or what he imagined was the luxurious retirement that awaited him.

Still, it had been tempting to kill Skwerl; particularly as he wouldn't shut up. Skwerl kept making claims that infuriated Ali Safi. He had gone so far as to say that he wasn't at fault for the death of Ali Safi's brother. Yes, he'd been in Now Zad, and yes, he'd been among the Americans on the raid.

"Then how can you proclaim your innocence?" Ali Safi was seething.

"Imperfect intelligence." With cuffed hands, Skwerl sipped his Diet Coke.

"Imperfect?"

"Gul Bacha was there . . . we weren't wrong about that. Mistakes were made."

"Mistakes . . . ?" Ali Safi came to standing, so he hovered menacingly over Skwerl. "*Mistake* isn't the word I'd use."

"What word would you use?"

"*Murder.*"

Skwerl rolled his eyes. Gul Bacha had killed Americans. He'd been a high-value target. How was he supposed to know Gul Bacha was trying to switch sides? And what about Dickhead Mike? If Gul Bacha and his men were so innocent, he said, how come they'd killed one of his own? "Notice I said *killed*," Skwerl added. "Not *murdered*. For someone who's spent his life in a country at war, you don't seem to know much about it. On and on Skwerl went, and while he spoke, Ali Safi was only able to ignore him by fantasizing about the moment he would end Skwerl's life.

He and Uncle Tony had plotted this out in detail. There was another room in the hotel where Cheese would be taken along with the plates. Assuming they were authentic and in good condition, Ali Safi would deliver Skwerl to this hotel room with strict instructions that neither he nor Cheese leave until their train's departure that evening. Eventually, Skwerl and Cheese would grow hungry. Uncle Tony had paid a series of bribes to members of the hotel staff— from the doorman to the receptionists to the concierge. The entire hotel worked for him, and when Skwerl and Cheese ordered lunch to their room, Ali Safi would intercept it. He would dose whatever they ordered with the last of his polonium-210.

Ali Safi could see it clearly. He would swipe a key card that Uncle Tony had already given him. Both Cheese and Skwerl would have collapsed, either on the floor or in their beds. There would be no sign of struggle, two 50-microgram doses would ensure that, death coming within minutes. Like he'd done with H in Marseille, Ali Safi would lay them out in a dignified manner. Unlike in Marseille, he doubted the overtaxed Ukrainian authorities would launch much of an investigation—if any at all. Still, he would take certain precautions. Whatever identifying markings he found on Skwerl or Cheese, he would remove with a razor, like with the meat tag he had found on H.

Yes, he could see it all.

There was a knock at the door. It was their breakfast, brought to them by a different white-jacketed waiter than yesterday, a rather large man, bald and with a beard. He was clumsy with the trolley, saying little, and spilling a glass of water as he reached for the bill. Ali Safi signed it, then rolled the cart into their room. He was pleased to notice that Skwerl hadn't ordered much, hardly anything in fact, just a coffee and some toast. Perfect, thought Ali Safi, he'll be starving by lunch.

PLATES COVERED EVERY SURFACE OF THE HOTEL ROOM. THEY lay on the floor, on the desk, across the twin beds. Uncle Tony was inspecting each one, documenting any imperfection. The most minute chip or scratch warranted a photograph and then an entry into a notebook he'd brought along for the occasion. It was a time-consuming process. Cheese helped, handing Uncle Tony specific pieces from the collection when he asked for them, and, eventually, repacking each of the plates into the aluminum suitcase. By this time, it was late morning and Uncle Tony still hadn't said anything about whether the plates met his standards. Finally, Cheese asked.

"We're good," said Uncle Tony. He gestured for the house phone, which sat on a side table between the twin beds. Uncle Tony dialed a short number and said, "Bring him up."

Cheese sat on the edge of one of the beds.

Uncle Tony hung up the phone and sat across from him as they waited.

"What will you do with all your money?" Cheese asked.

"*My* money?"

"Skwerl says these plates are worth millions."

"This money isn't for me." Uncle Tony started to laugh.

Cheese was confused. "Then why else would you . . . ?"

"Wait, you think I'm going to buy a villa, or a boat, or a jet . . ." Uncle Tony was really laughing now, and then, when he realized the punch line to this joke, which to him was even more hysterical, he keeled over. "You think I'm going to retire . . ."

Cheese gazed back at him stonily.

"I'm sorry." Uncle Tony wiped tears from his eyes. "I'm not laughing at you. Just the idea of me with $60 million in my pocket, retired, living like an oligarch on some riviera, well, let's just say that I thought Skwerl knew me better . . . Maybe you guys thought I was going to buy one of those megayachts in the port of Marseille?" As he said this, Uncle Tony started to laugh again, but caught himself.

"What are you going to do with that money?"

A beep came from the door, the sound of the key card reader.

Ali Safi stepped inside. Standing beside him was Skwerl, rubbing his wrists, as if they'd only just been uncuffed. When Skwerl saw the suitcase and Cheese, his shoulders slouched.

"Cheese was just asking me what I planned to do with the money."

Skwerl wasn't amused. "Spend it on tattoos and creatine for all I care."

"Would you care if I told you that I planned to pay you the original repossession fee for the Challenger? That's a million bucks."

Ali Safi shot Uncle Tony a disappointed look, which he ignored. Based on their plan, neither Cheese nor Skwerl would live long enough to collect that fee.

"That's less than two percent of the value of these plates," said Skwerl. "How generous. I hope you enjoy the rest."

"The rest isn't for me," said Uncle Tony. "I have to say . . . I'm a little disappointed you thought I'd spend this money on myself. And how can you think you're being treated unfairly? You and Cheese are going earn a payday that's ten times higher than anyone else on this deal."

Skwerl gazed down at the aluminum suitcase. "How do you figure?"

"Payroll," said Uncle Tony. "You thought this was about my retirement? Guys like us don't retire. 'This life, it follows you,'

you're the one who said that to me, Skwerl. And you were right. DRCA has got five thousand troops on the zero line who haven't been paid in months. These are our guys, our indig from all our old wars, and they're here, right now, killing Russians. What's more righteous than that? And we're going to screw them out of their pay? Sorry, not happening. I've got a buyer for these plates. The $60 million is going to our guys, to keep them paid, to keep them in the field, to keep that whole section of the front from collapsing. If the Office and the White Russian won't pay our indig, if the HPSCI staffers won't do the right thing, then guys like us have to figure it out because you don't retire from this job, never. Those plates are our payroll, Dumbshit."

"The name's Skwerl."

"If you say so." Uncle Tony grabbed the aluminum suitcase. "C'mon," he said to Ali Safi. "Let's get out of here."

SKWERL AND CHEESE SAT ON THE BED, WAITING. THEY HAD hours until they would leave for the station and board their train back to Chelm. They began with small talk. Skwerl wanted to hear how Fareeda was. Cheese assured him that she was fine, that her captivity hadn't proven too traumatic, that Ali Safi had, in his strange way, tried to make it as comfortable as possible. Skwerl asked about Sinéad. Cheese assured him that she was also fine, though she was worried about him. Skwerl glanced at the phone. "Probably best to wait until we know we're safe before I call."

"Probably, I think we're—"

Before Cheese could finish, Skwerl stood from the bed and clocked him on the jaw. Cheese rolled to his side, bouncing off the bed and onto the floor. Slowly, he got to his knees. "Are you insane?"

Skwerl was shaking out the knuckles on his right hand. "When you lost it about Fareeda, I said that I'd tag you later, and today you deserve it. You're the one who's insane. You come here alone, with the plates, and with nothing but Uncle Tony's word that he won't kill you—or kill us both."

"That's what I was trying to tell you." Cheese rubbed his jaw, sitting back down on the bed. "I think we're through the worst of this. I got an email from Sheepdog before I left."

"You mean from Uncle Tony?"

"No, I mean from Sheepdog, or what I think is the actual Sheepdog. The email was sent to you, too." Cheese pulled out his phone and tossed it at Skwerl.

" 'Measures have been taken to ensure a resolution to this breach . . . ' What does that mean?"

"Not sure," said Cheese. "It was a big risk traveling here. Without that email, it might not have made sense to come and get you."

"Thanks, I guess . . ."

"Hear me out. Uncle Tony wants those plates. Ali Safi wants you dead. If I had come here to exchange you for the plates, that would mean that Ali Safi wouldn't get what he wants—revenge. Do you think Ali Safi is going to let you out of here alive?"

"So we're dead men?"

"Not according to Sheepdog . . . 'Measures have been taken,' remember."

"What measures?"

"I don't know," said Cheese. "But I had enough faith in those measures to get on a plane, then a train, to try to get you home. We need to play this thing through."

As for what that might entail, neither knew.

They still had several hours to pass until their train. An uncomfortable silence settled between them as each imagined the possibilities contained within those hours. A lot could happen.

Skwerl stood from the bed. He opened his arms, a gesture of apology, for the mess this had all turned into. He was inviting Cheese to come in for a hug.

"It's two slaps on the back, right . . . ?"

"That's right," said Skwerl. "Two slaps."

They returned to the edge of the bed. Eventually, Skwerl asked Cheese whether he was hungry. It was coming up on lunch. Cheese was starving, and so they ordered room service.

UNCLE TONY SAT ON THE SOFA IN HIS JUNIOR SUITE, HIS FEET propped up on the aluminum suitcase, watching TV. More grim news from the front line. Equipment shortages. Ammunition shortages. Personnel shortages. Russian probes near Kharkiv, Chasiv Yar, and Vuhledar, and rumors of an offensive. Uncle Tony wasn't fool enough to think that the entire war hinged on DRCA making payroll for five thousand of its soldiers, but he'd also been around long enough to know that in war it's the little victories that lead to the larger ones, and that the obverse was often true. Today, he had scored a little victory. He was allowing himself a few moments to savor it.

But Ali Safi was killing the mood. He was pacing the length of the hotel room, blocking Uncle Tony's view of the TV.

"Why don't you sit down?"

"You're really going to pay them the million?"

"Not if you do your job."

"Then why mention it?"

"Would you rather they think they're *not* going to get out of here alive?"

Ali Safi continued to pace, blocking Uncle Tony's view of the TV.

"If you're going to do that, do it over there?"

Ali Safi moved behind the sofa. He went up and down the room a couple of more times, muttering to himself, "If you fuck me over . . . if you do . . . I wouldn't if I were you . . . but if you do . . ." while shaking his head side to side.

Uncle Tony finally muted the TV. He planted his feet and stood from the sofa, so he was facing Ali Safi. "Quit it . . . nobody is going to fuck you over."

Before Ali Safi could respond, the phone rang. Uncle Tony crossed the room. "Hello? . . . Yeah . . . Okay, got it." He hung up and turned toward Ali Safi. "They just ordered room service . . . happy now?"

Ali Safi hardly broke stride from his pacing as he rushed out into the hall.

The door hadn't even closed behind him before Uncle Tony took out his phone. He dialed another number. It answered on the first ring. In a low voice, he said three prearranged words, "Go get them," and then immediately hung up.

Uncle Tony settled back on the couch. He turned on the news again, kicked his heels up on the aluminum suitcase, and allowed himself to savor another little victory.

THERE WAS A KNOCK AT THE DOOR.

"That was quick," said Skwerl. Not even five minutes had passed since he and Cheese had ordered lunch. Carefully, he crossed the room while Cheese sat up from his bed. Skwerl fastened the bolt and chain across the door. He glanced back at Cheese, who nodded, and then he opened it. Through the gap, Skwerl glimpsed a waiter wearing a white jacket. He was tall, muscular, bald and with a beard. When he said, "Room service," Skwerl recognized the heavily accented voice from earlier that morning, when Ali Safi had ordered breakfast.

Skwerl shut the door, unfastened the bolt, and allowed the waiter inside. Except the waiter didn't have a tray, a trolley, or anything.

"Where's our lunch?" asked Skwerl.

"Come, we go." The waiter stood in the vestibule, gesturing toward the door.

"I'm not going anywhere . . . Where's our lunch? . . . Who are you?"

The waiter reached into his pocket, to remove something.

Skwerl lunged at him. But in a single, violent movement, the waiter delivered a perfect crossbar, slamming his forearm against Skwerl's neck, pinning him to the wall by his throat. Cheese was up from the bed now, racing across the room. The waiter had at least a hundred pounds and a half-foot on him. This hardly seemed to discourage Cheese. Since stepping inside, the waiter had had his back to him. Cheese used this opportunity to leap onto him from behind, clawing at his face. When Cheese grabbed a fistful of the waiter's beard and tugged as hard as he could, the waiter cursed in some unintelligible language. Then he howled, "Polish whiskey!" bending forward at the waist and flinging Cheese off his back and onto the floor.

When Cheese looked up, he caught a first glimpse of the waiter's face. He recognized him. "Fuck Putin?"

The waiter released Skwerl's neck. "Fuck Putin."

"Tomas? What are you doing here?"

Skwerl was on his hands and knees gasping. "You know this guy?"

"I met him on the train," said Cheese, before firing off a rapid series of questions: "You work at the hotel? . . . Weren't you headed to the front? . . . Why did you disappear from our sleeper car?"

Skwerl interjected with a question of his own: "Where's our lunch?"

Tomas couldn't understand any of this. He reached into his pocket again, pulling out the large Samsung, which he'd been trying to remove when Skwerl had lunged at him. He flashed his palm like a traffic cop to silence both Skwerl and Cheese, so their voices wouldn't blend with his as he spoke into Google Translate. He quickly finished, pushed a button, and the English came out in that robotic voice:

"You . . . assholes need to . . . come with me . . . we have to switch rooms . . . if you want . . . to live."

WHEN ALI SAFI STRODE THROUGH THE KITCHEN OF THE InterContinental, no one made eye contact with him. The cooks, the busboys, the waiters, they all pretended he didn't exist, as if there was nothing odd about this stranger's sudden appearance. Uncle Tony had paid handsomely for their inattention. He had also paid handsomely for the restaurant staff to leave the lunch trolley for room 636 unattended.

At this midday hour, the kitchen was abuzz with orders shuttling into the main restaurant where ministry officials, generals, and oligarchs huddled over their place settings. They would linger long after their meals had been cleared, their moods buoyed or sunk by the latest news from the front. Typically, room service orders were rare at lunch, and today was no exception. This made it easy for Ali Safi to spot the trolley with the Diet Cokes.

Ali Safi wheeled the lunch trolley into an alcove by the service elevator. This placed him out of sight of the restaurant staff. He then reached into his pocket and slid on a pair of rubber surgical gloves. He unfolded a partially crushed N95 mask and put it on. For eye protection, the best he had was a pair of reading glasses he'd bought from the hotel gift shop. He hardly looked the part of an assassin. Lastly, he removed from his pocket a heavy lead-lined bag, no larger than the type used for a sandwich. It was rolled shut with two rubber bands, which he removed. He opened the Velcro seal and inside was a Pyrex vial. A fine grey powder, tasteless and entirely soluble, had congregated at its bottom: this was the last of the polonium-210.

Ali Safi lifted the steel warming lids on the two entrees. They were the exact same: a burger and fries. He had no desire to kill Cheese, a fellow Afghan, a legendary pilot, a man who, in truth, he admired and whose wife he'd gotten to know, albeit under less than ideal circumstances. Ali Safi had hoped there would be some easily recognizable distinction between their two meals— like, say, if Skwerl had ordered a hot dog and Cheese a kebab. Such a distinction would've allowed him to spare Cheese. But now

Ali Safi had no choice.

Ten micrograms was a fatal dose. Ali Safi sprinkled ten times that on the burgers and into the Diet Cokes. He dropped the empty vial into the lead-lined bag. He removed his gloves, glasses, and mask and pitched them in a nearby trash can. He left the trolley by the service elevator. One of the hotel staff would soon deliver it.

There was nothing Ali Safi could do now but wait.

He was hungry so went to the restaurant. He sat at the bar and, after reviewing the menu, determined that the best thing on it was a burger and fries. He ordered that and a Diet Coke.

THE BURGER WAS PRETTY GOOD, THOUGH THE FRIES CAME OUT soggy. Ali Safi left most of them on his plate. Gradually, the restaurant had cleared out, until only a few of the lunch crowd remained. To kill the time, Ali Safi had found a couple of newspapers, but none in English. He'd read through *Der Spiegel* first, mostly looking at the pictures, and then moved on to *Le Monde*.

A few more tables cleared, and for the first time Ali Safi noticed two odd-looking fellows seated in the back. One was rather large, thick-necked with a buzz cut, wearing a black suit, white shirt, and black tie, like a powerlifter who'd joined a blues band. He stood, taking some instructions from the other guy, who was equally fit, though slimmer. The one in the black suit left, while the slimmer fellow lingered at the table. The waitstaff delivered him an ashtray even though several *No Smoking* signs hung around the restaurant. He lit a cigarette and exhaled a ribbon of smoke from each nostril. Beside him was the aluminum suitcase.

Ali Safi asked for his bill, but before it arrived, the man stubbed out his cigarette and, wheeling the aluminum suitcase behind him, headed for the door. Ali Safi buried his face in his newspaper. However, this didn't dissuade the man. He shouldered up to the bar and asked, "Parlez-vous français?" Ali Safi folded down the top page of the newspaper. He exchanged a vacant stare with this man, who added, "You are reading *Le Monde*."

"None of the papers are in English."

"Or in Dari . . ." said the Frenchman.

Ali Safi drew silent.

"I recognize you . . . from Marseille."

"I'm fairly certain we've never met."

"I still recognize you . . . You are Uncle Tony's friend, no?"

"I am."

"Ah, but this was a trick question." The Frenchman glanced down at his suitcase, considering it a moment. "Uncle Tony, he does not have friends."

"Is that so?"

"Yes, of course. But don't feel badly. It is the same for me. I am also one of Uncle Tony's 'non-friends.' When I saw you across the restaurant, I thought I would introduce myself. Now we can say that we have met."

The bartender arrived with Ali Safi's bill. "I'm glad you did," he said, as he charged his lunch to Uncle Tony's room. "Would you like to have a drink?"

"Unfortunately, I can't stay. I wish we had more time, but my driver, he is waiting." The Frenchman extended his hand. The two of them shook. He said, "Bonne chance, mon ami," and then wheeled his suitcase out of the restaurant.

IT WAS TIME. ALI SAFI CROSSED THE LOBBY FROM THE restaurant to the bank of elevators. He rode up to the sixth floor. The chime rang and the door opened. He glanced up and down the corridor. It was empty, aside from a trolley of discarded food sitting outside room 636. Ali Safi fished around in his pocket. He felt his disposable straight razor blade first and then the key card he would use to open the door.

As Ali Safi stepped into the vestibule, he kept the door handle depressed so he could ease the latch soundlessly into the metal catch. With equal care, he lifted the door chain, placing the bolt into the slide, lest a member of the cleaning staff, a waiter, or anyone else interrupt the next few minutes of hurried work. He returned the key card to his pocket and removed the razor blade, pinching it between his fingers as he stepped into the modest room.

He expected to find two bodies, their blue-lipped mouths open like fish, eyes rolled back into their heads, fingers clawed into the palms—predictably grim stuff.

Except the room was empty.

Ali Safi crossed it in two steps, checking either side of the beds. Still, nothing. Now he was beginning to panic . . . The trolley was outside . . . the food scattered on either plate, seemingly eaten . . . the dose so large it should've killed them both in minutes . . . They couldn't have just vanished . . .

A final possibility occurred to him: the bathroom.

Skwerl and Cheese were strong. They might have had enough time from the onset of their symptoms until their vital organs shut down to rush into the bathroom, to vomit or gulp water, not that either would have done much good.

Ali Safi glanced in the direction of the bathroom. For the first time, he noticed the door was edged in light. He flung it open.

Out of his peripheral vision, he caught a dark flash, followed by an explosion of white light in his face like a thousand micro starbursts. He was toppling backward, into the vestibule. His body hit the carpeted floor with a thud that knocked the wind out of him. When he took a breath, he felt a stab of pain in his nose, like someone had jabbed a sharpened pencil up each nostril, and he could hear a wet gurgling sound before he tasted the blood trickling down the back of his throat. Towering above him, his silhouette framed by a single ceiling light, was the waiter from that morning. He wore his white jacket and had stepped from the bathroom, shaking out his fist after a good punch. "See familiar face?" said the waiter in broken English.

"Uh . . . you . . . you brought breakfast this morning."

The waiter stepped on Ali Safi's hand, twisting on the ball of his foot like he was crushing out a cigarette. Ali Safi released the razor blade that he'd forgotten he was carrying. He noticed the waiter's shoes, which weren't shoes at all. They were combat boots with rubber soles and heavy treads.

The waiter picked up the razor. He slid it into his pocket, a souvenir. From that same pocket, he removed his Samsung. He spoke into it and pressed a button. The translation app on the phone said, "Do I look . . . familiar now?" The waiter smoothed down his beard with one hand, pulling it taught, allowing Ali Safi to better discern his jaw, which was hinged at a perfect right angle. His long nose. His wide eyebrows. He did look vaguely familiar, but Ali Safi still couldn't quite place him outside the context of this hotel. The waiter stuck his thumb into his mouth. He flicked his wrist in an upward motion, which made a clicking sound. He slid a flesh-colored palate, a retainer of sorts, wired with four fake teeth, out of his mouth. One of his two front teeth were among the fakes. He smiled at Ali Safi, whose jaw went slack. He looked like he'd seen a ghost.

"Victory Tooth?"

The waiter shook his head no, while speaking into his Samsung. "Both of us played . . . hockey . . . He was . . . my little brother . . . and you are . . . a fucking deserter." The waiter reached into the small of his back. He removed a pistol, which he leveled on Ali Safi, who began to speak in rapid fire: . . . *He and Tooth had planned to split the money . . . Stealing the plates had been Tooth's idea . . . Tooth had gotten drunk . . . When he fell through the ice it'd been an accident* . . . and, finally, "I didn't kill your brother."

The waiter seemed to understand this last point without translation. He spoke into his Samsung. "I don't . . . believe you."

Ali Safi found himself thinking of Now Zad. How many times had Skwerl proclaimed his innocence? And how many times had Ali Safi said that he didn't believe him? As he tried to take a deep breath, he coughed, choking on his own blood. In a weak, defeated voice he asked, "What do you want?"

"... Payback."

Ali Safi shut his eyes. "So kill me."

"I will ... let ... the fucking Russians ... do that."

Ali Safi opened his eyes. The waiter gestured toward the bathroom with the muzzle of his pistol. He wanted Ali Safi to clean himself up.

Bent over the sink, he allowed the blood from his nose to trickle into the warm running water. The waiter silently watched him, holding his pistol at the hip. Through the mirror's reflection, Ali Safi was able for the first time to get a good look at the model, a palm-sized Sig Sauer P938 ...

... Uncle Tony's favorite model.

SKWERL SAT PERCHED ON THE WINDOWSILL OF THEIR NEW hotel room. He'd been there for a couple of hours, peeking out between the curtains. He had a view of the semicircular driveway where the doormen in their grey-and-gold livery attended to arriving guests. Cheese had encouraged Skwerl to sit further back, lest the wrong person catch a glimpse of him. But Skwerl had insisted on keeping an eye on the front entrance. For his own peace of mind, he needed to see Ali Safi hauled away.

As Skwerl waited, he was hoping for the arrival of an ambulance and a team from the morgue, so was disappointed when a pair of muddy Toyota Hilux pickup trucks arrived. A half dozen goons wearing a mix of camouflage uniforms and black leather jackets stepped out of the trucks. They idled at the hotel's entrance, mingling with the doormen.

"There he is," said Skwerl.

Tomas had appeared outside. He marched behind Ali Safi, driving him forward by his bound wrists, which rested in the small of his back. Tomas had exchanged his white waiter's jacket for a camouflage uniform. Cheese, who had also come to watch by the window, recognized the uniform from the train. Two of the soldiers, on seeing Ali Safi, immediately grabbed him by either arm. They led him to the first of the two pickup trucks. As they pushed him into the backseat, he resisted for a moment, taking a stutter step. He seemed to say something desperate, a final plea. The soldiers laughed open-mouthed while the doormen turned away, busying themselves with one task or another.

One of the soldiers reached up and palmed Ali Safi's head like a basketball, pushing him down into the backseat. Another had walked around to the far side of the truck so that Ali Safi would be sandwiched between these two muscled apes for the duration of this journey. Given the mud on the two Hilux trucks, it seemed this was a journey that would take them back to the front, a drive of six or seven hours. As Ali Safi disappeared into the truck, Skwerl turned away from the window.

"That's the last you'll see of him," said Cheese. "The penalty for desertion is death."

"You really think they'll shoot him?"

"I don't think his 'comrades' plan on him lasting long. They'll either shoot him or feed him to the meatgrinder. Maybe he'll take some Russians with him first."

Outside, the soldiers were backslapping Tomas, welcoming his return and congratulating him on a job well done. Tomas handed a ticket to the bellman, who a few moments later returned with two bags, the same ones Tomas had carried on the train. He strapped on his body armor, which had the red-and-white Latvian flag Velcroed to its chest. That flag was noticeable on the body armor of several others, as well as the Georgian five-cross flag and the Finnish blue cross.

The trucks sped off.

Skwerl stepped away from the window and climbed onto his bed. "Why do you think Tomas came back?" he asked wistfully.

Cheese seemed confused. "Revenge for his brother, like he told us."

Skwerl made a face. "Revenge for Victory Tooth? Naw, I'm not buying it. The guy gets drunk, puts on some too-small figure skates, and falls into a frozen river. His brother sounds like an asshole."

"So why do you think he came back?"

"For money."

"Maybe . . . but you heard Uncle Tony. He said we're making out the best on this deal. Tomas couldn't be getting more than low six figures."

"That's more than enough," said Skwerl. "Think about it . . . he rides the train in, snatches Ali Safi, delivers him to his old pals, gets their back wages paid, and then he hangs out on the zero line like a hero before heading back to Riga, or wherever he came from. That's not a bad couple of weeks' work."

"You think Uncle Tony needed a bag man and found Tomas?"

"Maybe," said Skwerl. "Or maybe Sheepdog found Tomas."

Cheese slid his phone out of his pocket and again read, " 'Rest assured that measures have and will be taken to ensure a resolution to this breach.' "

"Those measures," said Skwerl, "were Tomas and the goon squad."

"Which means Uncle Tony works for Sheepdog?"

"Right now, it seems we're all working for Sheepdog."

"So who's Sheepdog?"

Skwerl had no idea. Cheese sat on the other bed and the two of them stared at the ceiling. After a while, Skwerl said, "When you think about it, of everyone here—you, me, Tomas, Uncle Tony— Ali Safi was the only one who wasn't in this for money."

"What do you mean? He stole the plates."

"Yeah, but not for money. For revenge. Against me. He was never in this for money and that's what made him dangerous. Ali Safi should've known better. Guys like him always get screwed over."

"You mean guys who aren't fighting for money?"

"I mean guys who show up at a basketball court wearing their football pads. I mean guys who don't understand the rules of the game they're in."

On the bedside table between them, the phone rang. Skwerl picked up—it was Uncle Tony. A car would be downstairs in ten minutes to take the two of them to the train station. "Also," he said, "if you guys check your bank accounts, your payment for this job should have just hit."

Skwerl didn't have a cellphone, but Cheese did.

Cheese logged on to his account . . .

. . . His mouth hung slightly open, and he sat there staring at his phone.

Skwerl cupped the receiver with his palm. "Cheese?"

He shut his mouth and nodded at Skwerl, who got back on the phone. "Received . . . thanks, Tony."

Uncle Tony hung up. Skwerl placed the receiver back in its cradle. He and Cheese left the InterContinental for the station, where they found their train home. It was right on schedule.

Chapter Eight

SECRETS WE KEEP
FROM OURSELVES

SKWERL HAD TRIED TO CONVINCE SINÉAD THAT SHE DIDN'T need to work anymore, that he could support her. When she'd asked how he planned to do this, he'd simply said, "Sheepdog." When she'd asked who Sheepdog was, he'd had no answer. "When you find out who Sheepdog is," she'd said, "maybe I'll considering working fewer client hours and scaling back operations at Knotty Pleasures, but until then I don't think our livelihood can depend on an anonymous email account."

This wasn't to say that Sinéad was ungrateful. Not losing out on the half million dollars had been transformative. It had allowed her and Skwerl to pay off both the mortgage on their farm and all remaining payments on the Acura, to invest in a new Twisto 6-E multi-braid (the "Ferrari of single braid rope machines," according to the ICI, the International Cordage Institute), and to launch an Amazon paid marketing campaign that, in a single month, had increased Knotty Pleasure's annualized revenue projections by 31.7 percent.

The money had proven even more transformative for Cheese and Fareeda. It allowed him to quit his job at the Esso station. During the last trimester of Fareeda's pregnancy, they had moved east, placing a down payment on a home twenty minutes from Skwerl and Sinéad, a farm in Amish country, Ephraim's old place.

Ephraim had plans of his own. He'd decided to move west to

Colorado. Just Shane needed an extra set of hands at his place and had offered Ephraim a job. There was even talk of the two of them working with Skwerl and Cheese again. To Sinéad, it seemed that everyone was moving on—or, if not moving on, then moving into their right place.

Except for Jay.

Weeks after his return, he wasn't sleeping well. On multiple nights, he'd toss around in bed, waking Sinéad. When she would ask what was wrong, they'd have a version of the following conversation:

"Why hasn't Sheepdog reached out with another job?"

"I'm sure he will."

"What if he doesn't?"

"Then you'll figure out something else."

"If I asked Uncle Tony for work, he would have to give me something. His boss doesn't know about DRCA and the $60 million. If I threatened to tell her, who knows, maybe he could set me up in the QX program, like he did with Mac."

"Do you really want to work for Uncle Tony again?"

The conversation would end there on most nights. Sinéad would roll onto her side and Skwerl would either fall asleep or he'd lie very still so Sinéad could sleep. But on other nights, a second and greater concern would arise, overwhelming Skwerl. At this point, Sinéad would know that it'd take quite a bit more work for either of them to get back to sleep.

"What if he's still alive?" Skwerl would ask.

Sinéad didn't need to ask who he meant. She would simply say, "He's not." She would remind Skwerl of what he had told her, how members of the International Legion had dragged Ali Safi back to the front, how the punishment for desertion was death, and how if Ali Safi hadn't been executed by his former comrades, they had certainly fed him into one assault or another so that he might take a few Russians with him before being butchered himself.

Skwerl's erratic behavior didn't overly concern Sinéad—he was erratic by nature. But on this issue, she wanted to put his mind at rest.

WITHIN DAYS OF SKWERL RETURNING, SINÉAD HAD RESUMED seeing her clients. This included Representative Charles Mangrove. He'd long had a special request: a double session. Given the rigorous nature of her practice, Sinéad had a no double sessions policy. They were too punishing for her and for the client; it was a liability issue. But also, Sinéad was having trouble with her back. While Ephraim was still in Colorado, she had returned his buggy to his farm. Using one of her own whips, she'd driven Ephraim's pony nearly two hours on an unpadded box seat, and afterward, her ass was killing her. The pain moved to her spine. Turned out it was a herniated lumbar disk, between her L5 and S1. But Mangrove was proving relentless. He kept pestering her about a double session. When Sinéad finally agreed to three hours on a Saturday night, she said she was doing it as a special favor to him but that he should be forewarned: she would be asking a favor in return.

"Anything," he'd said gleefully, and she planned to take him up on it.

Thirty minutes before Mangrove arrived, Sinéad began her warm-up routine, some easy biking on her newly purchased Peloton, followed by deep knee bends and stretching with a focus on her lower back, shoulders, and hips. The last fifteen minutes she used to dress. Corset, thigh-high boots, bikini bottoms—all black leather. Over-the-elbow gloves in red latex. Lipstick to match the gloves. Hair pulled into a ponytail. Her equipment was already laid out—paddles, whips, gags, restraints (leather, stainless steel cuffs, and, of course, rope)—so that when he arrived in his BMW and parked it in the barn, she was waiting at the top of the stairs. She threw him a bathrobe, called him a pig, and told him to change so they could get to work.

Three hours later, and after having resuscitated Mangrove three times with smelling salts, Sinéad stood over him and said, "Time's up." He lay on his back, spread-eagled on the wood floor in a puddle of his own sweat, staring at a ceiling fan turned to full power. She tossed him back his robe. Unlike their last session, he wasn't bleeding. Bruised, yes. Welts, everywhere. Twitching, a bit. But otherwise, fine. This was a great relief to Sinéad, who promised herself that she'd never run the risk of a double session again.

"Now it's time for you to do a favor for me." Sinéad hopped on an inversion table. She flipped herself upside down, sighing as the pressure came off her back.

Mangrove tried to sit up but couldn't. Instead, he rolled onto his side. He came onto all fours and then plopped into a sitting position, clutching his robe to his naked waist. "Okay," he said, in an exasperated, almost amazed voice, as if he couldn't quite believe the ordeal he'd endured. "What is it?"

"A name: Ali Safi."

"Him again?" He tilted his head to the side, so he and Sinéad were eye-to-eye.

"You've got access to the casualty reports coming out of Ukraine. I want you to run his name. He'd likely be in the southeast, somewhere around Kherson. He should be listed among the dead."

"That's it?"

"For now."

Mangrove made a face. He picked himself up off the floor. "Okay," he said. "I'll get back to you." Then he put on his robe, cinching it around his waist. Before he went to the bathroom to change, he turned to Sinéad and said, "That was amazing. I swear, you almost killed me."

TWO WEEKS LATER, A MANILA ENVELOPE ARRIVED IN THE mailbox, delivered by hand. Sinéad knew who it was from. She stepped into the house and sat at the kitchen table. She sliced open its top. Inside was a photocopy of an official document, riddled with signatures and certifications of authenticity, all written in Cyrillic.

Paper-clipped to the back of the document was its translation in English:

> *For valor and gallantry above and beyond the call of duty, the President of Ukraine, authorized by an act of Parliament, takes pleasure in awarding to Private Ali Safi the Hero of Ukraine medal, posthumously. Private Ali Safi of the International Legion distinguished himself by extraordinary heroism in action along the Kherson sector near Dar'ivka. When preparing for a frontal assault against an entrenched Russian position, Private Safi's platoon was ambushed moving into their trenches. Pinned down by an intense machine-gun crossfire from a knoll two hundred meters on their flank, Private Safi's platoon began sustaining heavy casualties. On his own initiative, Private Safi crawled toward one of the hostile weapons. Reaching a point 25 meters from the enemy, he charged the machine-gun nest, firing his rifle, hurling grenades, and killing three enemy soldiers. While his comrades moved up to help him consolidate his advance, Private Safi observed an entire enemy squad maneuvering to launch a second ambush. Before the enemy could initiate this attack, Private Safi stormed their position. Although Private Safi failed to take the position, his single-handed assault and personal sacrifice allowed the surviving members of his platoon safely to withdraw. Private Safi's extraordinary heroism and devotion to duty are in keeping with the highest traditions of military service and reflect great credit on him, the International Legion, and the Armed Forces. Glory to Ukraine! Glory to the heroes!*

When Sinéad finished reading the citation, she turned her attention to the rest of the packet. It included two witness statements, neither longer than a few paragraphs, signed at the bottom by soldiers with multisyllabic and consonant-heavy names. These statements detailed Ali Safi's actions and seemed to be the basis on which he was receiving this award.

This was good news, thought Sinéad. It proved Ali Safi was dead. She called Skwerl. She wanted him to come home and see these documents for himself, except he wasn't answering his phone. That morning, he'd gone to Cheese's house a short drive away. Fareeda was due at the end of the month, and these past two weeks, he and Cheese had been preparing for the baby's arrival. When Sinéad couldn't reach Skwerl, she decided to drive over there herself.

Her arrival was announced by barking, a new puppy, a scruffy brown-and-white rescue. He ran figure eights around Sinéad's legs when Cheese opened the front door. Cheese had brought the puppy home for Fareeda only a few days ago. He joked that it would probably save him money given the donations Fareeda kept making to the ASPCA. When Fareeda announced her intention to name the puppy "Tony," Cheese had objected. "Like *Uncle Tony*? . . . No way." But then she'd corrected him, "No, like *Antoinette*."

Upstairs, Cheese and Skwerl had been hard at work in the nursery, a converted home office that Ephraim had once used for prayer and personal reflection. They were painting it a gender-neutral yellow as Cheese and Fareeda had wanted the baby's sex to remain a surprise.

"What's up, Toots?" Skwerl was perched on a ladder with a tray of paint and roller balanced beside him. He leaned down to knock her a kiss. Cheese resumed his painting, bent over in a corner doing detail work on the trim with a brush.

Sinéad held up the packet. "I've got proof that Ali Safi is dead."

Skwerl and Cheese wiped their hands on their paint-speckled pants. They gathered around Sinéad. She handed Skwerl the packet. He read the citation and then passed it to Cheese. Skwerl then read the witness statements, which described Ali Safi's final moments:

> "... the orcs had us pinned down a second time. Private Safi was already ahead of our main body. I could see him running up the line of their trenches, dodging back and forth until he reached the machine-gun position. He jumped over its top firing his rifle. There was a large explosion and he vanished in a cloud of smoke. The machine gun then went silent. We called out for him, but he didn't come. Not long after, we received orders to withdraw. Our attack had been called off ..."

The second witness statement, although written from a slightly different perspective, also described this moment: the loud explosion and how Ali Safi had vanished in a cloud of smoke.

Skwerl handed the packet back to Sinéad and said he needed to finish his work.

"What's the matter?" she asked. "This is what you were looking for."

"I know, it's just ..."

"Just what?"

"'A loud explosion ... a cloud of smoke ...' That's it? Are we sure he's dead?"

Sinéad felt an urge to throw the papers in Skwerl's face. The citation said the medal, Hero of Ukraine, was being awarded posthumously. What more proof did he want? A body? It was almost as if he needed to believe that Ali Safi was still alive, like he couldn't let him go. She wondered if Skwerl was, perhaps, suffering from stress-induced delusions. Or, if that wasn't his diagnosis, maybe he was just determined to be a pain in her ass.

Before she could say more, Skwerl interjected. He wanted to know what Cheese thought. Cheese finished reading over the remaining witness statement. "Alive or dead," he said as he handed the statement back to Sinéad, "there is one thing that, without a doubt, this citation proves: Ali Safi is a hero."

With that, Cheese picked up his brush. As did Skwerl. The two of them resumed their work, painting the nursery.

UNCLE TONY HAD TO WEAR THE PLASTIC BOOT ON HIS FOOT for nearly two months. Running was too painful. He couldn't swim, either, as his doctor wanted him to avoid the pool, lest the wound get infected. He could lift weights but, given his age and ever-slowing metabolism, he knew he had to throw some cardio into the mix, otherwise he'd have to restrict calories with no drinking, no desserts, no carbs (there was no chance). So this left one option: cycling.

Pedaling on a stationary bike in the gym seemed an unimaginable humiliation for a used-to-be-commando, so on a spectacular morning, sunny and warm, he had walked into the bike shop on M and 34th Streets in Georgetown and purchased an entire road biking package—a starter-level Cannondale, a pair of size 11 Shimanos with clips, a helmet, and a water bottle. The bike tech had tried to talk him into a Lycra cycling suit, but that was where Uncle Tony drew the line. He would cycle in regular workout shorts and his cotton SEAL Team 4 T-shirt. This is what he was wearing a couple of weeks later when his tire popped twelve miles into a fourteen-mile out-and-back on the C&O Canal.

Fortunately for Uncle Tony, he would only need to wheel his bike two miles into Georgetown where he could get a patch for his tire before cycling the final mile home. He entered the shop covered in sweat and stepped straight up to the counter, explaining to the technician on duty what had happened and asking how quickly he could get the tire patched up. The technician didn't answer at first. He had another bike on a rack, its high-end frame all swooping, rounded angles, space-aged and predatory. The technician wore a pair of headphones attached to what appeared to be a set of tuning calipers. As he spun the rear wheel, he held the calipers to its rim and shut his eyes. He was listening for hidden sounds, as if he were trying to divine water from the bare earth. Suddenly, he opened his eyes. A look of inspiration passed over him. He picked up a hex key and began tightening a few of the spokes.

"Give me twenty minutes," he said, finally answering Uncle Tony.

Twenty minutes wasn't *right away*, which was the answer Uncle Tony had been looking for, but it was good enough. He took a seat in the corner of the shop. Next to him, a customer flung open one of the changing room curtains. He wore one of the Lycra outfits they had tried to sell Uncle Tony. "What do you think?" the man asked his wife. "I'm into it." He rotated his body in front of a full-length mirror. Front and back, he was all awkward bulges. Uncle Tony watched as this poor woman tried to answer.

Five minutes later, as the man was at the cash register buying his outfit, Mac strutted into the store. The technician handed the man his receipt and announced to Mac that his bike was almost ready, just a couple of minutes more. Mac stepped toward the seats in the corner of the shop, and that's when he noticed Uncle Tony. "I wouldn't have thought to see you here?"

Uncle Tony glanced down at his bike. "It's helping with my rehab."

"I heard about your foot."

"What'd you hear?"

"I heard you told the White Russian you dropped a weight on it at the gym. But I heard other things, too . . . I heard it was a .357 in Kyiv."

"Who'd you hear that from?"

"I've got my sources."

"Your sources are mistaken, big surprise." Uncle Tony held up his foot, rotating it at the ankle as if it were a jewel cut to catch light at different angles. "It was a 9mm in Marseille." The two shared a laugh, but then Uncle Tony's expression turned grim. "You and I are overdue for a sit-down. I already left a couple of messages for you over at Cyberdyne. What gives?"

"Sorry, I haven't returned the call. It's been crazy busy."

"You're a bad liar."

"What do you want me to say, Tony? You're a little hot right now."

"*Hot?*"

"Yeah, hot. You get shot in the foot in Kyiv . . . or Marseille . . . or wherever. Our European partners, the ones who work with DGSE, are saying you single-handedly kept the five thousand members of the International Legion from deserting. People talk, Tony. They might not know exactly what you've been up to, but they know you've been up to something. The only person who seems completely clueless is your boss. And if she finds out . . . well, it's just . . . you're a little hot right now, and until you cool off, I don't want to lose my job if you lose yours."

"That's not gonna happen."

"You sound awfully confident."

"People only see what they want to see in this business. The White Russian doesn't want to know what I've been up to. And who's going to tell her?"

"Your friend Skwerl paid me a visit while you were gone," said Mac. "I don't think he'd have a problem telling her."

"I can handle Skwerl."

Mac shifted in his seat. He looked longingly at his bike. The technician was making a few final adjustments. "Whatever you say, Tony."

"Don't you get it? The White Russian doesn't *want* to know. She doesn't want to know about the Marie Antoinette plates, or

DRCA, or Cyberdyne, or Ali Safi. She doesn't want to know about my foot, or your friend Dickhead Mike, or the FISA Court. She has no interest in those details. *Plausible deniability,* ever heard of it? In our business, the customer doesn't want to know everything about everything—that's not intelligence, that's just information. Intelligence is telling someone everything they want to know about a specific thing. As for those things that they don't want to know, well, you better be damn sure not to tell them. We deal in secrets, Mac, but the biggest secrets we deal in, the ones that *really* matter, are the secrets we keep from ourselves."

Before Mac could say anything, the technician took off his headphones. "Man, this Ventum One is cherry. You're all set." He placed the tuning calipers on his workbench. He hoisted down Mac's bike from the rack and wheeled it in front of the cash register. Mac asked him to charge his account.

The technician then grabbed a small patching kit and crouched next to Uncle Tony's front tire. He licked his thumb, rubbing away the dirt and grime so he could get a good look at the puncture. "This'll only take a second," and, true to his word, the technician slapped a patch over the tire, reinflated it, and Uncle Tony was ready to leave with Mac.

They stepped outside. Mac's Ford Bronco was double parked by the curb. Its black coat gleamed as if he'd just had it cleaned and waxed. He offered Uncle Tony a ride home as he hoisted his bike's frame onto the rack's twin arms.

"Naw, I'm okay," said Uncle Tony. "But listen, I want you to come see me—it's time."

Mac tugged on his bike, to make sure it was secure. Once he was convinced of this, he turned and said, "Alright, we'll get something scheduled."

They shook hands. Mac pulled away in his Bronco, weaving through traffic. Uncle Tony rolled out onto M Street. His bike felt a bit wobbly beneath him. He pedaled carefully, muttering to himself about this being a stupid fucking way to stay in shape and an even stupider way to get around. Uncle Tony hoped the thin rubber patch on his tire would hold. He didn't want to find himself stranded, yet again.

WHEN IT BECAME CLEAR THAT THIS LATEST PUSH ALONG THE southeastern front would fail to yield the territorial gains the Kremlin had hoped for (and that Kyiv and Washington had feared), Uncle Tony was summoned to Congress. Win or lose, the outcome always seemed the same: he would wind up sitting in the basement of the Rayburn Office Building, at the U-shaped table in the SCIF, surrounded by HPSCI staffers. These Toms, Marys, Johns (and two Janices) would pepper Uncle Tony with questions, demanding he answer with absolute rigor on certain subjects while ensuring they remained assiduously in the dark on others.

Although Congressional testimony was, by far, one of Uncle Tony's least favorite parts of his job, he was in a good mood that morning. He attributed this to a little thing: when he had pulled up to the lot on the Capitol grounds, he'd found his preferred parking spot unoccupied. The Capitol police officer had waved him in, no questions asked. He had parked and, as he jogged across the four lanes of Independence Avenue, he noticed that his foot was feeling better too. Once inside the Rayburn Building, he even bypassed the elevator, opting for the stairs.

After greeting the pasty-faced staffers who, per usual, seemed to have no idea that outside a glorious day had dawned, Uncle Tony began his briefing. It started with a slide show that broke down the last month's fighting by sector along the zero line. The story it told was one of Russian miscalculation, as the Kremlin had clearly misjudged the readiness of the Ukrainian units they'd faced. Uncle Tony zoomed in on certain sectors. The Russians hadn't thrown quite enough troops at the defensive positions to break through; however, the margin of Ukrainian victory had proven uncomfortably slim.

Nowhere had this proven more true than around Kherson. Along a fifteen-mile front, five thousand members of the International Legion had held off an attacking force of approximately twenty-two thousand Russians. This was below the 5:1 or even 6:1 attack to defense ratio that Russian "Deep Battle" doctrine mandated for success.

"These numbers," Uncle Tony explained as he circled the figures with a laser pointer, "are proof of a miscalculation within Russia's high command."

One of the staffers, Uncle Tony thought his name was Tom, asked, "Weren't these defending troops threatening to desert a little while ago if they weren't paid?"

"That's correct."

"What changed?"

"Well, for starters, it would appear they got paid . . ." Uncle Tony knew not to say more than that. The staffers didn't want the details.

"Good thing you and your colleagues managed to sort that out."

Uncle Tony took a deep, calming breath. "Yes, we managed."

"And if we'd had a thousand less or even five hundred less troops there . . . ?" The staffer's already pale face turned an even lighter shade—he'd realized the answer to his own question.

"The Russians would've broken through." Uncle Tony zoomed out, to a slide that showed the roads leading from Kherson to Mykolaiv and then north, to a chain of poorly defended cities that would have placed the Russian army within striking distance of Kyiv.

The room went silent.

"But they didn't break through," said Uncle Tony. "Next slide."

This second part of his presentation, without battle maps, was visually less accessible than the first, but it was every bit as significant. Uncle Tony had sent over several binders' worth of read-ahead materials, labyrinths of wire diagrams and column after impenetrable column of Excel spreadsheets, all of it documenting current U.S. covert action in Ukraine and its intricate systems of logistical and financial support. Before he could begin briefing these documents, another staffer interrupted. Unlike Tom (at least he thought that was his name), Uncle Tony recognized this staffer immediately: Janice.

"Tony," she began, "this is amazing work by the Office. But I've got a quick question before we move on."

"Sure thing, JA-niss." (He nailed the pronunciation.)

"It's come to my attention that the Ukrainians have decided to award the Hero of Ukraine medal posthumously to a member of the International Legion, an Ali Safi. Are you aware of this?"

"I am."

Janice's eyes dipped to her desk, and she consulted a sheath of papers. "His citation is quite something," and she held up the document. She read a few lines—thus entering them into the Congressional record. "Are you also aware that he was an employee of DRCA on sabbatical to fight with the International Legion?"

"Yes, I am aware."

"I figured you were." Janice opened a binder. "In your read-ahead materials, I saw this month's casualty lists. I was surprised Ali Safi wasn't among the dead given his posthumous award."

"Those lists are prepared by Ukraine's High Command for Military Administration," said Uncle Tony. "Typically, there're quite a few clerical errors. But I can look into it for you." He flipped his presentation to the next slide.

But Janice wasn't done.

"A clerical error in Kyiv . . . okay, if you say so. But when I checked his 201 file, I saw that you were the one who archived it after the Office terminated its relationship with DRCA. As you'll recall, we discussed archiving 201s when you last testified before this committee. You served as Ali Safi's case officer, correct?"

Uncle Tony glanced around the U-shaped table. The other

staffers had fixed their attention on him, waiting for an answer. "I managed the Office's relationship with DRCA. Anyone working for them would have me listed as their case officer. But that was only in an administrative and purely programmatic capacity."

"Thank you for clarifying," said Janice. "Because I thought it was unusual that after you had archived Ali Safi's 201 that another case officer would replace you."

"What are you talking about?"

Janice extended her hand, offering Uncle Tony the 201 file. He took it and, sure enough, he was no longer listed as Ali Safi's handling case officer. He had been replaced by Alejandra Fedorov, the White Russian.

"Do you know why your boss made this change?"

Uncle Tony shut the 201 and handed it back to Janice. "No idea," he said. "You'd have to ask her."

"That won't be necessary." Janice tucked the file among the myriad other documents she had stacked in front of her. "I'm sure there was good reason, and, given the Office's recent success, that reason is really beyond the purview of this committee." She then ceded her remaining time to the other staffers.

Uncle Tony spent another two hours answering questions in the basement of the Rayburn Office Building. He touched on programs managed by the Office in five of the world's seven continents. He explained counter-narcotics operations in Sinaloa, the establishment of anti-Chinese resistance networks in the Spratly Islands, the targeting of Islamic extremists in the Sahel, but all the while his mind remained elsewhere. He was fixated on what Janice had shown him. That minor change on Ali Safi's 201 file . . . What did it mean?

Uncle Tony finished his briefing. He traversed the three lengths of the U-shaped table shaking hands with the staffers. He left the basement, ascending the stairs to the lobby and the light of day. When he crossed the four lanes of Independence Avenue back to his car, it was at a slow walk, not his carefree jog from that morning.

He pulled out of the Capitol parking lot and, on the drive back to Tysons Corner, the gears in his mind continued to turn:

If the White Russian had been handling Ali Safi this whole time, did that mean she had been the one to dispatch him to the lobby of the Grand Hotel in Lviv, to make the approach about them working together?

What about the polonium-210? It was a Russian poison, one the White Russian could come by easily enough. Had she acquired it on Ali Safi's behalf?

And the Marie Antoinette plates, had Ali Safi really stumbled across these by accident? Or had the White Russian learned of them and recognized an off-the-books opportunity to fund a program that she downplayed but knew to be essential?

In Kyiv, at the pizza parlor, Uncle Tony had been so focused on not betraying the reason for his visit, he had thought little about asking the White Russian the reason for hers. Was she also there to make sure the International Legion would hold their positions, that this latest Russian offensive would fail?

But something didn't add up: Sheepdog.

Where did Sheepdog fit in?

When Uncle Tony finally arrived at the Office, he sat in the parking lot, with his hands frozen at ten and two on the steering wheel, like he was listening to a particularly gripping story on the radio when in fact he was racking his brain for a single, elegant explanation to everything that had happened.

Nothing was clear to him, except his determination to uncover Sheepdog's identity.

SEVEN DAYS

"WHAT'S IN A NAME?" SHAKESPEARE ASKED THAT, AND THEN he went on to say that a name really didn't matter that much, that what you call a thing isn't really so big of a deal. A rose by any other name still smells the same, right? It's still a rose, right? Nope . . . Wrong . . .

A name matters.

In our business, it's everything.

Take Skwerl. If he had known Dickhead Mike's real name, he might not have had his breakdown. When he'd called out to him in Now Zad, saying, "Stay with me, Dickhead, stay with me . . ." over and over, for some reason that had broken him. If that had never happened, then Skwerl would've stayed working at the Office. If he'd stayed at the Office, he never would've needed to make a living off the books, and he wouldn't have reached out to Cheese to do the same. Skwerl's life and Cheese's life hinged on the fact that Mac, years ago, decided to call Sergeant Mike Ronald, Dickhead Mike.

So what's in a name? Quite a bit.

Today, Skwerl and Cheese are discussing names. They're in the hospital cafeteria where, three floors above them, Fareeda is napping. Just this morning, she gave birth to a daughter. It isn't only Skwerl and Cheese who've gathered here, but Sinéad, too. The three are sipping coffee, waiting for Fareeda to wake up. The baby doesn't have a name yet and, according to Islamic custom, Cheese and Fareeda will wait seven days to name her, something Skwerl is struggling to understand.

He says, "Are you going to try different names during the week, like call her Susie on Tuesday and Rhonda on Wednesday and see how it goes?"

"No child of mine will be named *Rhonda*."

When Skwerl asks if they plan to give her an American name, Sinéad elbows him in the ribs, and says, "Tell me, Jay, what exactly is an American name?"

Cheese's cellphone rings. It's Just Shane and Ephraim. They're out in Colorado, calling from the Iridium on Just Shane's property. They want to congratulate Cheese. When they also ask about the name, Cheese explains, yet again, how his daughter will have no name for seven days. They seem more understanding than Skwerl. They do ask, however, whether Skwerl or Cheese has heard about any new work, perhaps another jet or boat, something expensive that will earn the four of them a healthy commission. Just Shane and Ephraim have officially joined as minority partners in Skwerl and Cheese's fledgling repossession business where they'll lend a hand with "logistical support," as they're calling it. For a percentage of every commission, they've agreed to set up safe harbors—like they inadvertently did in Colorado—for future jobs, though those future jobs have still yet to materialize, news that dampens the otherwise celebratory mood.

After the call with Just Shane and Ephraim, the three continue sipping their coffee. Sinéad openly wonders about Sheepdog and whether another job will ever materialize given the challenges of the last one. Cheese says nothing, but Skwerl's eyes widen. To him, it's an article of faith that an email from Sheepdog will appear, addressed to him and Cheese, as members of the *network*, outlining a lucrative new opportunity.

"Have a little faith," Skwerl says. "If it weren't for Sheepdog, I'd be lying in a morgue in Kyiv, just another unclaimed body in a freezer." Skwerl levels his gaze on Cheese, adding, "And so would you."

"You don't even know who Sheepdog is," says Sinéad.

"I know enough, Toots," and Skwerl relays his theories, how perhaps Sheepdog had had a hand in these events from the start. Maybe it was Sheepdog who had first tipped off the White Russian on the location of the Marie Antoinette plates. Few could boast an operational history on par with the White Russian, one of the most skilled case officers the organization had ever produced; and so maybe Sheepdog knew the type of intricate operation she was capable of organizing, one that would monetize those plates and get DRCA paid. Maybe she was the one who had orchestrated Uncle Tony and Ali Safi's meeting in that hotel lobby in Lviv. It was often said that for an operation to succeed, it required three things: money, time, and a skilled case officer. But there was never enough money. And there was never enough time. And so the success or failure of every operation depended on the case officer. As for Ali Safi, Skwerl wonders if he was ultimately a bit player, a patsy, with an easily defined motive, one of the oldest around: revenge. Skwerl sees Sheepdog's hand in everything. The polonium-210 that killed H. Grillot appearing as a willing buyer of the plates. Tomas's appearance on the train. The job had a unified logic, one that indicated a singular architect, and that architect must have been Sheepdog. Each of them became a piece that Sheepdog moved around his or her board.

Cheese's phone rings. It's Fareeda. She is up from her nap, as is the baby. Skwerl drops the subject of Sheepdog. They stand and clear their empty cups, filing out of the cafeteria in silence, each seeming to consider Skwerl's theory of events. This whole time the three of them have been speaking freely, unaware that they aren't alone. The hospital CCTV relies on a Wi-Fi network with only basic WEP encryption; also, a cellphone with a known IMEI can be coopted easily enough as a listening device. This is basic tradecraft, which Skwerl knows even if the others don't. He seems to be ignoring this. Or maybe he suspects he's being observed and wants to be overheard? He hustles out the door behind Sinéad and Cheese.

The cafeteria is entirely quiet now that they've left. Skwerl's theories seem to hang in the air. His story, particularly as it pertains to Sheepdog, isn't a wholly accurate rendering of events. But as you've seen, it's pretty close. Skwerl generally has the gist of cause and effect. He understands the nature of the game he is in.

As to the future, Skwerl isn't wrong. Another job will come. To be precise, it will come in seven days. A name is an important thing. Unless you're in our line of work, a person gets only one, and so Cheese and Fareeda should have the chance to pick their daughter's name carefully, without any undue distractions.

The next job can wait. How can I be so sure of it, and of their future? It's because of my name. You might be wondering what that is, but chances are you've already guessed it . . .

Acknowledgments

With thanks to my network: PJ, D, Big Daddy; and to my love, Chui.

A Note About the Author

Elliot Ackerman is the *New York Times* bestselling author
of the novels *2054*, *Halcyon*, *2034*, *Red Dress in Black and
White*, *Waiting for Eden*, *Dark at the Crossing*, and *Green
on Blue*, as well as the memoirs *The Fifth Act: America's End
in Afghanistan* and *Places and Names: On War, Revolution
and Returning*. His books have been nominated for the
National Book Award, the Andrew Carnegie Medal in both
fiction and nonfiction, and the Dayton Literary Peace Prize,
among others. He is a contributing writer at *The Atlantic*
and a Marine veteran, having served five tours of duty in
Iraq and Afghanistan, where he received the Silver Star, the
Bronze Star for Valor, and the Purple Heart. He divides his
time between New York City and Washington, D.C.

A Note on the Type

The text of this book was set in Sabon, a typeface designed by Jan Tschichold (1902–1974), the well-known German typographer. Designed in 1966 and based on the original designs by Claude Garamond (ca. 1480–1561), Sabon was named for the punch cutter Jacques Sabon, who brought Garamond's matrices to Frankfurt.

Composed by North Market Street Graphics,
Lancaster Pennsylvania

Printed and bound by Berryville Graphics,
Berryville, Virginia

Designed by Betty Lew

Love books? Hate waste?
Then read on . . .

If you've finished with this proof but don't want to keep it, you unfortunately can't give it to charity or pass it on*. But, don't worry, you can recycle it.

Here's how:

Step One: if the cover, front or back, has any laminations, varnishes, or foils**, please tear it off and put it in your non-recycling rubbish.

Step Two: place the book in your recycling (after checking how your local recycling treats books at **recyclenow.com**).

You're done.

If you'd like to be greener still, then next time ask for a proof in a digital format.

We're making our books more recyclable

To find out more about our sustainability commitments including our journey to net zero, please visit greenpenguin.co.uk.

* They are not the final text and as such are available only for a limited time.

** These can contain metals and plastics.